HIS MADDENING MATCHMAKER

Virginia Heath

MILLS & BOON

First published in Great Britain 2023
by Mills & Boon, an imprint of HarperCollins*Publishers* Ltd,
1 London Bridge Street, London, SE1 9GF

www.harpercollins.co.uk

HarperCollins*Publishers*
Macken House, 39/40 Mayor Street Upper,
Dublin 1, D01 C9W8, Ireland

His Maddening Matchmaker © 2023 Susan Merritt

ISBN: 978-0-263-30500-5

02/23

MIX
Paper | Supporting
responsible forestry
FSC
www.fsc.org   FSC™ C007454

This book is produced from independently certified FSC™ paper
to ensure responsible forest management.
For more information visit: www.harpercollins.co.uk/green.

Printed and Bound in Spain using 100% Renewable Electricity
at CPI Black Print, Barcelona

For Jean Fullerton and Clare Flynn.

It was an honour fighting in the trenches beside you last year.

Chapter One

❧⟡❧

May 1818

He was all alone in the corner again. Seemingly oblivious of the crowd or the music although Isobel wasn't the least bit convinced of that. Staring with too much determination into his glass as if nothing else existed. Trying to disappear into the plaster—as usual—despite standing a good head and shoulders above everyone else in the room. As if he firmly believed, if he willed it hard enough, that a man of six feet and six inches could simply fade into the background.

'You are never going to find yourself a wife like this.' Ned jumped at the sound of her voice, then regarded her with the same peeved and put-upon expression as he always did whenever he acknowledged her. 'You look like an old curmudgeon here on sufferance.'

He slanted her a peeved glance. 'I'm not looking for a wife and I am here on sufferance.'

Isobel Cartwright rolled her eyes heavenward and prayed for strength.

He was the same at every village assembly. Unsociable, unapproachable and uneasy, and it was getting worse with each passing year. Once upon a time, he at least made the effort to join in and once in a blue moon even deigned to dance if he was cajoled into it. But nowadays he took the phrase keeping himself to himself literally, and as much as it annoyed her to think it, she found it all worrying. Years of all work and no play had made Ned Parker a very dull boy indeed.

'Whose sufferance?' She glanced around the village hall to the sea of cheerful locals who all looked forward to the first Saturday in every month. Excuses to dress up and make merry were pitifully thin on the ground in Whittleston-on-the-Water so the assembly in this ancient, high-beamed ramshackle appendage of St Hildeth's church was always a highlight. 'Nobody here is ever formally invited, and I cannot imagine anyone insisting on your scintillating presence or even missing it if you failed to turn up. Therefore, it is a mystery to me why you always turn up like a bad penny the moment the doors are flung open and stay until the last song is played.'

'Habit,' he said with a resigned huff. 'My father insisted it was imperative to be neighbourly and that edict has become ingrained in my conscience no matter how hard I try to ignore it—and my blasted neighbours.'

'Maybe if you joined in, you'd enjoy it?'

'I sincerely doubt that.'

'Ask someone to dance.'

'No. I loathe dancing.' Which was a shame as for a big man he was a surprisingly competent partner.

Not that she would ever tell him, of course. Any more that she would ever let on how much she missed the close friendship they had once shared or how much she still grieved for his father too. Caleb Parker had meant the world to her, and his loss had left a big hole in her heart. One that was made bigger by the withdrawal of his vexing son from her life on the back of it. It was sad—more than sad actually—but she and Ned had ceased trading niceties as soon as they hit adulthood. If she would have let him, she was convinced he would have ceased bothering with her completely, exactly as he had everyone else. That she still forced him to see her was a source of a great deal of irritation to the both of them, although undoubtedly for entirely different reasons.

'Perhaps have a conversation with someone

then? With one person this evening, at least. Mrs Outhwaite's niece is pretty...' Mrs Outhwaite's visiting niece, in Isobel's humble opinion, was perfect for Ned. She was a quiet country mouse who had grown up on a farm and at five and twenty was obviously in as dire a need of a husband as he was a wife.

'I'm talking to you, aren't I?' Typically, he ignored her subtle hint about the newcomer, just as he had ignored all of her recent subtle hints about his romantic future. 'By my reckoning, and your logic, that's my one done now till next month.'

She made no attempt to hide her exasperation with him. The man wasn't only the size of an ox, he was as stubborn as one. 'You are only talking to me because I made the effort, although heaven only knows why as you are hardly a barrel of fun.'

'Then go find your fun elsewhere, Izzy. There are at least fifty other people here to gossip mindlessly with.' He always pretended to abhor gossip but still always seemed to know it just the same. 'Save your scintillating conversational efforts for someone else who'll appreciate them...' He flapped one meaty paw in the direction of the refreshment table where a crowd of locals were chatting. '...and take your unsubtle matchmaking efforts with you. Or better still, go find a willing man to flirt with as that seems to be your favourite sport.' He jerked his thumb in the direction of Mr Bunion, the local solicitor's socially ambitious new apprentice, who had a peculiar penchant for lacy cuffed shirts and had breath so rancid it had almost burned her eyebrows off when she had danced with him earlier. She might be desperate for a husband to whisk her away from Whittleston—but she wasn't that desperate. 'He's male, single and has a pulse, so clearly fits all of your *discerning* criteria.'

Ignoring the typical insult about the sorry state of her own romantic future—and past—she pasted on a sunny smile and, for his own good, forged ahead. 'Mrs Outhwaite's niece is called Rose. Isn't that a pretty name?'

Deadpan, stony silence.

'*Miss* Rose Healy. Her father is a farmer too. Just like you, so you have heaps in common.'

He shook his shaggy head in disgust. 'You're wasting your breath, Izzy. As I keep repeating...' He huffed out more frustration than her well-intentioned and undoubtedly charitable efforts deserved. 'I don't have the time for your nonsense. When I want a wife, rest assured that I'm quite capable of finding one for myself.'

It was her turn to scoff in disgust. 'Now who is talking nonsense? You couldn't find a wife yourself if your life depended upon it. You are gruff, surly, unapproachable and scruffy—and that is on one of your good days—and it will take quite a bit of work for you to turn any lady's head the way you are now.' She swept a critical gaze down the long length of him, which to be fair wasn't the least bit unpleasant no matter how much she forced her expression to pretend that it was, before she frowned at his thick, dark beard. 'It will likely take several weeks for me to physically transform you into any fit state to go courting. I dread to think how many months it will take to teach you some social niceties to improve your ornery character. You need me, Ned Parker, or you will die alone.'

'And again, I'll remind you that I don't have the time for courting and even if I did, you'd be the last person I turned to for advice on how to do it.' He folded his arms and glared. 'If you are such an expert on the subject, kindly explain why every fellow you set your cap to fails to put a ring on your finger.'

She ignored that dig too as she refused to mull on her own dismal failures at courting. It forced her to admit that there was something intrinsically unlovable about her that ultimately made all men reject her when she would much rather bury her head in the sand on that score. Admitting that was tantamount to admitting defeat when she was a firm believer in that if at first you don't succeed, you should try and try again. That she had done more than her fair share of trying with absolutely no success whatsoever was by the by. 'Then more fool you as I have a proven track record of helping lonely people find love.' She pointed to Lord and Lady Hockley, smiling soppily at one another on the dance floor. They were still clearly in the besotted newlyweds stage despite several months of marriage. 'I take full credit for getting those two together.'

'Of course you do!' His bark of laughter was rarer than one of his begrudging smiles. 'Because it takes a special sort of arrogance to take *full credit* for something which was practically a fait accompli from the first day they met. At best, you had a small hand in it, Izzy. A very small hand indeed and only because your own charms had no effect on Rafe.'

How typical of Ned to notice yet another one of her spectacular failures on the marriage mart. 'A small hand was all that was needed. A gentle nudge to encourage them towards the right path and you have to admit, I did that with aplomb.'

Up until that moment, Isobel had had absolutely no idea that she had a talent for matchmaking or that she enjoyed it quite so much. She had been too busy trying to attract her own mate so that she could escape this suffocating village and, more importantly, leave her father's oppressive and soulless house.

That one success had given her the taste for more, given her a blessed sense of purpose for a short while in a miserable few months devoid of any now that even her father had escaped his own oppressive and soulless life, and straightaway Ned had been the obvious next candidate to bestow her innate gift upon. She missed the old Ned and wanted him back and in the absence of any candidates who might whisk her down the aisle now that Mr Bunion had been crossed off her empty-again list, doing something wonderful for her former best friend was the next best thing while she waited for one to turn up. 'Obviously, with you, more of my effort would be required than was needed with Rafe.'

Ned would make a wonderful project to help pass the dreary time she was currently marching since her father had closed his shop. He had only ever allowed her to serve behind the counter at Cartwright's for an hour every day while he went home to eat—but she had lived for those hours her entire adult life. Meeting all the new people who stopped at the inn while their horses where changed, gossiping with the locals, convincing them all to buy things they did not even know that they needed had been the highlight of every day. She had become so good at it that many of the regular customers timed their visits to coincide with her being there and many used her recommendations to quietly persuade her father to stock the items—because obviously he would never have ordered them if he had known the suggestions came from her.

As his profits increased as a result, Isobel got the greatest sense of satisfaction knowing that she had had a direct hand in it, but that had been her secret. Hers and *her* customers, who saw through her father's fake chirpy façade and much preferred her.

When he had informed her that he intended to open a bigger and better shop elsewhere with her brother, she had begged him to keep the one here in Whittleston open so that she could run it. She had even confessed to her hand in some of the most lucrative recent decisions to convince him that she was worthy of the task but, typically, all to no avail. In fact, she still kicked herself now that she had played it all wrong. She should have buried her true emotions and denied him the power to wound her so. She should never have declared her interest and instead said good riddance to the dratted thing because shop work was beneath her. Perhaps if she had appeared elated that he was granting her more empty hours to fill with frippery, he might have *punished* her for her inherent laziness and insisted she earn her keep by working there from dawn to dusk.

She would have loved that!

But alas, Cartwright's had closed at Christmas, and it still left a gaping void in her life.

Hence the challenge Ned presented was too good a distraction to ignore. Oh, how she longed for some actual purpose again! A reason to get up. Something to distract her mind to wandering back into the murky depths of her past and all the unpalatable mistakes she had made which shamed her beyond measure. Mistakes which, thankfully despite all the gossip and speculation that swirled about her, the majority of Whittleston-on-the-Water were still unaware of. Yet still they kept her up at night.

Unless she buried her head in the sand and distracted herself from them.

To that end, she eyed Ned thoughtfully. 'Considerably more of my efforts will be required to get you up to scratch.' She glared at his beard, convinced it served as another barricade for him to hide from the world behind when she had made it her mission to drag him back kicking and screaming into it. He was three years shy of thirty, which for a man was the prime time to settle down. Any older and it was in danger of remaining a crusty, old bachelor for ever. 'All those whiskers will have to go to get you to appeal to the ladies, and a good haircut wouldn't go amiss either. Some smart new clothes and a few lessons in being charming and mark my words, the pretty Miss Healy will be all yours.'

'I've no interest in appealing to Miss Healy.' But his gaze wandered to her regardless before he snapped it back with a put-upon expression which furrowed his ebony brows.

'But surely you want to appeal to someone, Ned? Even if that's only to beget some heirs to bequeath your precious farm to one day. Otherwise, why did you bother with all the palaver of buying it from Lord Hockley? You're in your fields from dawn to dusk toiling away and for what? And more importantly for who? You certainly cannot leave it all to one of your sheep or that big, sloppy dog of yours. What on earth would Falstaff do with a farm on the banks of the Thames?'

'What business is my land of yours, Izzy?'

'It isn't my business, but as much as I loathe you, I still hate to see you so unhappy.'

'I'm not unhappy.'

'But you are not happy either, are you, Ned?'

She folded her arms and stared at him this time. 'I know that for a fact too, as with every passing year you become more cynical and curmudgeonly and that doesn't happen to happy people.' Although she was a naturally happy person and the same seemed to be happening to her now that Cartwright's was gone. 'Don't you get lonely? Crave some human companionship? Someone to be there when you get home at night. Someone to talk to?' All things she craved too and always had, but most especially these last few months. Some people were cut out for loneliness. Isobel most definitely wasn't one of them. There was only so much solitary reading or embroidery or busying herself on nothing important that a woman in her prime could do when she had always preferred to be out and about and in the thick of everything. 'Some burly sons to work your land beside you?' All men wanted sons. Daughters, however, as she knew to her cost, not so much. 'You never used to be so unsocial and insular.'

She blamed the flood for the unhealthy change in him.

The Great Flood of 1809 which had wreaked havoc all along the River Thames but had hit the Parker farm the hardest hereabouts. It one fell swoop, it destroyed all of his crops and most of his livestock. Poor Ned had been just eighteen then and already struggling to manage after his father had died only a few months before. The sudden failure of Caleb Parker's big heart had come as out of the blue as the tidal surge had, but it was the flood which had plunged him into years of horrendous poverty and that experience had changed him. The optimistic, mischievous, kind-hearted boy she had grown up with had been swept away by the tidal wave of grief and those raging flood waters, exactly like his livelihood, and had left a jaded, guarded and overly cautious man in its wake. Only Ned's stubborn pride had remained intact, and he had wielded that to his own detriment, refusing any and all offers from the community—and her—to help him in his hour of need.

Then, she had veered between having the utmost respect and admiration for his work ethic and determination to fix it all himself and wanting to bash him over the head with one of his shovels for being so foolishly intractable and insular.

Still did, truth be told.

He was as impossible still as he was enormous and as stubborn as a whole herd of mules put together.

In the absence of a shovel, she threaded her

arm through his, enjoying the defined shape of the solid muscles despite them being Ned's. 'No man is an island and even you deserve someone.'

'Must we talk about this again? Your incessant nagging is getting tiresome.'

He made a valid point as, so far, all the nagging in the world hadn't done one jot to get him to see sense. 'You are right.' He was deaf to her nowadays. 'I am all done with talking and believe some decisive action is required or nothing about your depressing situation will ever change.' Before he could stop her, she gripped him tight and waved at Mrs Outhwaite, who was standing with her niece by the refreshment table. When Mrs Outhwaite waved back, Isobel instantly gestured for them to come over. Obviously, that was all it took to have them both headed their way, because most people usually tended to avoid conversations with the uppity harbinger of doom Mrs Outhwaite so an actual invitation from someone willing to volunteer to converse with her was rarer than hen's teeth.

Ned's substantial bicep tightened beneath her fingers as he tried to tug his arm away, but she clung to him for grim death until it was too late for him to politely escape. Even then, she still held on in case he still made a break for it. As big as he was, he had always been surprisingly nimble, and he had never been one for doing anything he did not want to.

'Good evening, Isobel.' As grateful as she was to be summoned, Mrs Outhwaite still managed to greet her with a disapproving expression. 'What a *bold* gown you have chosen for this evening.'

As 'bold' was clearly a reference to the barest hint of her cleavage on display on her latest freshly altered gown, Isobel squared her shoulders so that it protruded some more and was rewarded by the familiar puckered lips of disdain which the older woman always used so well around her. 'I do so adore turquoise, don't you? It is bright and cheery and is determined to stand out. Much like me.' Isobel was what she was and was largely at peace with it because all attempts at changing herself had thus far proved futile. That the way she was also infuriated her father was a bonus. Therefore, she had long taken the attitude with every person who openly disapproved of her, and she happily included her mostly absent nowadays father in the number, that she might as well be hung for a sheep as for a lamb. Hence, when she had found this previously simple second-hand gown on her travels, she had remodelled it. She had cut the neckline lower to comply with the latest fashions and raised the hem to match, before she had cheered it up with some reused trim.

'Less is always more.' Mrs Outhwaite loved finding fault in people, especially Isobel, who had plenty of them. 'It always amazes me that your father never taught you that.'

To have taught her that, her father would have to care that he possessed a daughter in the first place, and he hadn't managed that in all the years she had been alive. Isobel might as well have been born invisible as far as he was concerned. She was certainly inconsequential and most definitely an inconvenience to him, and always had been. He had wanted another son to help build his empire, not a troublesome daughter who had left him a widower and thus slowed the pace that lifelong ambition down. Or so he always claimed. They would have to differ on that score as he had always blithely lived his life at his own speed and hadn't seemed to care one jot where she was or what she was doing at the time.

'Alas, but he has tried, Mrs Outhwaite.' If one assumed that occasionally bemoaning how much his wayward and still unmarried daughter cost him if they happened to collide once a week when he returned home was trying. 'But as you know, I have always been too wilful and rebellious to listen to him.'

Refusing to allow that man to crush her spirit despite everything he had done to crush it was a petty revenge she was proud of.

She smiled at Mrs Outhwaite's niece, who, to her credit, was obviously mortified by her aunt's blatant rudeness. 'I assume you have been introduced already to Ned Parker, Miss Healy?' She gestured towards the stiffened brute on her arm, knowing full well she hadn't because he avoided all social interactions like the plague.

Miss Healy smiled somewhat shyly. 'I have not yet had the pleasure, Miss Cartwright.'

'Then we must rectify that immediately as I believe the two of you have a great deal in common.' Isobel let go of his sleeve only to push him reluctantly forward. 'Ned here is a farmer, Miss Healy. A very successful one hereabouts.'

Ned couldn't have looked more uncomfortable if he tried as Miss Healy bobbed a curtsey and he inclined his head. 'It is a pleasure to make your acquaintance Miss Healy.' And with that, he stepped back, clearly all out of polite conversation now that he had managed to choke out that short, uninspiring sentence.

Good grief, but he was hard work!

Instead of rolling her eyes at him, Isobel offered her most friendly smile at the young woman.

'How are you enjoying your stay in Whittleston-on-the-Water, Miss Healy?'

'Very much, so far.' Miss Healy returned the smile of her own then, wonder of wonders, smiled shyly at Ned again as if she rather liked what she saw. But just like him, had nothing further to elaborate with beyond her single sentence, and just like him looked as though she would rather be anywhere in the world but here.

Good heavens above but they were both clearly as socially awkward as each other! Further proof that they would make a perfect pairing as this conversation was already like pulling teeth.

'Why don't you tell Miss Healy what sort of farm you keep, Ned?' Isobel would squeeze blood out of this stone if it killed her, and perhaps, if she actually got them chatting, they would stay chatting. After all, from little acorns, oak trees grew and a journey of a thousand miles had to begin with a single step, albeit a step caused by an almighty push.

'I grow wheat and barley mostly. Keep a few sheep.' He rocked on his heels, ill at ease after that uneffusive monologue, making Isobel want to whack him around his thick, stubborn head because she knew he could talk if he wanted to. He frequently had plenty to say to her, even if it was mostly all criticisms about her bothering him when he had to work.

Miss Healy smiled in response but failed to follow up with a single syllable, so clearly it was down to Isobel to fill in the pained gaps. 'What sort of farm does your father keep in Suffolk, Miss Healy?'

'Much the same but...'

'But obviously significantly bigger.' Always one to brag, Mrs Outhwaite interrupted her niece's tentative answer. 'My brother's farm is at least twice the size of Ned's. In fact, it might even be bigger and the yields from his fields are probably thrice fold. The soil of Suffolk is famously fertile. So much more superior to the chalk and clay we have here in Essex. And he has cows as well as sheep. Chickens too. It is a very impressive farm. A very impressive and *sizeable* farm indeed.'

'It certainly sounds it.' And because that was that topic all done, Isobel scrambled around for another. 'You have a brother, do you not, Miss Healy?'

'Yes... Daniel...he's...'

'He's a lieutenant in the cavalry.' Mrs Outhwaite plumped up like a peacock even though she had already bored absolutely everyone in the village, ad nauseum for years, about her magnificent, uniformed nephew. 'And has been such an exemplary officer, we fully expect him soon to be promoted to captain.' With that, the village braggart bestowed upon them all one of her most pious, and therefore most reliably annoying facial expression. 'Soldiering is more than a career for dearest Daniel—it is a *vocation*. Isn't it, Rose? We are all exceedingly proud of his sacrifice for our great nation.'

Before Ned groaned aloud, as he was prone to do when Mrs Outhwaite blew her family's trumpet, Isobel spoke for them both again. 'As indeed you should be. He sounds like the most wonderful nephew and brother.'

'Oh, he is!' Mrs Outhwaite jumped in again before her niece could respond. 'He is the absolute best of men. First rate in every way. Clever, witty, resourceful and handsome. The whole family adores him! My dear brother, especially, is so proud to have raised such a fine boy.'

Isobel suppressed the urge to ask if the sainted Lieutenant Daniel Healy could also walk on water too, as the way Mrs Outhwaite droned on about him reminded her too much about the way her father idolised her significantly older brother. However, responding with sarcasm, no matter how well deserved, would not help with her quest to get Ned better acquainted with Miss Healy, so she bit her tongue as much as she could. 'He sounds like a credit to your entire family as well as the army, and one can only hope that one day he graces Whittleston-on-the-Water with his inspiring presence so that we may all thank him for his selfless service to our nation. Don't you, Ned?'

He nodded solemnly, but she could see the rare flash of amusement dancing in his chocolate eyes at her gushing insincerity. Mrs Outhwaite, however, was oblivious to it and grinned from ear to ear.

'And hopefully you shall soon, Isobel, as he is taking some well-earned leave and has promised to visit his sister while she is here. Is that not the most excellent news?' The older woman clapped her hands like a delighted child. 'I am assured Whittleston will be graced with his presence as soon as he has concluded his business in the capital. We expect him towards the end of this month, don't we, Rose?'

'So he says,' said Rose, undeniably unconvinced that that was the case, and something about her tone piqued Isobel's interest. 'But you know Daniel.'

'What business detains him in London, Miss Healy?'

'The business of being a handsome and single

officer on some well-earned leave in the capital, Miss Cartwright. I adore my brother but he
has always been a shocking ladies' man and he
has always cut quite the dash in his regimentals.' A comment which was accompanied by a
wry smile that automatically made Isobel like
her. 'And knows it.'

'He does look exceptionally handsome in his
regimentals.' Mrs Outhwaite primped again as
if she was entirely responsible for her nephew's
superior appearance too. 'He shall have to beat
the young ladies off with a stick when he arrives
here, as Whittleston has rarely seen the like of
such a fine gentleman like Daniel.'

'Who doesn't love a man in dashing regimentals.' Isobel certainly had always had a soft spot
for one. Enough of one that she had completely
had her foolish head turned by one years ago
when she had pinned all her hopes of escaping
this village upon him. 'I do hope that he arrives
in time for our next monthly soiree. Whittleston-
on-the-Water is sadly lacking in handsome, single
gentleman, as I am sure you have already gathered from their sparsity at this little assembly.'
Miraculously, Miss Healy's eyes darted to Ned
again. Only briefly but not brief enough to disguise the fact that she thought the brute somewhat
appealing. 'There is always a shortage of decent

dance partners here. My card is pathetically half full. I sincerely hope that yours has fared better else you will surely die of boredom before the end of the night. There is nothing worse or more depressing than not dancing at an assembly.' She nudged Ned with her elbow to ensure he knew that dig was meant for him.

'Can you believe that nobody has yet asked Rose?' The tone suggested Mrs Outhwaite took her niece's empty dance card as a personal slight. 'We have been here almost ten minutes already, too.'

While Rose coloured prettily and looked at her hands mortified by that admission, and Ned remained mute, Isobel saw her chance.

'Then that will not do at all, Miss Healy, will it Ned?' Isobel elbowed his annoyingly solid arm again. 'You must rectify that immediately and take Miss Healy for a spin around the floor.' In case he argued, as he looked set to do at any moment, she pushed him hard towards her. At his obvious reluctance, poor Miss Healy blushed crimson.

'You really do not need to feel obligated, Mr Parker. I am quite content to watch the proceedings from afar.'

'It would be my pleasure, Miss Healy.' Begrudgingly, jaw clenched, he held out his big hand

to his foisted partner and forced a smile. 'I would
be honoured to dance with you.'

'Then in that case…' Miss Healy took it and
beamed up at him. 'I should be delighted to take
a turn with you, Mr Parker. Thank you for reluctantly asking.'

As he turned to lead her to the floor, Ned shot
Isobel a few subtle daggers over his ridiculously
broad shoulders. He was livid at her machinations, she could tell, but she was unrepentant because if ever a person needed a nudge towards
romance and happiness it was him. Even so, she
couldn't resist one parting jibe to remind him
how hopeless he was beneath his Sunday best
and how inept with women he would be without
her help. 'Be sure to guard your toes, Miss Healy,
as Ned's enormous, clumsy feet will likely crush
them otherwise.'

Ned shot a few more daggers her way when
the first bars of the next dance were played because it was a waltz and he hated the waltz most
of all, but for Miss Healy's sake he still went
along with it. Miraculously, Ned even managed
to smile at his partner as he pulled her into the
hold, and even said something which made Miss
Healy giggle as she gazed up at him with more
than a hint of feminine interest as he twirled her
around the floor.

While Mrs Outhwaite chewed her ear off moaning, and with no waltzing partner of her own, Isobel had nothing better to do but watch them dance.

They looked well together.

Exactly as she had hoped they would.

Which was…good.

Of course it was good.

He might not realise it yet, the big, insufferable clod, but Ned deserved and needed a wife and Miss Healy was perfect for him. Therefore, there was absolutely no reason to feel so suddenly unsettled about thrusting them together. And certainly no reason whatsoever to feel so uncharacteristically…envious.

Chapter Two

It was late morning by the time Ned had completed all his most pressing daily chores, so he was starving by the time he began the trudge back to his farmhouse.

He had been salivating for a good hour at the thought of the thick wedge of cheese and half loaf of bread awaiting him in his pantry and was desperate for a big mug of tea to appease his parched throat. He fully intended to take a full half hour to enjoy both in his favourite armchair while he finished reading last week's newspaper. That half an hour of rest beckoned like an oasis in the desert, and he would relish every minute of it in blissful peace because he deserved it. It felt as if he had been working like a dog nonstop for months, which was ironic when even his actual dog could not stand the pace Ned had set any more. Falstaff had stuck with him till nine while he'd tended to the sheep, then had quietly abandoned him somewhere between the pasture and the top wheat field. Ned knew already he'd be spreadeagled on the hearth rug, snoring his ugly big head off.

He envied him. It was a sorry state of affairs indeed that his mutt had a better life than he did. While Falstaff had napped, he'd repaired a fence, tracked down two escaped chickens and hoed a quarter of his fledgling spring barley field, so he had earned this break.

After that, he had a mountain of neglected jobs to do which were now bordering on urgent. It would be dark before his day finished despite it starting an hour before dawn, but it couldn't be helped. The tail end of lambing season was always the same and it would take him till May to catch up. Then he'd have a scant few weeks of respite before the shearing began and his winter barley had to be harvested in July, closely followed by the wheat in August. Autumn would be taken up with ploughing before he sowed his fields with the more crops and the never-ending cycle would begin again. He was enslaved by the seasons, but such was the life of a farmer, so he tried not to allow it to grind him down now that his cursed land was finally making a decent profit for the first time in living memory.

Yet it still did because the cycle was increasingly relentless if he wanted to turn a profit, and all his days had begun to merge into one neverending soul-destroying ordeal of work. The irony wasn't lost on him that the more he did, the more profitable the farm became, the more he had left to do to improve on that, so Izzy's insightful question last night did little to ease his worndown mood. In fact, it had niggled him ever since she had asked it. Because now that his head was finally above water—both literally and figuratively—what the blazes was he still working so hard for?

Sadly, Ned knew the answer.

He was compelled to.

He feared that if he didn't, it could all go to hell in a handcart in an instant and he would lose everything again.

It didn't matter than nine years had passed since the flood had taken his livelihood and all his savings. It didn't matter that he finally owned the land his family had toiled upon for over a hundred and fifty years so there was no longer any chance of eviction. It didn't matter that he finally had some money put aside to tide him over for at least a year if the river ever decided to be so vindictive again. Nor did it matter that he knew he was being irrational and obsessive about his financial future—the scars of his past were too deep and still too raw to put aside just yet. He worked his fingers to the bone out of fear—pure and simple—to create the most substantial buffer between him and disaster as was humanly possible. He did that because he had experienced both crippling poverty and hopelessness and could not face the prospect of ever experiencing either again.

Which was all well and good, but if his current monotonous and unfulfilling life was a taste of what his future looked like, with all the relentless, lonely drudgery and the seasons all merging in perpetuity, then it frankly depressed the hell out of him.

He was seven and twenty for pity's sake, yet inside already felt a hundred years older, and lately that had bothered him. Life was passing him by and, worse, he was allowing it. Willing it even. No man was an island. A farmer *did* need a wife to come home to and he did need a family to share both the workload and the spoils with. He could try to ignore it till he was blue in the face, but the ache in his heart seemed to get bigger with every passing year. It increased at twice the speed of his bank balance, and he was sick and tired of feeling so alone and burdened that he found little joy in anything any more. As much

as it pained him to make Izzy right about anything, nothing about that was going to change
unless he put some decisive effort into changing
it. And maybe, just maybe, he would do exactly
that very soon.

Or soonish.

Or he would at least give the topic some serious thought the second the farm gave him some
time off. Once the harvest was in. And sold. The
fields replanted ready for the next harvest. The
next generation of lambs were born.

And his three aged and useless Tamworth pigs
sprouted wings and flew.

Those three bottomless porcine stomachs
should have been turned into sausages by now
but he couldn't bring himself to send them to the
butcher's. They were the last animals his father
had bought the day before he had keeled over
in their paddock and, pathetically, he was too
sentimental to break that last link he had to the
man who had loved this land with every fibre
of his being. That his father had blithely spent
his last few pounds he had on the swine with
no knowledge of farming pigs beyond his whim
to give it a go, also served as a visible, daily reminder of the grave dangers of acting on impulse.
He had adored his father, missed him daily, but
was damned if he would ever make the same

mistakes, even if that did, as Izzy had lamented, make him a very dull boy indeed nowadays.

Frustrated, Ned huffed out a sigh at his own failings as he approached his house, then swiftly let out another when he spied a visitor hurrying down the lane towards him.

Even from this distance, and simply because of the way her basket swayed in time with her seductive hips, he knew it was her before Izzy sent him a cheery wave and quickened her pace.

He didn't bother heading up the lane to intercept her before she ruined his already miserable morning, as he knew she'd be coming in whether he wanted her to or not. Izzy had been turning up here at least twice a week since she was five to bother him, and nothing he could do or say, or even propriety could stop her. So he left his front door open after Falstaff, the traitor, bounded out of it, and braced himself for the inevitable interrogation.

He was setting the kettle to boil when she skipped in, still tickling his devoted mutt's ears.

'So...?' In typical Izzy fashion, she deposited her basket on his kitchen table and tossed her pretty straw bonnet beside it, then plonked her bottom on one of his chairs as she stared up at him in anticipation while Falstaff stared up at her as if she was his everything. She had always had the canny knack of looking at home in his home, but it would be a cold day in hell that Ned ever admitted how much that had always unsettled him. Or how much a part of him still appreciated her unannounced visits or her continued friendship despite his lack of friendliness.

'So what?'

'So what indeed, Falstaff?' She rolled her cornflower-blue eyes at his besotted dog in exasperation before she lifted them to his. 'So... you danced with Miss Healy last night and then spent a good half an hour cosied up in a corner chatting to her...'

'So I did.'

'*And?* Did you like her?'

'She seems nice enough.'

The blue eyes rolled again. 'Nice enough to chat to or nice enough to want to get to *know* better?'

He knew what she was alluding to but wasn't ready to admit that either because he wasn't sure how he felt about that yet. Miss Healy was nice. Very nice in fact, but likely as out of his league as the vexing woman currently laying siege to his kitchen. 'It's impossible not to know somebody better after chatting to them for half an hour.'

'So...?'

It was his turn to roll his eyes. 'So what, Izzy?

I chatted to the woman. It wasn't as if I had much choice in the matter after you practically threw me at the poor thing, so it seemed like the polite thing to do not to abandon her at the first chance.' Which wasn't strictly true, but about as much of the truth as he was prepared to concede to her.

In actuality, despite the mortifying start to the proceedings, he and Miss Healy had had had a rather decent chat, all things considered. After some prompting during their awkward dance after he had apologised profusely for Izzy's part in it, she had found her voice and then they had found some common ground discussing farming.

He had been particularly interested to learn that her father had spent the last few years experimenting with planting turnips rather than leave his fields fallow after two years of harvest. Especially after Miss Healy was quite adamant that her father was subsequently getting better wheat yields on the back of it. Ned had read a few articles that claimed as much, but to hear about the results on a farm where it had actually been put in practice was fascinating. Certainly fascinating enough to convince him to give it a go himself. At least in a controlled, small manner until he was convinced that it would work. The way Miss Healy put it, he'd be mad not to when the method not only grew good wheat, it also provided another crop to take to market. Or to use to feed his animals over the long winter months. Sheep, according to Miss Healy, adored the taste of turnips. Both the tops and the bottoms, and the bottoms could be kept for months if stored correctly.

They had barely scraped the surface of her father's top tips for effective turnip storage when Mrs Outhwaite had stolen her niece away, determined to introduce her to all the 'decent gentlemen of the village.' The unsubtle implication, of course, was that a former subsistence tenant farmer was neither decent enough or gentleman enough to fraternise with any of her flesh and blood. Mrs Outhwaite would never forgive him for the years he suffered holes in his boots, as if those holes were entirely his fault. Which, he supposed, they sort of were. Up until the flood, he'd never had cause of questioning his father's habit of spending rather than squirrelling money away, so he hadn't been brought up to worry about tomorrow. He'd been brought up to believe that something would always turn up because his father was an eternal optimist, just like the vexing minx stood before him. He did now though. Tomorrow kept him awake at night despite all the reserves he religiously squirrelled away every month while he waited for it.

'Did you think she was pretty?'

He pondered it for a second then shrugged. 'I suppose so.' Because Miss Healy wasn't unattractive, she just wasn't as attractive as the woman currently sat at his table. But then again who was? Izzy was, and always had been, far and away the prettiest woman Ned had ever set eyes upon and that was a hard yardstick for anyone else to measure up to.

The halo of pale blonde ringlets she had been born with had grown into an artfully arranged riot of golden curls that a Roman goddess would envy. Her figure had ripened in all the right places too. The perfect, symmetrical features that had charmed him so as a boy had only improved with maturity and the ridiculous big blue eyes were more than capable of stealing a man's breath away if he let them. Which Ned didn't, because as much as his idle mind occasionally wished otherwise all alone in the middle of the night when she'd invaded one of his dreams, Izzy wasn't for him. She had been made effervescent, for a life filled with excitement rather than the day-to-day drudgery of farm life and someone like him would only hold her back. She had never made any secret that she intended to marry outside of Whittleston and well either. She was so determined escape its suffocating and judgemental confines for ever.

Nor had the minx ever passed up any opportunity to try to turn that dream into a reality when an unattached new gentleman wandered through their village. Although why one of those many fellows hadn't snapped her up was a mystery to him. Unless women outside of Whittleston were better looking than she was, which he sincerely doubted, or more vivacious or more entertaining. Not that he left its environs very often, but when he had, he still hadn't found one who held a candle to her. Not even in that hellhole they called London where females were as plentiful as the stars in the sky. Still she managed to burn the brightest.

The meddling menace.

'You *suppose* she is pretty?' She shook her head as if he had grown two of them. 'Attraction doesn't require quite so much thought, Ned. It is either there or it isn't. It should hit you like a thunderbolt.' She clasped her hands dramatically to her pert bosom. 'Like Cupid's dart that pierces your heart and changes it in an instant and leaves you weak at the knees.' Exactly like his father, she had always been more hopeless romantic than pragmatist too. Always leapt before she looked and rushed headlong into everything without a moment's pause for thought, whereas he was the opposite. Ned always weighed up the pros and the cons and all the potential dangerous risks before he leapt, and even then he didn't so much leap as creep. He couldn't afford to be reckless, like Izzy was and his father had been. Recklessness, as he had learned the hard way, left you wide open to outright disaster and almost cost you everything, and that was not something he was prepared to do again without several layers of contingency.

When he finally got around to finding himself a wife, he wanted one with a strong character and back, not weak knees. That was another of his optimistic father's mistakes which he had learned from. Caleb Parker had married the first woman who dazzled him, probably thanks to those damned daft thunderbolts, and she hadn't been cut out for farm life either. It had made her so miserable she had escaped it the first chance she got with a travelling businessman within months of Ned's birth. He didn't miss her. It was impossible to miss what one had never had or known, nor did he harbour much malice towards the woman beyond ambivalence, but the short-lived marriage of his parents had always served as a cautionary reminder against reaching beyond your means. Between that and the flood, he knew his place and it wasn't up with the stars.

'Ah…well, there was no thunderbolt nor any darts.' He fetched two cups from the cupboard and the teapot from the side in time for her to jump up and relieve him off them as he had hoped, because, as his dear departed father always said, nobody made a better brew than Izzy Cartwright.

'That doesn't mean that there is no hope for you and Miss Healy.' Izzy always squinted when she measured out the tea leaves. Always jiggled the spoon gently until the mound upon it was the optimum size before she deposited it in the pot. 'Obviously, a thunderbolt is the romantic ideal, but it is also true that many couples grow on one another in its absence.'

'Like mould on an apple? Now that is romantic.'

She ignored him to rummage in his pantry before she waved his half a loaf at him in disgust. 'This is stale, Ned! How many times do I have to tell you that bread doesn't last much longer than two days?' And then, in typical Izzy fashion, she retrieved a fresh loaf from her basket because she never visited him without stopping by the bakery first. He'd wager all three of his barren pigs that there was a cake in there of some sort too, as she always arrived with something sweet and usually ended up devouring half of that herself. 'There is also every chance that the thunderbolt might still come—given time to percolate.' For a woman who stormed through life like a whirl-wind, nobody ever cut a straighter slice than Izzy did and he never tired of watching her carve two precise and equal squares which would also end up being buttered identically. 'There is no rhyme or reason to *l'amour* and no definitive way that it should be achieved, so let's not give up on it happening just yet.'

'Give up on what?'

'On you and Miss Healy.' She waved the breadknife at him. 'I think you and she make a splendid pairing. As I knew that you would.' She inhaled deeply, mightily pleased with herself. 'I smell rose petals in your future, Edward James Parker. Rose petals and wedding cake.'

If he'd had something in his mouth, he would have spat it out in shock. 'Were you dropped on your head as a child, woman! You force me to dance with a stranger and now expect me to take vows beside her!'

'Well, you conceded that she is pretty, and she did grow up on a farm.'

'So obviously, based on those two things alone we should get married and live happily ever after.' For all her precise measuring and slicing, Izzy's warped logic, however, was always unfathomable. 'You came to that ludicrous conclusion simply because we had a little chat and a dance.'

'You had a *long* chat and *you* danced. For you, that is unheard of.' She swapped one knife for another smaller one and plunged it in the butter. 'Unprecedented even. Ergo, it must mean something. I saw the way that you looked at her...' The hand with the butter knife went to her curvaceous hip, her expression daring him to deny it. 'You were smiling, Ned Parker. *Smiling*. When you stopped smiling at everyone years ago. From where I was stood, it looked to me like you might have even been flirting a little.'

While she likely made a valid point about his lack of smiles, because last night's had felt odd, she was floating in the realms of fantasy if she imagined he had been flirting. The very idea was laughable when even if he had been tempted to— which he obviously hadn't—he wouldn't have the first clue how to do it without cringing with self-consciousness. Unlike the charming, effervescent and flighty vixen currently tormenting him with her nonsense, Mother Nature had designed him to be a blunt instrument. One who ploughed fields, heaved sacks of grain, spoke plainly when it was necessary and clamped his jaws shut when not. He was pretty sure he did not possess a single flirtatious bone in his big, ungainly body.

'And I am certain that Miss Healy was flirting back, Ned. She was definitely interested in you.'

Two golden brows wiggled suggestively. 'In the feminine sense. She didn't stop surreptitiously staring at you afterwards either.'

He scoffed at that, because clearly she was now just being plain daft. Well-heeled, well-educated and affluent young ladies like Miss Healy did not look at labouring lummoxes like him with feminine interest. At least not for more than an illicit roll in the hay. For anything more they looked to 'decent gentlemen' of their own ilk that their aunts approved of. 'Only a fanciful fool like you could misconstrue a conversation about turnip rotation into one of seduction.'

'Why on earth would anyone want to willingly chat about turnips while they were flirting?' She pulled a baffled face then shook her head to dislodge it as she held up her palm. 'Never mind. Each to their own. I've given up wondering how your strange mind works. The subject of your scintillating conversation is irrelevant because at least you had one.' The buttered bread was deposited on a plate, topped with cheese and the second slice, before it was slid in front of him at the same time as another slice of cheese was covertly smuggled to Falstaff behind her petticoats. 'We must build upon that and strike while the iron is hot. I think the best way forward—'

Ned raised his own palm. 'To clarify, there is

no *we* in this situation.' As much as her neat sandwich beckoned, her nonsense needed to be nipped in the bud. He knew Izzy too well not to know that she would go off half-cocked and cause him all sorts of mischief if he didn't clip her wings beforehand. Poor Miss Healy had enough on her plate being Mrs Outhwaite's niece, so she didn't deserve any fanciful matchmaking nonsense. 'If I ever decide that I wish to further my acquaintance with Miss Healy—and I'll confess here and now that I haven't given that idiotic idea a first thought let alone a second—then I shall go about it in my own way and without your interference.'

'Suit yourself.' Feigning insult, she sashayed towards the whistling kettle and used a rag to grab it from the range, then poured the boiling water into his teapot in aggrieved silence until she could stand it no more. 'Die alone an embittered old bachelor. See if I care. But after the *enlightening* conversation I just had with Miss Healy in the market square, I really think that you should give it some thought.'

He knew he was going to regret it but asked anyway. 'And why, pray tell, was it enlightening?'

'Why do you care? When you've made it plain you are more interested in rotating stupid turnips than you are in furthering your acquaintance with the beguiling and obviously beguiled Miss Healy.'

One of these days he was going to strangle her with the ribbons of her own bonnet, but instead he tossed the flowered straw frippery towards her. 'I don't care, I've decided, so leave me to my luncheon in peace.' For good measure, he pointed to the still-open door. 'Get out of my house and never come back.'

She responded to that with a grin which only got wider as she sunk into the chair opposite him. 'She asked me all manner of questions about you.'

Ned decided it would probably be best if he allowed her to say what she had come to say until she had exhausted herself, as she would anyway regardless of whether he wanted to hear it, so stared at the heavens for strength as he snatched up his food. As her mouth opened to speak, he took an enormous bite, ensuring his was so full there was no possible way he could respond to any of her futile machinations. The least said, in her case, was always the soonest mended.

'It turns out the apparently shy Miss Healy can be quite talkative without her aunt around.' Izzy beamed as she poured them both some tea. 'She wanted to know how long you'd lived here in Whittleston.'

Refusing to so much as pretend to care, Ned chewed without the slightest flicker of interest.

'She asked about your farm…'

He refilled his mouth and chewed some more.

'Then she asked about your character for a bit and seemed impressed by what I told her, although Lord only knows why because I told her the honest truth.' He would have yawned but it would have meant spraying her in crumbs, which she probably deserved but good manners prevented him from unleashing. 'And then she said that she thought that you were a very nice and a very kind man.' She paused for dramatic effect, and when she received absolutely no reaction whatsoever, leaned forward. 'She likes you, Ned. Isn't that wonderful?'

When he took another bored bite of his sandwich, she groaned before gilding her wholly imagined lily further. 'It is categoric proof that she is interested in you. In the feminine sense.'

'It really isn't.'

'Open your eyes, Ned! Admit for once that I was right!'

'Even a stopped clock is right twice a day.'

'The "very" was a hint that she is attracted to you and an unsubtle one at that because she used the word *very* twice in one sentence. A *very* kind and *very* nice man, and she smiled wistfully as she said them.' Izzy leaned on her hand as she smiled wistfully at him. 'And she asked me to thank you for dancing with her, even though you didn't really want to, and for taking the trouble to talk to her and make her feel welcome when you had no reason to. Those were her exact words. Verbatim.'

'I think that maybe your ears and mine hear things differently, Izzy, as I'm not getting any alleged attraction from all that, merely her thanks that I didn't embarrass her by refusing after her awful aunt embarrassed her and then you embarrassed her further when you thrust me at her. You are a *very* intrusive and *very* annoying nuisance.'

'But you did not see her eyes when she said all that, and the covert message in those eyes spoke volumes.' He rolled his again as she batted her long lashes to ensure she got the message that he thought she was talking complete codswallop, to which she laughed at him as if he truly knew nothing. 'If you bothered to engage with the world, Ned, you would know that that is the way all proper young ladies approach a potential courtship. With subtle looks and thinly veiled words. Anything more overt would be frowned upon as brazen at this delicate stage in the proceedings.' Which was a rich explanation coming from someone who had always been as brazen in the pursuit of courtship as Izzy.

'Oh, we're at a stage already are we.' He shook

his head in disbelief. 'And on the back of one chat about turnips and just two mentions of the word *very*, to boot. I'd best get my wedding suit pressed in readiness for the nuptials then, especially as you can apparently sniff the confetti and wedding cake in my future.' He jabbed his finger in the air between them. 'I am not a fan of most people, but you are, without a doubt, the most maddening individual I have ever met.'

'Courtship is a dance, Ned. She has executed the first steps and now it's your turn to parry.'

'I hate dancing even more than I hate clueless, maddening matchmakers poking their deluded noses in where they are not wanted.' He stood and gulped down his tea, all done with her silly flights of romantic fancy for the day.

Two uses of the word *very* in one sentence indeed!

Suddenly, it made perfect sense to him why none of the gentlemen she had thrown herself at over the years had ever snapped her up. The woman lived in cloud-cuckoo-land. 'There is only one thing that I hate more than dancing, and that's someone who forces me to dance. I let you bully me into it last night, Izzy, but it will be a cold day in hell before I allow you to do it again.'

Chapter Three

'And now the sudden, impromptu visit to Whittleston-on-the-Water makes perfect sense.' Mrs Fitzherbert shook her snow-white head at the letter in her hand which had come from her friend in Suffolk. A friend who conveniently only lived five miles away from Miss Healy's village. 'The poor girl.'

It was post day in Whittleston-on-the-Water, and as she had every day the mail coach arrived since she was a little girl, Isobel had picked up Mrs Fitzherbert's letters for her from the postmaster's office next to the smithy. As the oldest matriarch of the village seemed to know everyone for a hundred miles, there was always a stack of them, and they were always a great source of entertainment to the four women present. So entertaining that at Isobel's instigation they now had a standing appointment to take tea together at the old lady's house every Monday and Wednesday after the coach had made its deposit, where they always put the world to rights afterwards. Fridays, Isobel merely delivered the letters when she collected Mrs Fitzherbert and then the four of them simply gossiped about everything in them at the sewing circle instead.

Growing up motherless, Isobel had always been free to do as she pleased during daylight hours while her father had worked. Like the other ladies present, who also hadn't had the privilege of being born to the gentry, nobody ever batted an eyelid that she wandered around the village without a maid. Nobody did because most couldn't afford a maid. It was a different story when night fell and propriety dictated that no decent woman was seen out unaccompanied, so in return for the prompt thrice-weekly delivery of her mail, Mrs Fitzherbert had returned the favour by being Isobel's chaperone. An arrangement which suited them both because Mrs Fitzherbert had always marched to the beat of her own drum and took great pleasure in being the worst chaperone in the world.

'Jilted!' Beside Isobel on Mrs Fitzherbert's brocade sofa, Sophie frowned as she poured more tea. 'What sort of monster would do such a thing to a gentle soul like Miss Healy? And at Christmas too. That seems doubly cruel when her fiancé's affair had *obviously* been going on for some time.' Enough time for Miss Healy's treacherous best friend to be pregnant enough for there to have been no doubt that she was in the family way if it had set tongues wagging weeks before the planned wedding.

'No wonder she fled to her aunt's.' Sophie's beloved aunt, and Mrs Fitzherbert's oldest friend, Miss Jemima, shook her own head sighing. 'As we all know from bitter experience, there is nothing more brutal than village gossip. The scandal must have been soul-destroying for the poor dear. Especially to have endured four whole months of it.'

'Which beggars the question as to why she left it so long to leave. After four months, the scandal should be waning by now.' Village scandals, in Isobel's extensive experience of them, tended to blow over in half that time if you brazened them out. Quicker if something else occurred locally to set the cat amongst the pigeons.

'Maybe it isn't the scandal which has chased her away. Maybe it is the aftermath of it.' For the second time in as many minutes, Sophie rubbed her belly idly. 'Her fiancé was a local man and so was the woman he ran off with. If they stayed put, then they will soon be birthing the child that they made behind Miss Healy's back. Perhaps that has had some bearing on her sudden desire to visit Mrs Outhwaite for the entire summer?'

As a theory, it made perfect sense. Poor Miss Healy. It was one thing to be publicly humiliated or abandoned, as Isobel was only too aware. Another entirely to then have your nose rubbed in it. At least all her romantic failures had had the good grace to leave Whittleston after they had crushed her desperate spirit. She couldn't imagine how horrific it would be to keep colliding with them on the street and be reminded what a stupid fool she had been to have put such stock in them in the first place. 'Things must have been unbearable for Miss Healy to willing suffer Mrs Outhwaite for months on end. My entire world would have to implode before I spent a whole day in her company, let alone a summer.' Everyone nodded at Isobel's pithy comment. 'My heart doubly bleeds for her. I've never met her hideous former fiancé, but I already loathe him on her behalf.'

'So do I, but at least the wretch did the decent thing by one of his women and his unborn child, but I sincerely doubt poor Miss Healy would see it that way.' Sophie rubbed her belly again, adding fuel to Isobel's suspicions that more than Miss Healy's replacement was currently in the family way. Knowing her friend's history, she decided it was best not to query that yet. Sophie had lost her first pregnancy early on a decade ago, so would be understandably cautious a second time around. 'She must have felt thoroughly humiliated. I think I too would have preferred to suffer a whole summer with Mrs Outhwaite than all the pitying stares and whispers of my neighbours.'

'There is that.' Growing up, Isobel had suffered enough of those to last a lifetime. 'Some gossip is just too awful to bear.' If some of her misguided youthful mistakes ever leaked out, she sincerely doubted she'd ever be able to look anyone in the village in the eye again for the shame of it all. Not that she would need to. If proof ever found its way to her father that she wasn't as white as the driven snow, he had promised her that she would be disowned in a heartbeat.

'We should probably keep the unfortunate tale between us for the time being, as I suspect she has already suffered enough.' Miss Jemima was always the most sensitive of the four of them. 'We don't want to set idle tongues wagging here in Whittleston too and add to her misery. She came here to escape it, not suffer more of the same.'

'Agreed,' said Mrs Fitzherbert with a decisive bash of her crystal-tipped cane as if they had just passed a law. 'Unless Miss Healy or Mrs Outhwaite volunteer the information themselves, we must play dumb. What happened in Suffolk should stay there. Miss Healy deserves to recover and grieve from his treachery in peace. If she is sensible, she will soon realise that she had a lucky escape and thank her lucky stars that he showed his true colours before she shackled herself to him for eternity, for a man like that would never have made her happy.' Which was precisely Isobel's preferred way of dealing with her own perennial romantic disappointments. 'Hopefully she will eschew bitterness that way and find a better one, as her finding great happiness elsewhere is a much more fitting revenge.'

'Onwards and upwards,' said Sophie with a clenched fist in the air. 'A mantra which has always served me well.'

As she had always been of the same opinion herself, Isobel nodded, more convinced than ever that Miss Healy needed a man like Ned to help her to get over the dud who had discarded her. For all his faults, Ned wasn't the sort of man who would have an affair behind a woman's back. Despite his surly demeanour and lack of charm, he was about as upright, loyal and noble a man as it was possible to be. The sort who did not shy away from his responsibilities or make false promises. His word was his bond. There was right and there was wrong with Ned, no matter what the circum-

stances, and nothing in between. He was a very
different kettle of fish to Miss Healy's duplicitous former fiancé and the perfect antidote to all
her current woes.

Isobel was waiting for a gentleman of a similar ilk herself. Unfortunately, as far as new single gentlemen were concerned, there had been
a drought in Whittleston these past few years.
The only two viable recent candidates had been
Lord Hockley, who had only ever had eyes for
Sophie, and the foul-breathed Mr Bunion, who
really needed to keep his eyes to himself. Mean-
while, she wasn't getting any younger and would
soon be past her own prime if nobody came along
to change that.

A depressing thought that always induced
panic if she entertained it for too long, so she banished it a second before Mrs Fitzherbert's cane
thudded against the parquet again.

'Her duplicitous former fiancé will get his
comeuppance in the end. Of that Miss Healy must
console herself. No sin goes unpunished for ever.'

'You are quite correct.' Miss Jemima was also
a firm believer in fate. 'What goes around comes
around and there are plenty more fish in the sea.
The change of scenery will do Miss Healy good,
and one never knows, she might just find the real
man of her dreams here over the summer.'

'Wouldn't that be marvellous.' As much as Ned had told her to mind her own business, getting him and Miss Healy together would now not only be a charitable favour towards him but a favour to Miss Healy also *and* the perfect way to right a wrong.

However, knowing Ned's stubbornness as well as she did, after his unreasonable reactions to all her matchmaking attempts thus far, she would have tread carefully. He would batten down the hatches at the first hint of any more machinations and poor Miss Healy was probably all done with men in the short term. Therefore, although it would take longer, some subtlety and some patience were required. This would need a long, discreet and considered game. But what was the hurry when she had all summer? It wasn't as if she had anything better to do with her time, so the distraction of several months of restrained matchmaking would give her something meaningful to focus her attention on and another much-needed excuse to get out of her father's soul-destroying silent-as-the-grave house. 'Does anyone know when Miss Healy plans to return to Suffolk?'

Mrs Fitzherbert pondered that for a moment. 'I seem to recall Mrs Outhwaite saying September, but as it was said in the midst of one of her droning, self-aggrandising soliloquies, I could be mistaken. I tend to glaze over when that woman lectures.'

'Don't we all,' said Sophie before she frowned again. 'Poor Miss Healy. To have to endure an entire summer of Mrs Outhwaite on top of everything else. Hasn't she already suffered enough?'

'You make a valid point, Sophie dear.' Mrs Fitzherbert's expression was a cross between pity and horror. 'We should also extend to her the hand of friendship, as she has already been through quite the ordeal and anything we can do to make her stay with her dreadful aunt more bearable is the only decent thing to do.' Her ancient, gnarled finger pointed at Isobel. 'You are about the same age as the poor dear, so why don't you befriend her on our behalf first so we can lure her into our fold.'

'I have already started. We conversed at the assembly and again the day after.' When Isobel had specifically lingered longer than usual in the market to hunt Miss Healy down to gauge her opinion of Ned. That Miss Healy had thought the big clod a very nice and very kind man now all made perfect sense in light of how abominably she had recently been treated by another of his sex, so surely that was another point in his favour? 'In fact, we had a very pleasant chat last time I saw her so I would be more than happy to befriend without any other agenda.'

Never mind that being Miss Healy's friend also gave her a good excuse to champion Ned too while nudging them both in the right direction. It was always satisfying to hit two birds with the one stone. Three if it included making a new friend to kill time with. Like cheerful bonnets, a girl could never have enough decent friends to take tea with, and the more times she took tea, the less hours she spent in her father's oppressive house.

'I shall call on her when I leave here and extend the invitation.' Already the prospect thrilled her. Not only was this a nice thing to do for two people who deserved some luck, selfishly, it would also break of the monotony of her own life. And good gracious it had been monotonous of late! So monotonous, her trademark cheerful smile was in grave danger of slipping.

'Excellent. Then invite her to the sewing circle tomorrow and then we can all become better acquainted with Miss Healy. We should also invite her to take tea with us soon—obviously without her dreadful aunt as she is the last person I wish to waste any of my dotage on.' Mrs Fitzherbert turned up her nose. 'I am all for being a good

Samaritan, but nobody can be expected to be that good. Especially not at my age.'

'Why don't you come and sit over here with us?' Isobel gestured to the already seated Sophie as soon as Miss Healy arrived at the Friday sewing circle two days later. 'Let us leave the matrons to their chatter.'

'By that she means moaning,' said Sophie in a stage whisper, 'as there was a great deal of consternation at the market yesterday because the fishmonger has put sixpence onto the price of his dover sole. Most of them do not buy dover sole this early in the season because it is so expensive due to its scarcity, but apparently it is the principle. Daylight robbery is not tolerated in Whittleston.'

'So I heard.' Miss Healy's pretty eyes were filled with mirth. 'My aunt is so incensed she has instructed my uncle to write a scathing piece in his newspaper urging people to fish for their own sole in the Thames if the fishmonger continues to extort money to feed his greed.'

The Outhwaites owned the *South Essex Gazette*, which was printed and distributed all around the Thames estuary every Saturday morning. It was a typical local rag filled with a mixture of news and gossip from their immediate environs and the out-of-date news which Mr Outhwaite shamelessly lifted almost word for word from other local newspapers and, most especially, from the *London Times*. He did that, so he claimed, for the benefit for the two thirds of his readers who did not receive their own copy of *The Times* a day later than the Londoners did. But even that wasn't fast enough for all the best news to travel from the capital, and being only twenty-five miles from the city, the most effective route for speedy communiques was always the many carriages that trundled through the village down the London Road stuffed with passengers who ate at the inn. Which left the *Gazette* largely read entirely for the endless local gossip, speculation and, more often than not, Mrs Outhwaite's outraged personal opinions on everything from the vulgar, improper fashions being imported from town to the price of fish.

'I've always wondered…' As the very best friends always shared confidences, Isobel thought she would start with Miss Healy how she meant to carry on—by being her flippant, often inappropriate self. '…does Mr Outhwaite write those outraged articles himself or does your aunt do it for him?'

'It seems to be a more collaborative affair.' Miss Healy dropped her voice so that only the three of them could hear. 'In that he writes them while she stands over him dictating the words.' Her naughty smile said that she was well aware of all of her aunt's many faults.

'I knew I sensed her acidic tones in last week's rant about hemlines. They should trail along the floor, apparently, irrespective of what the current court fashion for cutting them to show the slipper has to do with it. Personally, I cannot fathom what is quite so shocking about a glimpse of ankle— but then I am a great fan of fashion and not easily shocked. To my mind, if the royal family can cope with the sight of an ankle, so can Whittleston.'

'Were do you stand on the Great Ankle Debate, Miss Healy?' Sophie had never been any better at behaving properly than Isobel had.

'Well, my lady…'

'Call me Sophie, please, as I am still not used to my awful title any more than my husband is his because neither of us ever expected to have one.' With a toothy grin she pointed across the table. 'And this is Isobel.'

Miss Healy beamed. 'Well, *Sophie* and *Isobel*, I think the answer to that all rather depends on the ankle, as some should most definitely remained covered. And you must both call me Rose.'

'You make a valid point, *Rose*.' Isobel grabbed the bag of quilting patches and selected three as a token effort in case any of the benevolent sewing circle stalwarts tried to remind her that this month, they were supposed to be making eiderdowns for the needy. She was an accomplished needlewoman. On her paltry allowance, she had had to teach herself to be or go naked as her father rarely paid for her to visit the modiste. However, for all her handiness with a needle, eiderdowns did not hold her interest in the same way that a new gown did. 'I feel much the same when it comes to tight breeches. Some men can pull them off and some really can't. Lord Hockley—Sophie's husband, Rafe—for example, always wears his well. Whereas Mr Peabody the magistrate really doesn't have the figure or the knees for them.'

'Did you notice Mr Bunion's breeches at the assembly?' Sophie pulled a face as she threaded her needle. 'I swear that they looked a bit purple under the chandelier. I've never seen purple breeches on a grown man before.'

Isobel's nose automatically wrinkled at the mention of Mr Bunion. 'Perhaps he had them made to go with his garish lavender waistcoat?' There had been a peculiar musty scent clinging to that too.

'Oh, I quite liked that, but then I only glimpsed it from a distance. I noticed that you two both danced with him though, so was it unpleasant close up?'

Before Isobel could answer, their new friend Rose did. 'His vile waistcoat wasn't anywhere near as unpleasant as his breath.' And then she coloured as if she had accidentally offended one of them. 'That was mean of me, I apologise. I forgot myself.'

Isobel threw her head back and laughed, so loudly it earned her a scathing look from Mrs Outhwaite. 'Oh! Please don't as his breath was truly rancid the other night. It was so potent, I had to step outside in the fresh air afterwards to stop my head from spinning. He asked me for the waltz afterwards.' She made an unladylike gagging sound which made the other two giggle. 'Obviously, I had to pretend I was otherwise engaged.'

'Obviously.'

'And please, you are always safe to forget yourself around Sophie and I. In fact, we positively insist upon it as I dare say we will forget ourselves around you with predictable regularity. I, for one, would find it practically impossible to change the habit of a lifetime.'

'That is true.' Sophie jabbed her needle into

the two hexagonal quilting patches she had sand-wiched together. 'Isobel is *always* the one to say what everyone else is thinking but doesn't dare speak, and is famously unsubtle as I am sure you already realise. I saw the way she forced you and Ned onto the dance floor when clearly neither of you wanted to go there.' Her friend's mock chiding look made Rose smile. 'But she always means well.'

Unoffended, Isobel decided to use the change of topic to her advantage to test the waters. 'At least Ned doesn't smell like Mr Bunion! You have to concede that, Rose.'

'He smelled lovely.' She smiled. And a tad wistfully too. 'Not at all like a farmer usually smells.'

'That is because he is obsessively fastidious about bathing, isn't he, Sophie?'

'Indeed. He takes a bath in front of his fire every evening and goes through bars of soap like they are going out of fashion. Three this month according to Mrs Derwent the apothecary's wife.' Her friend chuckled. 'We all know each other's business here in Whittleston and, as you can doubtless tell, have to be creative to find some-thing decent to gossip about.'

Isobel dropped her voice to just above a whis-per. 'He got the blacksmith to make him a special bathtub a couple of years ago that the big brute can fit in with ease, but I was sworn to secrecy by the blacksmith's wife at the time, so please don't either of you let on to Ned that I told you. And whatever you do, make no mention of the fact that he has a standing order at the apothecary for expensive London bath salts. He would be mortified to think that we all thought him soft for enjoying a relaxing soak in the tub when he cultivates the image of a robust and hardy man who does all his ablutions from the frigid pump water in his yard. There is a deceptive softness beneath that huge, hard, rough-around-the-edges exterior, Rose. He might be a man of few words but still waters run deep.' That Isobel, for some inexplicable reason, now had a vivid and distracting image in her mind of Ned's big body naked and sluiced with water was suddenly unsettling in the extreme. Yet she couldn't shake it now that it was lodged there and worse, didn't particularly want to. 'He is one of the good ones.'

'I could tell that straightaway.' Their new friend smiled again, and Isobel took that as a very promising sign indeed. 'It is refreshing to meet a man who listens and asks questions rather than lectures. Another admirable trait Mr Bunion lacks. He talked incessantly about himself throughout our dance. The only thing he asked me was about the size and success of my father's farm.'

'That is because Mr Bunion, for all his gentlemanly aspirations and manners, lacks the funds to go with them and is on the lookout for a wife who he hopes does. Or so the solicitor's wife confided in me at the market last week.'

'Oh, good grief,' said Sophie with a shudder. 'Perish the thought. Who on earth would want to be Mrs Bunion? No right-minded woman would want to be named for ever after a deformity of the feet! Especially not to a man who also smells like them! However, I suppose you could forgive the dreadful surname if he wasn't so obnoxious, but he is. He has been fawning all over me and my husband since he arrived here.'

'He fawns a lot,' offered Isobel, cringing for effect to add more colour to the story. 'Yet seems oblivious how much it irritates people.'

Sophie also cringed. 'He is oblivious of how his extended presence irritates people too. We made the mistake of inviting him in for tea when he called last week and then had to suffer him for two whole hours after he outstayed his welcome.' Then, remembering their mission, she smiled at Rose. 'But enough about him. On the subject of tea, you must come to Hockley Hall tomorrow with Isobel here. I am in the midst of redecorating the place after the previous, and miserly, lord of the manor left it to go to rack and ruin, so she is helping me choose some new wallpapers. I would value your honest opinion too, especially now that you have forgotten yourself, as I've seen so many, I am overwhelmed by the responsibility of it all and I fear I do not have the eye an ancestral manor house deserves.'

'Why don't we make a day of it? We could then take Rose for a tour around the area to help her find her bearings?'

A tour that Isobel would make sure included the Parker farm.

Chapter Four

Ned squished the stunted, rotten tuber with his boot and concluded his brief but optimistic experiment with new potatoes was an unmitigated failure. At least this close to the river it was. He had read that the plants were thirsty, but clearly they weren't thirsty enough for the clay beneath his feet so he would have to rethink, yet again, what he did with the most useless field that he owned.

This particular field has always remained idle for as long as he could remember. The only plants that thrived here were the native reeds, wildflowers, buddleia bushes and marsh grasses and as pretty as that all was in the warmer months with the mighty Thames as its backdrop, they hardly constituted a viable crop. Even if the sheep did like to snack on the flowers.

He stabbed his spade in the ground and rested his arms on it to ponder whether to dig them all up now or leave them to die of their own accord when he spied Izzy in the distance. Unusually, this time she came with others, and it was Sophie who waved first while Archie, her childlike but fully grown brother-in-law bounded towards him with his puppy in tow. Then, if he was not mistaken, it appeared that Izzy had dragged Miss Healy along too.

Because of course she had!

Quite by coincidence, he'd wager, was how she would justify that unmistakable bit of meddling if he queried it—which he wouldn't. With Izzy, feigning ignorance was always more blissful than bashing your head against a brick wall trying to make her listen. Clearly she currently had it in her pretty but vexing noggin that he still required her services as a matchmaker, and clearly nothing he had to say about it would make a blind bit of difference.

The blasted woman was the bane of his life!

'Hello Ned!' As was his way, Sophie's brother-in-law Archie flung himself at him the second he was close enough to, hugging him before he remembered that men shook hands as a general rule. Ned didn't mind and slapped him heartily on the back. Archie was Archie and you couldn't help loving the irrepressible scamp even if he had no boundaries.

That exuberant greeting done, the unlikely Lord Archibald Peel then dashed after his dog, who was already rolling about the ground with his sire Falstaff, to join in the fray. 'Fred's got big.'

An understatement. At just five months he was two thirds the size of his enormous father and wasn't anywhere close to growing into his vast paws. He had a sneaking suspicion the mutt might even finish off bigger than Falstaff, but like him he was also as soft as butter on the inside despite his fierce-looking exterior. In his experience, the biggest always were the softest and Ned counted himself in that number. For all his grumbling and his incessant frustration at his inconvenient conscience, he had never been able to ignore a friend in need or a damsel in distress or even a wounded animal as the mad, hissing swan currently hidden in his barn while its broken wing healed was testament. That damn thing was going through his chicken feed at a rate of knots, and thanked Ned daily for his charity by charging at him with his tiny razor-sharp beak.

'My brother is still convinced you purposefully gave us a dog who is part wolf,' answered Archie, giggling as the excited dogs licked him. 'Or part werewolf.'

'There is no such thing—but just to be certain, you'd best keep him out of the way of a full moon.' He winked at Archie before turning back towards the approaching ladies with his blandest smile. 'What brings you three all the way out here?'

'We are showing Rose around the village.' It was Sophie who answered, acting as if that was all that they were doing.

'Then you've missed it as the village is a mile that way.' He pointed towards the mismatched cluster of thatched roofs to the west of them.

'No tour of the village is complete without a meander along the riverbank.' Izzy said that with all the innocence of a woman who firmly believed she was cleverer than him, when they both knew that it was a long riverbank and was just as pretty in the opposite direction where the view was unencumbered by his farm. 'Besides, it is such a lovely day that none of us wanted to be cooped up inside. Did we, Rose?'

So Miss Healy was apparently Rose to the vixen now was she? Izzy was nothing if not tenacious and if one door closed, she fetched herself a sledgehammer and smashed out a new opening to get inside anyway, irrespective of whether or not she was welcome.

'No indeed.' Miss Healy blushed prettily. 'I am so glad Isobel brought us to the river. Your views are stunning, Mr Parker.' She stared out at it as if she meant that. 'I've always loved the water, but alas there is none near me in Suffolk. You must find this vista very soothing.'

He did. To be fair to his most useless field, it had always held calming properties so he wasn't completely devastated that his spuds had failed.

'When we were children, Ned and I used to sit over there and watch the sun go down every summer.' Izzy smiled at him as she pointed to the wide, ancient tree stump on the highest part of the bank, and that smile warmed him with the same familiar intensity as her bewitching smiles always did. The menace's smiles were potent that way. 'Do you remember that, Ned?'

'Vaguely.'

Of course he remembered! He couldn't sit on that stump and watch the sunset nowadays without recollecting those halcyon days sat there beside her.

She had been a fanciful dreamer back then too. Always plotting and planning something daft and outlandish, whether that be sailing the seven seas in search of adventure or finding a foreign prince and living happily ever after in his castle to spite her disapproving father. Ideas too big and grand for Whittleston-on-the-Water, and too impractical for a shopkeeper's daughter who had been born there, yet she had woven such engrossing fantasies that he could have sat and listened to her spin them for hours.

That and watch the way the setting sun played with the various shades of gold in her hair.

'I recall you bothering me and my father incessantly back then.'

She had been the archetypal unloved waif and stray as far as her own family were concerned but had been loved unconditionally by his father in their stead. For Caleb Parker, Izzy was the daughter he never had. A kindred spirit, and she twisted him around his little finger in a way she never managed with her own sire. His had never understood why George Cartwright was so oblivious of his daughter's delightful existence that she was left entirely to her own devices growing up. The cold skinflint had certainly never invested in a nanny or a governess to feed her inquisitive mind and relied instead on his succession of servants to see to her basic needs. Beyond that, she had always been left to flounder and find her own amusement in between breakfast and dinner while he worked in his shop, and more often than not that had brought her here to them even though her father and his had always disliked one another.

But that fool George Cartwright's loss was

their gain, his father had always said when she turned up sad and lost, as she was his personal little ray of sunshine, and he needed his daily dose of it.

When she left, always somehow looking more lost than ever at the prospect of going to a home where she wasn't wanted, without fail his teasing father had always told Ned that he was looking forward to the day she became part of their family properly—as his daughter-in-law. He was so convinced of that he would never hear otherwise when his only son assured him that it was never going to happen—for so many reasons he couldn't even begin to count them. The biggest of which was Izzy's lifelong desire to escape Whittleston. Just like his faceless mother had, Izzy thought this place a prison and he would not attempt to be anyone's gaoler. That was a hiding to nothing if ever there was one. Some things were meant to run free and others were meant to stay put. Ned was hopelessly in love with this land that she hated. Or hopelessly chained to it. Either way, he was going nowhere.

'You both just need to do some growing up first' was always his father's stock response whenever Ned reminded him that oil and water never mixed, and that was always accompanied by a knowing wink. 'But I know the pair of you will get there in the end.' His father had always been a hopeless, impractical dreamer in that respect—exactly like Izzy. Which probably explained why they had always got on so well.

'What's happened to your potatoes?' Miss Healy's voice snapped him out of his pointless reverie.

'Rot or blight or likely both.' He shrugged. 'Either way they don't like clay and I'll confess I'm a novice when it comes to potatoes. Hence I only planted this small square of them.'

'Because he is overly cautious and averse to risk.' Izzy tossed in that comment as if were an insult. 'He likes to do everything at the excruciating pace of a tortoise. A big, lumbering, irritating, cogitating, overthinking tortoise.'

'According to Aesop, the tortoise always wins in the end.' He shot her a bored but unrepentant look, because he was the tortoise, Izzy was the hare. 'You should give thinking a go one of these days.' She responded by poking her tongue out at him.

Miss Healy laughed then frowned at his failed crop. 'Did you plant them on straw?'

'Several inches of the stuff and I even dug the life out of the trench and mulched it with more a week before I planted them to break up the soil.'

To his surprise, she crouched down and

scooped up a handful of his claggy soil and squeezed it in her palm. 'It does hold a lot of water. How deep did you plant them?' She tossed the mud and began to examine one of the spindly stems that remained.

'About ten inches.'

She sat back on her heels. 'If you are intent on planting this land with potatoes, I would halve that next time and pile more dirt above as the stem begins to grow. Force the plant like rhubarb to lift it away from the soggiest clay.' A suggestion which made perfect sense now that he heard it but which hadn't occurred to him until this precise moment.

'That is useful advice, Miss Healy, thank you.'

'It is not so much advice, Mr Parker, as another novice's best guess, as I've no experience of potatoes either. But as most of the Suffolk potato farmers seem to use that method, it might be worth a try. I certainly wouldn't risk digging up all of your pretty meadow here on the back of it. It would be a shame to ruin your beautiful sunsets with an ugly, failed potato crop.'

Always one to make something out of nothing, Izzy was beaming at the exchange. 'It must be refreshing, Ned, to be able to talk about farming with someone who shares your passion for it.'

He suppressed the urge to roll his eyes as he

knew, to her mind, she was being subtle and was blissfully unaware that she had always used a mallet to crack a walnut. Because she couldn't help herself, she then turned to Miss Healy.

'And you are right, Miss Healy, Ned's land here by the river is stunning. Thanks to Constable and his lauded *Hay Wain*, everyone always goes on and on about the beauty of Suffolk but in my humble opinion nothing is prettier than the banks of this estuary.' As she swept her arm out to encompass it, the sun caught the gold in her curls and set them shimmering and he found himself hoping that she meant the compliment. Because if she meant it, then surely she couldn't bear to leave it for ever? *Good grief, he was an idiot sometimes!* When Izzy left, he sincerely doubted she would ever look back, let alone come back to visit.

'We are so convenient to London here too, Rose.' She pointed upriver. 'A mere two hours by road and you are in Bond Street and its even less if you go via the river. But obviously, you'd need to live by the river, like Ned here, to justify buying a boat.'

'Do you own a boat, Mr Parker?' Miss Healy seemed impressed at the prospect while blessedly oblivious to the sales pitch her new best friend was giving her on his behalf.

'I don't—and have no plans to purchase one.' He added that last bit specifically for Izzy and for good measure, glared at her to let her know that he was on to her. 'It takes a skilled sailor to navigate the currents of the estuary—not a farmer.' Boats and shopping indeed! Trust her to try to impress Miss Healy on his behalf with things he put no stock in. 'You can count the number of times I've been on a boat on one hand.'

'At least you have had the pleasure, Mr Parker.' Miss Healy glanced wistfully at the busy waterway again, and the merchant ship floating past on its lazy journey to the city docks. 'My brother often claims that there is nothing more invigorating than the feel of the salty breeze against your skin as you fly across the water. Sadly, I have never experienced that joy.'

'Then we must remedy that soon.' Sophie pointed to one of the barges hugging the edge of the shore. 'We shall hire a Thames barge for an afternoon or find a wherryman to take us across the river to Kent. Gravesend is a nice place to visit.' She pointed towards it across the wide stretch of water to allow Miss Healy to get her bearings. 'Especially on a sunny day. Pocahontas is buried there.' Alongside the several thousand plague victims who had given Gravesend its cheerful name.

'Oh, that would be lovely!' Miss Healy beamed at the suggestion. 'I have never been to Kent either, so it will be a true voyage of discovery. Although to be fair, anywhere out of Suffolk feels like an adventure to me. I've not been to many places at all. Sadly. But such is the lot of a farming family. There is always some chore or another that ties you to a land—as I am sure you can confirm, Mr Parker.'

He nodded, and because he couldn't resist a dig at his tormentor, added, 'Some of us can only dream of having nothing to do because we have to work for our living.'

'Which Ned does by working all the hours God sends, never mind that he could well afford to hire some help to ease his load and allow him to have a life outside of his fields. Is your father the same, Rose?' Ignoring his pithy response, Izzy seemed determined to try and find as many things that he and Miss Healy had in common, as if those similarities alone proved that they were destined to be together like she claimed.

'He used to be until my mother put her foot down several years ago after he collapsed from exhaustion. She raged that she wasn't keen on being a young widow left to raise her children alone and was convinced Papa's obsession with doing everything himself was sending him to an early grave. Thankfully he listened before too much damage was done, hired several men to assist him and the farm went from strength to strength too on the back of it. Many hands, it turned out, do make light work exactly as the old proverb says. Papa still likes to get his hands dirty, but he no longer works from dawn to dusk and even has the time for hobbies nowadays too.'

'Thank goodness your father had a sensible wife to listen to and that her sage advice also proved to be so fruitful.' If that barbed comment wasn't unsubtle enough when Izzy had been nagging him for years to do the same, she couldn't help herself from embellishing it further. 'Ned is still a bachelor—without a sweetheart in sight— because he's always too busy working his land.'

'All work and no play apparently makes Jack a dull boy.' Miss Healy smiled shyly.

'That is exactly what I keep telling him! Being single—' The invisible walnut mallet came down again with a vengeance. '—Ned currently does not have the obligation to listen to anyone.' Izzy shook her head at Miss Healy in an unspoken that-man-needs-a-wife kind of way before she tried to sell him to her some more. 'But his stubborn determination to work himself to death as his dear father did aside, one must give all credit to him, for he has achieved wonders with this land since he inherited it. Enough to have been able to afford to buy it outright and completely modernise everything in just nine short years. It is a very different farm to the one he grew up on, I can tell you, and that is all down to Ned. Nobody could fault his work ethic or his dedication to his responsibilities.'

Now she was complimenting him! When she never did anything but bother him usually. He would have blinked in shock, but his mortified internal cringing prevented him from doing anything other than stand rigidly still. The only part of him that could move was his toes which were curling inside his work boots. He was going to kill her when he got her alone. Wring her swan-like neck until her beautiful cornflower-blue eyes bulged out of their perfect almond-shaped sockets!

'To do so much on your own in such a short space of time does indeed deserve credit. Farming is not for the faint-hearted.' Miss Healy smiled his way and distracted him from committing murder. It was a nice smile. Genuine and friendly but nowhere near as impactful as her vexing companion's had always been—more was the pity. Izzy's smile, or her clever wit or her sunny presence always held the power to dilute his frequent desire to strangle her. Worse, he missed that smile if he didn't see it and if she left it too long between her unwelcome visits, he began to pine for it. He had decided long ago not to analyse why that was.

After all, self-preservation was always preferable to self-discovery and ignorance was supposed to be bliss. Especially when her destiny lay far away from this village and his responsibilities rooted him here.

Thankfully, Miss Healy's curiosity once again dragged his mind away from Izzy. 'What modernisations have you done?' She was smiling again, and he tried his darndest to focus on it and force himself to enjoy it.

'Well, I…'

'What hasn't he done? Perhaps, in view of your mutual interests in agriculture, you would prefer to see them rather than just hear about them?' Izzy linked her arm through Miss Healy's before she could answer as if that answer was a fait accompli. 'I am sure Ned will not mind. In fact…' She glanced his way as if butter would not melt in her meddling mouth. 'I am sure he would enjoy accompanying us on the tour as he can explain his changes far better than I can, and I can tell that he already values your unique insight. What he has done to the house is lovely too—if one excuses the spartan tastes of a bachelor. If ever a house needed the homely touch of a woman, it is his...' She practically marched Miss Healy off as she listed his virtues.

Reluctantly, and now completely self-conscious and irritated, Ned now had no choice but to trail after the minx as she took it upon herself to show her new best friend Rose his land while no doubt still unsubtly lamenting his lonely, wifeless existence.

Being Izzy, and therefore a magnet to all males irrespective of whether they were man or beast, Archie, Falstaff and Fred followed behind in obvious and devoted admiration as if she were the Pied Piper of Hamlyn. All hoping for a smile or a word or the beguiling brush of her manipulative fingers to make their day complete.

In rebellion, because that was the only weapon he currently had to combat the menace, Ned dawdled back as far as he could so that he didn't have to listen to her nonsense. So far back it made Sophie stop and wait for him to catch up.

'I feel that I am missing something here.' Never one to either mince her words or fail to get to the crux of the matter, she gestured to the two ladies headed towards his house with a jerk of her head. 'But suspect you aren't similarly afflicted, just as I also suspect that, whatever it is that Isobel is up to, you aren't particularly happy about it.'

Ned huffed out a sigh of frustration. 'She's got it into her thick head that me and Miss Healy are made for one another, and she refuses to be swayed from that path.'

Sophie chuckled. 'That explains why she was so keen that we all take a stroll along the river-bank this afternoon, and why she forced the pair of you to dance at the assembly.' At his put-upon expression, she shrugged. 'As annoying as that likely is, at least she's chosen a decent candidate for you. Aside from the inescapable fact that the pair of you do have a great deal in common, Rose is rather lovely—or do you not think so?'

'She's nice enough but that is by the by.' It was impossible to contemplate Rose with the exasperating Izzy nearby. No matter how lovely her smiles or how much they had in common. 'I've already told the hoyden that I'm not interested in her services as a matchmaker! Told her and re-iterated it, so I don't appreciate her carrying on behaving as if she's been appointed mine regard-less.' Trust Izzy not to listen to a damn thing he said! 'She's being so blatant about it too, it's em-barrassing. She couldn't have hammered home my bachelor status hard enough with her "not a single sweetheart on the horizon" quip and now she's waxing lyrical about my property as if Miss Healy is a prospective buyer for both it—and me.'

'If it's any consolation, I don't think Rose has worked out that that is Isobel's motive. If she did, I think she would run a mile—'

Ned stopped dead, affronted. 'Well, thank you very much for that gushing endorsement!' He wasn't that bad a catch, surely? Despite his reluctance to be caught like this. 'Some friend you are.'

'Not running a mile from *you*, idiot, more the matchmaking.' Sophie's apologetic smile turned into a more calculating version. 'But your reaction does beg the question that if you are offended by the idea that Rose wouldn't be interested, which you clearly are, then maybe Isobel is doing you a favour in piquing the lady's interest on your behalf?'

'I'm not a prize bull up for auction.'

'Is that your only objection—or is there some other which Isobel is unaware of?' She gazed toward the menace and then back at him frowning. 'Is there a chance you are not interested in Rose—or any other woman for that matter—because your interest lies *elsewhere*?' Two expressive brows rose in challenge as her finger flicked to Izzy. 'You do seem to watch her often.'

'Izzy!' He scoffed at that ridiculous implication. 'Aside from the fact that you are barking up the wrong tree entirely with that asinine theory.' For good measure he scoffed some more even though something about the accusation was making his mind whir in panic and his heartbeat ratchet up to nineteen to the dozen. He knew he was prone to watch her—but was he so prone he did it enough for others to notice? 'I am more than capable of finding my own woman without anyone's help, thank you very much.'

'Are you?' Instead of seeing things from his point of view, Sophie snorted in derision. 'Because you have such a proven track record with the ladies, Ned. So much of one that the entire village was only gossiping about one of your legendary romantic liaisons…well…never actually.' She quirked one brow in challenge. 'When, precisely, was the last time you indulged in one?'

He'd walked headlong into that pothole, he supposed, and with entirely the wrong person. Lady Sophie Peel—*née* Gilbert—was one of the few people who knew him well enough to spot a lie fifty paces. 'It wouldn't be decent to say.'

It would also be humiliating to admit to as it had been a long time since he had indulged. Practically a lifetime, or at least that's what it felt like. He tried not to count the days, months and years since his last dalliance with a woman but was only too aware of the number nevertheless. Nine years was a depressing eternity to go without. Buried so far in his past it would be a wonder if he still remembered what to do with one between the sheets.

'A convenient excuse to avoid the question if ever there was one, when I've known you for a decade and, unlike the rest of the village, know that you stopped doing *odd jobs* for that colonel's wife the same January the militia left Whittleston.' There had never been any flies on Sophie. She was right too, damn her, because that also coincided with the same January when his entire world had collapsed. And, by worrying coincidence, the same winter that he had practically caught Izzy in flagrante with a handsome army officer in the churchyard.

He hadn't found the time for women after that.

He'd been too busy being angry at everything and struggling to survive, and by the time he had ceased struggling and his anger had abated, he had focussed all his energies into ensuring that he never had to struggle ever again. Either way, he had lost the habit and likely his former confidence with the opposite sex with it.

'Perhaps it is time to get back in the saddle again, Ned?' Sophie's smile was tinged with both pity and understanding. 'And I say that as someone who withdrew from the prospect of love for more years than was healthy.'

'I'll get back on it when I'm good and ready.'

'I am sure that you will.' She didn't sound convinced. Likely because he didn't fully believe it himself. He had too much work to do and the need to do it consumed him in a manner that wasn't healthy either. 'But sometimes we all need a helping hand, Ned. I know I certainly did. It took a bit of misplaced jealousy to first realise I had feelings for Rafe. Misplaced jealousy which Isobel masterfully orchestrated, so as much as I revolted against her helping hand to begin with, I shall remain grateful for it to my end. Do bear that in mind while you are contemplating what to do about that saddle.'

She linked her arm through his and tugged him to follow the others. 'In the meantime, is there really any harm in going along with it just a little bit? Even if it is to gently ease yourself back onto that daunting saddle. Besides, what if she is right and Rose is the one? She was right about me and Rafe after all. Rose is only here in Whittleston for the summer, and you might miss your chance with her if you drag your feet. And if she isn't the one...' Worryingly, Sophie's gaze flicked briefly towards Izzy again, perplexed. 'She'll go, so you have nothing to lose while still regaining some of your old confidence.' Then she grinned. 'And, of course, the added bonus is that it will get Isobel off your back too as she can hardly interfere further if you are doing what she wants.'

'Are you sure we are talking about the same Izzy? If you give that woman an inch, she takes a blasted mile.'

'Maybe—but it will make her happy, Ned. We both know that that sunny smile and devil-may-care attitude hides a miserable home life that she is always desperate to distract herself from. Have you noticed she's not quite herself of late?'

'No.' Ned always tried his best not to notice her. But, of course, he could never resist a damsel in distress. Especially if that damsel was Izzy. 'In what way is she not herself?'

'It is hard to pinpoint beyond a feeling because she is so good at hiding it, but she seems a little lost to me. Her smiles aren't quite as convincing since Cartwright's closed, and she seems to be working doubly hard to distract herself from whatever is going on at home. Aunt Jemima thinks relations between Isobel and her horrid father have somehow deteriorated further.'

'But he's hardly ever home nowadays to bother her.' A state of affairs he had assumed Izzy would be cock-a-hoop about. She had seemed thrilled to bits when her father began to spend more and more of his week focussing on his new, bigger shop fifty miles away in Chelmsford because, as he remembered her saying vividly at the time, that was too many miles to travel back and forth in a day so she would be relieved the chore of seeing his miserable face over breakfast.

'Yet she is home constantly. Rattling around that house with nothing of import to do and nobody to talk to except the latest live-in maid who always seem to change like the weather because he pays them such a pittance. Haven't you noticed how she is going out of her way to fill her time lately?'

Ned shook his head, suddenly uncomfortable that he hadn't given much thought to why Izzy had upped her unannounced visits to his from two a week to three after Cartwright's closed its doors. Or why she stayed longer, even when he abandoned her to work, simply to play with Falstaff.

Sophie exhaled, clearly troubled. 'I haven't found a way to broach the subject with her yet, because I know she'll deny that there is anything amiss and only increase her efforts to behave as if that is the case out of her defiant pride, but she has definitely lost her sparkle since Christmas and I am worried about her.' And now, as much as he really didn't want to be, so was he. 'That is why I would urge you to let her help you, Ned, even if that help is unwanted and ultimately pointless. Be a friend to her in her hour of need. For me—please—and for Isobel. You never know, the experience might turn out be beneficial for the pair of you.'

Fiorella Mould

Chapter Five

Isobel always awoke with a spring in her step on market days. She was always up with the lark on a Tuesday, Thursday and a Saturday as there were a plethora of people bustling about the village to chat to and usually something to do afterwards, even if it was only carrying the older ladies' shopping home for them. Her bi-weekly teas at Mrs Fitzherbert's followed by her customary stroll to Ned's to bother him and the Friday sewing circle gave her excuses to not to stay at home on the other days. Saturdays were, of course, now the best days of all as alongside the arrival of the post coach and the market, the first in every month was always accompanied by the local assembly.

Sundays, however, had become her least favourite day as that was the only one in the week nowadays where she was guaranteed to have to suffer the insufferable presence of her father.

He was a stickler for attending church—not because he was a particularly God-fearing man but because he liked to remind the rest of the congregation how far he had risen in the world since he abandoned his birthplace for pastures new. From the owner of one humble, rented shop here in Whittleston-on the-Water, he now boasted the biggest one in the county after going into partnership with her sainted brother. The freshly opened Cartwrights' Emporium in Essex's capital, Chelmsford, part funded by her brother's well-to-do in-laws, was allegedly spread over three floors and people already apparently travelled from far and wide to shop there rather than inconvenience themselves with the long journey to London. Or so her father bragged to anyone in the churchyard who would listen. She hadn't been invited to see it yet. Neither had she ever been invited to visit her sainted brother's apparently fancy house close to it which he had lived in for the last eight years, so she held out little hope she would be welcomed to Chelmsford anytime soon.

Her brother resided with his impeccably behaved and terminally pregnant wife and three similarly idolised sons. Which gave her prickly father plenty of better excuses to rarely bother to come home between Mondays and Saturdays while he concentrated on his new business.

While that suited her just fine, because frankly the less time she spent with the old curmudgeon the better, it also made the dreaded Sundays particularly fractious. It meant that all his frustrations with his disappointing and disastrously still-unwed daughter were often aired in one big lump all on the one day. Usually over breakfast. It was impossible to predict whether or not a particular Sunday was Lecture Sunday or whether it was going to be one of the days during which he ignored her completely instead. He had always blown hot and cold with no rhyme nor reason, that was nothing new, but now that it was concentrated in one chunk it felt somehow worse than it ever had. That constant feeling of walking over the eggshells of uncertainty until she knew which way the wind blew was most unsettling. It was also exhausting and sucked all the joy from her usually joyous soul.

That alone was as good a reason as any to make sure she had escaped the house well before he had risen so that she could avoid him until they collided at the service.

The promise of a pretty spring sunrise was another splendid reason to leave her bed behind. After being reminded of the stunning sunsets on Ned's wild little stretch beside the river the other day, she was keen to watch one. She had always loved all his cheery meadow flowers too and since spring had most definitely sprung, her feet decided that was precisely where they were going to take her the moment she silently closed her father's front door.

The wrong side of six, the village was deserted as she wandered through it. The dawn silence only marred by the occasional sounds of activity within the dwellings she passed. As much as she loathed her current dull lot in life, the familiar noises she had grown up with still had the power to soothe her soul. The blacksmith pumping his bellows. The neighing of the horses who had stayed overnight at the inn and were impatient for their morning oats. The rhythmic ticking of the clock that dominated the front façade of the shops facing the market square which could never be heard during the bustle of the day when the sounds of other people silenced it. The only establishment already open for business was the bakery, and because the baker had been working already for many hours, the mouth-watering scent of warm, fresh bread and pastries reminded her tummy it was as empty as Cartwright's former shop window beside it.

On a whim, and because staring into that dusty window from her not so distant past still depressed her too much, she bought a loaf and a pork pie to graze upon while she watched the sun awaken over the Thames, then quickened her pace to the riverbank to ensure that she didn't miss it.

There were plenty of suitable places to sit and marvel in the morning, but the spot they used to share as children beckoned like a siren's song, so she did not linger on Ned's pasture despite the lure of the early meadow flowers poking their colourful heads through the morning mist, or the friendly new lambs frolicking amongst them.

As soon as she sunk down onto the old tree stump, she knew she had been right to come here. Not only did this place provide no reminders of her own oppressive home, the view was outstanding. The beauty of the sun's golden rays snaking across the tranquil river and bathing her little corner of the earth in light fair took her breath away.

Isobel happily lost herself in the spectacle, tilting her face so that the sunrise warmed her skin, and by default, buoyed her typical flattened Sunday morning mood too.

At least temporarily.

She would still have to sit beside her nit-picking sire during the church service and while away the hours in the house afterwards while she prayed for him to leave it.

'I see someone's avoiding her father.'

Ned's voice so close behind her made her jump. She had neither heard his approach nor sensed him or his dog, and surprise made her acknowledge the truth for once rather than brush it away as if she was unbothered by it. 'He gets more tiresome with each passing year.' She made a fuss of Falstaff as she said this prevent Ned from witnessing the despondency in her eyes at that depressing truth.

He huffed his sympathy rather than ask anything more as he, better than any, understood her situation.

From her earliest memories, there had always been a gulf between her and her father. She accepted it for what it was now without trying to rationalise it or figure out why, but as a child his coldness and distance interspersed with periods of unpredictable rage had weighed on her mind. Back then, she had done everything she could think of to change the cloying timbre of that relationship, all to no avail, and had poured out all her worries to Ned and his father almost weekly.

Back then, the Parker farm had been both her sanctuary and her solace. A place of fun, friendship and the sense of family which she received nowhere else. Caleb Parker had always been more father to her than her own had been, and Ned had always been so much more than a sibling. Despite the two years of difference in their ages, he had always been both her big brother and her best friend.

She supposed that they were still friends nowadays—after a fashion—but it wasn't the same. The strong bonds which had bound them together as children had waned in the intervening years. A great deal of that was his fault. After his father died ten days before the flood came, Ned had pushed her away along with everyone else to fester in his grief and financial despair. He barely acknowledged her existence for two whole years no matter how much she tried to force her way back into his life. Then he had buried himself in so much work ever since that Isobel had gone from being his best friend to an irritation he no longer had the time, nor the patience, for.

But she was honest enough with herself to know that her own behaviour had played a part in that too. Exactly like her father, Ned had disapproved of her flirty nature from the second her figure had begun to develop, while she had seen that as her ticket out of Whittleston and her father's soulless house. Unlike her father, Ned's issues with her behaviour came not from the fact that she flirted without much discernment, more that she was prepared to stop at nothing to convince a gentleman he should sweep her away from her miserable home life.

From her first shameful mistake, she could sense his silent disapproval. As if he too despaired of both her and her reliably poor choices and had now washed his hands of it all—exactly like her father had—except he never mentioned it. Somehow that was worse because she had no idea what he thought about it, and she tied herself in knots worrying about it.

Unfortunately, and despite the fact he did little to disguise that he only tolerated her these days, she hadn't found the same fortitude to be able to wash her hands of Ned. She still cared for the obnoxious, big oaf as much as she always had and still, much to her chagrin, craved his approval. And his counsel. And his dratted company for that matter too. He had always been her one constant. Her north star—especially when she was struggling to find her way through the quagmire as she was now.

Which probably explained why she had been pulled here today, pathetically trying to soak in every echo of their past to make herself feel better about her present. A present which seemed to only get worse with each passing year.

Despite all her best efforts to the contrary, her life hadn't gone to plan at all. She was supposed to be long gone from Whittleston-on-the-Water by now. Adored by someone who appreciated her and wanted her in his life. Have her own house. Her own home. Her own family to fill her days with meaning and purpose, love and respect, yet those things seemed to be further out of her grasp now than they ever had.

Originally, she had intended to be married at sixteen simply to be shot of it all, not stuck here trapped under her father's thumb for what now felt like an eternity. However, and thanks to her own stupidity, that hadn't happened and because she was too desperate to have learned from that first fateful mistake, she had repeated it too many times. Not always with the same reckless abandon as she had displayed with that untrustworthy officer who had allowed her to think he intended to put a ring on her finger, but always with the same disappointing outcome. The sad fact was that men she wanted to desperately run away with always wanted her—that was never a problem—just never in the for ever sense. Something about her sent the good ones running for the hills almost as soon as they met her and allowed the opportunists to take advantage before she realised what they were. Whichever category they fell into, however, rejection was all she had ever secured from the lot of them.

Which now left her apparently doomed to a life of spinsterhood and trapped. As lost today as she had been as that needy a little girl in constant search of affection and more of a disappointment to her father than she had ever been.

'When is the bastard going to find himself a church in Chelmsford and leave us all in blessed peace?' It was a typical gruff and unvarnished Ned thing to say. 'Or does he keep coming back to spite us because he knows that's what most of the villagers are willing the sanctimonious old sod to do?' He had never minced his words with her and, oddly, she had always liked that. Ned treated her like an equal because to him her pretty petticoats and well-practised allurements were invisible.

'If he did that, then he wouldn't be able to re-cite his favourite litany of all of my many mis-deeds since time immemorial.' Dear Papa did like to store them up to spring on her unawares and never differentiated between the things she had actually done and those he had conjured out of thin air. She had long given up trying to defend herself against the injustice of half of his griev-ances as that was pointless. If he was in the mood for battle, she was always guilty as charged, no matter how outlandish the charge was. 'I suspect, no matter how much he tells himself that he is doing his duty as a father until he can be shot of me, that the blistering lectures are his favourite aspect of parenting. He lives simply to verbally knock me down.'

Although, since he had abandoned her for Chelmsford, the tone of those unpredictable lectures seemed to have changed in the last few months. He still accused her of all manner of things which had no basis in fact—that wasn't new—and rued the day she had been born, but his threats to disown her had increased tenfold. His favourite new mantra was that it was only a matter of time before categoric proof that she was as sullied as he suspected found his ears, and then he could finally be shot of her. Finding that proof seemed to be the main reason for him coming here nowadays, and if he dug in the right places, Isobel wasn't convinced he wouldn't find it. He made no secret of the fact that he used his weekly visit to church to listen out for any whiff of gossip which included her. Then used that, and the maid's detailed weekly report of her precise comings and goings, to emphasise why she had reached the end of his rope now that he was finally going up in the world. As it was all her fault that no man wanted to put a ring on her finger, he was adamant that he should hardly be expected to fund her life in perpetuity.

More troubling, now that everything he held dear was miles away, he had also made it plain that he resented the expense of the house he was forced to keep here. As he was adamant he didn't want her anywhere near Chelmsford to sully his or her sainted brother's good name there, it increasingly felt as though her time beneath his roof—or any roof for that matter—was now limited.

Then what?

With nothing better than homelessness on the horizon, that now unsettled her most of all.

'I even think he writes his lectures down to practise in the carriage on the way home, as they have that same considered *sermon* feel to them. Last Sunday, he said that he suspected the only reason I was still unwed and was likely to remain so was because everyone knew that my behaviour has always "hovered on the hazardous brink of harlotry."' Isobel snorted as if that was water off a duck's back, still hurt by that cutting insult despite knowing that it wasn't completely undeserved.

She might be well shy of a harlot, but thanks to some shameful stupidity and her poor judge of a man's character, she was no blushing virgin either. Ned undoubtedly also knew that she was, as her father so often accused, soiled goods too, as he had once managed to be at the wrong place at the wrong time when she had allowed that first, deceitful officer to take liberties, but he still winced at the harshness of the comment in solidarity.

'Oh, Izzy.'

Because she couldn't cope with his sympathy, she brushed that off too in case she did the unthinkable and cried at the awful truth of that insult. 'That sort of alliteration never comes off the cuff, and I did not know that *harlotry* was even a word until he uttered it, so I know he had to look it up. Word smithery—like fatherhood— has never been his forte.'

Ned's eyes darkened with anger on her behalf, and she consoled herself that, despite hiding it well most of the time, he did still care for her. Perhaps not as much as he once had, but she would treasure the loyal sentiment regardless. 'That is an unconscionable thing for a father to say to his daughter.'

'To him, I have always been unconscionable.' She shrugged off that sad fact too. 'I wouldn't mind—but I haven't put a foot wrong in for ever, thanks to the dismal lack of opportunities currently on offer in dreary Whittleston for me here to misbehave.' That depressing truth aside, navigating the fine line between propriety and her own defiant pride had always proved impossible and she held out little hope that she wouldn't use up the last few inches of her father's rope before she found a husband to free herself from him. 'I am starting to lose faith that I will ever escape Whittleston.'

Rather than roll his eyes or say something sarcastic about how irritating she was, he huffed out another sigh and sat beside her. 'You are being unfair to Whittleston by lumping it in the same boat as your father. It isn't the village that has always made your life here difficult—it is him. I reckon you'd come to love this place again if he wasn't in it.'

'Perhaps—' Except her father did make one valid point. Her reputation did precede her here in Whittleston and village gossip was so rife newcomers always heard all about it if they stayed around long enough. Lately, and at her most uncharacteristically melancholic, she had wondered if a fresh start somewhere new might help wipe her somewhat smudged slate clean. It would be freeing not to be disappointing, tainted, flighty Isobel for a change. In a place where nobody knew her, she could redo things and be the respectable woman she wished she was. She wasn't without skills and might be able to find a position in a fancy shop or some such if she stiffened her spine and finally found the courage to tell her oppressive father, and his suffocating house, they could go to hell.

'I am bored of every day being the same.' So bored with it, it was becoming an effort some days to bury her head in the sand or maintain her customary optimism. As that admission left her feeling more exposed than she was comfortable being, she nudged him as she swiftly shifted the subject. 'What I need is the male equivalent of Miss Rose Healy to miraculously decide to spend the summer in Whittleston-on-the-Water. I need someone attractive, kind and intelligent who I have heaps in common with...'

Instead of clamming up and bristling, Ned shook his head while enough of a smile played on his lips that she could see it clear as the dawning day beneath his dense beard. 'You never miss an opportunity, do you, Izzy?'

'You have to grab them as they happen and hope for the best, as you never know when the next one is coming—or if it's coming at all—especially here in dull, old Whittleston where nothing ever happens. Rose is an opportunity, Ned.'

He was quiet for the longest time, staring out at the river with an odd expression on his face. Eventually he spoke but still did not look at her.

'If I did agree to go along with your hare-brained scheme, we would need to set some boundaries.'

It took all of Isobel's will to stop her jaw from gaping. 'Of course. Whatever you want.'

He turned and his eyes narrowed as they bored into hers. 'I mean it, Izzy. Strict boundaries, which if you cross, mean that I'll withdraw from your nonsense completely. I'm not going to be made either a laughingstock or pushed into doing something I do not want to do before I am good and ready to do it.' She had to bite her tongue to not say that they would both be ancient by then, because even with caveats, this was still a momentous and uncharacteristic step for Ned. 'I'll be honest up front and say that I currently have no feelings for Miss Healy beyond the fact that I like the woman—but I'm prepared to make a bit of an effort to get to know her better on the proviso that you stop behaving like a trip up the aisle is inevitable. I want no more talk of rose petals and wedding cake in my future.'

Stunned at that concession, she nodded. 'I understand. You want to dip your toe in the water first before you commit to the cause wholeheartedly.' As he did with everything. 'I can help with that, in fact, I think Rose would prefer a slow...' He placed his finger over her lips, and they seemed to blossom into life beneath it.

'I'm prepared to concede that I am out of practice with all the social niceties, and I'll also admit that I'm a bit sick of *being* an island and as bored with every day being the same as you are. To that end, I am prepared to allow you to help me fix those things. However, I am not prepared for you to interfere in any way with any relationship which may or *may not* develop between me and Miss Healy. Do you understand those boundaries?' Because his finger was still on her lips and was playing havoc with her nerve endings, she nodded.

'I want none of your nonsense, Izzy. No quips about how I need a wife or gushing speeches about my land or work ethic or character to try and sway her mind to your cause. I don't want to be forced onto the dance floor or for you to engineer situations to thrust us together alone. And I especially want no matchmaking. None whatsoever.' He withdrew his finger, but it did not help one jot because she could still feel his unsettling touch everywhere. 'Your only two jobs are to make me less awkward in social situations and to encourage me to engage with them. Are we clear on that?'

'Crystal clear.'

'Good.' He smiled then snatched up the basket with the same grin he used to bestow upon her when they were children. 'In return, if you want to watch my sunrise, you have to share your breakfast as penance for trespassing on my land. Because once again my bread is stale and I'm starving.'

Chapter Six

'I knew I was going to regret agreeing to this.' Izzy was waiting for him when he took his mid-day break the next day and, bless her kind and generous if somewhat irritating heart, she had been to the baker's shop. There was a fresh loaf, a pot of steaming tea, some sticky buns and his sturdy kitchen table was already set for two. 'I take it your father has gone away again?'

'Yes, and good riddance to him. Chelmsford is welcome to the sourpuss, and I am as free as a bird for the next six days.'

'Hence you are here, bothering me.'

Her smile was suddenly lit with excitement. 'I am here, as you well know, so that we can begin transforming you from a rough-around-the-edges, grumpy, single farmer into a charming gentleman in fit state for courting.' She looked him up and down with a comic frown. 'And good gracious, it is going to take some work. But first, we must create our battle plan, so sit.'

With much trepidation he did while he watched her reach for a stack of papers from her basket. 'Am I going to school, Izzy?' Because that hadn't been part of this hastily agreed deal. He was doing this to help the minx regain her sparkle, not give himself more tedious work to do.

'We are going to create a schedule, silly. Of upcoming social events which you must be present for.'

'The next assembly isn't for three weeks. I think I can remember that. In fact, as much as I despise them, I've never missed one yet. More's the pity.'

'There are more opportunities to mix with people than just the assembly, Ned. I am going to make a list and stick it somewhere prominent so that you know exactly where you need to be and at what time.' She held up a blank sheet of foolscap and a pen. 'That will be your battle plan.'

'Oh, good grief.' As much as that prospect pained him, Ned was pleased to see that this futile project was making her happy. She had an unmistakable glow about her today that hadn't been there yesterday. Yet he was still curious about yesterday and still furious that her awful father had called her a harlot the week before. A cruel, unforgivable, and undeserved jibe which had clearly cut her to the quick and which Ned still wasn't convinced he should have given the bastard a piece of his mind over. While she made neat little piles of whatever nonsense she thought he needed to take part in, he helped himself to the bread and tried to inject some nonchalance into the question he was desperate to ask. 'So… was this week's fatherly lecture as blistering as the last?'

'Not at all—thank goodness.' She seemed relieved by that. Too relieved for someone who was unbothered about the situation. 'Yesterday was one of our customary Silent Sundays where we managed to avoid one another like the plague for the duration. The misery guts spent the afternoon in his study scrutinizing the household accounts to check that I haven't been frittering away the measly allowance he expects me to live on, and his silly new yellow curricle left before three without him bothering to say goodbye. I danced a jig and the rest of my Sabbath was, as I am sure you can imagine, utter bliss.'

She sighed smiling as if it had been but for all her shrugs and proud, blasé mockery of her situation, her lovely eyes were still tinged with some of the sadness he had witnessed in them yesterday as she had recalled the insulting way her bullying father had spoken to her.

And there was no doubting George Cartwright was a bully. He might never have raised a hand to his daughter, but in some ways the mental torture he always put her through was so much worse as it was relentless. Her father had always made it his life's work to dull his daughter's natural sparkle—and Sophie was right. Izzy's wasn't half as bright as it usually was, and he would lay good money that Cartwright was at the root cause of that. Because he always was. Whenever Izzy was happy, like a malevolent puppeteer, her father did his darndest to dampen it, and when she was at a low ebb, he worked extra hard to send her to her lowest. Always whittling away at her self-esteem until she secretly believed she was worthless— exactly as he had done throughout her childhood.

Ned had never liked the man for exactly that reason—and so he always made sure his expression let the bastard know how much he disliked him whenever they collided just as his father had. He had loathed and despised George Cartwright with every fibre of his being and always had.

As the congenial Caleb Parker hadn't been one to hate, the simple fact that he had hated Cartwright spoke volumes. But then, they had a history which had predated the arrival of Izzy and

Ned, one which had gone way back to when they had both been boys. He had always seen through George Cartwright. Saw the cruel streak which he hid from most of the world behind his polished shopkeeper's veneer of charm. That dislike had deepened into a visceral hatred as they had grown older and his father had abhorred the way hers had treated Izzy's mother.

Like Ned's lifelong relationship with Izzy, his father had been a childhood friend of her mother. They had both been the children of tenant farmers who had played together in the fields. She had been little more than a child when her family had pushed her into a union with Cartwright because they perceived that becoming a shopkeeper's wife was a huge step up from the dirt-beneath-the-fingernails world they scratched a living from. But according to Ned's father, the marriage had never been a happy one. Her awful husband had made her life a misery behind closed doors exactly like he had his daughter's. The worst sort of bullies, as his father was so fond of saying, were the ones who took their meanness out on a woman and Cartwright was one of those to his core. He had been a cold, cruel and controlling husband, finding fault with everything and always lamenting that he could and should have held out for better.

His father could never forgive George Cartwright for crushing her mother's spirit, or forcing her to try to carry more children after she had struggled with birthing Izzy's brother, losing baby after baby and being worn down as a result. Yet even when the physician had warned the couple that another pregnancy would be dangerous, her husband had still bullied her into bearing him another son and had never displayed any sign of remorse that that quest had cost Izzy's mother her life. Nor any subsequent remorse for blaming Izzy for the apparently unforgivable crime of being the hindrance of an unwanted daughter. His father and hers had locked horns a time or two over that too, when he could stand the gross unfairness no longer, but it had always backfired on her.

But then a bully never much cared about the feelings of others, and there seemed little doubt that George Cartwright took perverse pleasure in hurting Izzy's. He happily abandoned her for Chelmsford when he closed his shop here in the village, yet he still took perverse pleasure in travelling all the way back here weekly to hurt her more—and that made Ned's blood boil. For all his size and physical strength, he had never been a violent man. If anything, the thought of it disgusted him. He rescued ungrateful, hissing swans and kept ancient pigs who served no other purpose beyond eating him out of house and home for pity's sake! But his fists kept clenching beneath the table exactly as they had yesterday thanks to that despicable harlot comment which he still wasn't over, and he had the overwhelming desire to immediately travel all fifty miles to Chelmsford to pummel the monster into pulp for hurting her yet again.

'On Friday, between four and six, the Reverend and his wife are hosting a cake sale and tea party in the rectory garden to raise money for the poor in the parish.' In his suppressed rage, he hadn't noticed that Izzy had spread a copy of this week's *South Essex Gazette* on the table between them and she was pointing at the upcoming events page. 'You should definitely go to that.'

'I can't take time out of my working day to buy cake! Not when I've got animals expecting their feed and fields to tend to. I can't risk leaving the young lambs in the pasture as the sun goes down with all the bloody foxes. There would be carnage.'

'But Ned…'

'There are no buts where my livelihood is concerned, Izzy, and I'm not working into the night because I wasted valuable hours drinking the vicar's tea. Even with a well-trained dog like Falstaff, it can take me over an hour to round up all those stupid sheep on my own, and at this time of year I have to do that before six if I want to be done by eight.'

'This is why you need to hire some help! You are spread too thin.'

He knew she was right. 'Well even if I did and they started tomorrow, I still wouldn't be able to go to the rectory this week. It takes time to train a hand in the particular ways of a farm and my time is too stretched as it is already to find the time to train a hand, let alone interview for one.'

She went to argue then clamped her jaw shut irritated at being thwarted. That lasted all of two seconds before a grin blossomed. 'I already have the solution! As your father trained me how to do all those things growing up, I shall help you. After the tea party is finished, with two of us, with Falstaff, can easily corral your lambs in their barn ready for bed and then we can still feed all your animals long before the sun goes down. As the *lovely* Rose so rightly pointed out only the other day, many hands make light work and your father always said that I possessed a knack with sheep.'

Pleased with herself, because she did have the knack, drat her, she wrote the rectory cake sale on the top of her list. 'You are also going to need to make the effort to attend church every Sunday. And before you say you've got too much do that day, as you inevitably will, that doesn't seem to prevent every other overworked farmer in this parish from sparing an hour to sit through the sermon, so that excuse will not wash.'

Church every Sunday was written above the dreaded rectory cake sale and underlined twice.

'Obviously, the biggest event in the dismal upcoming Whittleston spring and summer social season is the May Fair. The first of May is on a Saturday this year, so you we are going to have to plan that week's chores accordingly for you to be free for the entire day...'

'I can't be free for the entire day.'

She skewered him with her glare. 'With a concerted effort and my help beforehand, you can be free for most of it, and that is that. Every other local farmer somehow manages to attend church on Sunday. You are the only exception.'

As she had him there, he merely grunted and she grinned. 'That noise, right there, is proof that I am right!'

'Even a stopped clock is right twice a day Izzy.'

'Then it is decided! However, as I do not trust you to commit to the cause, I shall make a note that we need to plan that week together nearer the time to ensure that all that needs doing on the day are the feeds and putting the stock to bed.' She grabbed a little leather notebook from her basket and scratched herself a reminder, then tapped her pencil to her chin as she flipped through a few pages. 'We should probably arrange a day this week to go to the tailors in Hornchurch, else you'll have nothing new to wear to the fair or the assembly at the end of this month.'

'I am not going to the tailors. You forced me there last year and I've barely worn all those pointless smart clothes you nagged me incessantly into buying then.'

'You at least need a few dashing new waistcoats to liven your wardrobe up.'

'No.'

'But all yours are so plain and muted, Ned, when the new fashion lends itself more towards bolder brocades for the evening.'

'Then I shall be plain and muted and quite content to be so, Izzy, as wild horses will not drag me to that tailor's again this year and that is my final word on the matter.'

She huffed, then eyed his chest oddly before she stood and walked behind his chair to pull about with the seams of the tatty work waistcoat he was wearing. 'I've never made any gentleman's attire before, but this doesn't look too complicated, so how about we compromise? I shall make the dashing waistcoats for you and the only effort required by you is accompany me to the drapers in the next village to choose and pay for the fabric.'

'If I've got to compromise on dandified waist-coats that I do not want, to wear to stupid events I have no desire to attend, then all I'm prepared to do is pay for them—begrudgingly.' He pointed to the top drawer of the kitchen dresser. 'There's money in there. Help yourself.'

'Don't you at least want to choose the colours?'

'And what, pray tell, would be the point of that complete waste of my precious time, when you are going to pick what you want regardless of what I might have to say about it?'

Always one to strike while the iron was hot, Isobel walked the three miles to the drapers in Little Chafford as soon as she left Ned's and spent over an hour choosing the right fabrics. She had caught the shop at a good time as Mr Arnold, the proprietor, had just taken delivery of a cart-load of new stock which included several bolts of fancy brocade. Amongst them were two that would look splendid on Ned—a rich deep bur-gundy woven with a swirling feathered pattern that cried out for a big chest to display it on and a gold and blue stripe which would complement his dark hair and eyes perfectly. After an age trying to choose between them, and because he hadn't set a budget and his top drawer had been stuffed with more money than she had ever seen in one place, she decided it was worth the risk of incurring his inevitable wrath and bought both.

Next, like a woman on a mission, she hurried to the haberdashers at the other end Little Chafford's eclectic high street before it closed and bought jolly buttons and matching thread and hurried back to Whittleston eager to make a start that very evening.

It was only when she returned home to a completely empty house that she realised that she should have taken one of his smart but muted waistcoats from his wardrobe to use as a template as she had no clue how to start. While her eye for shape and size was excellent, she was used to making feminine garments for herself and not an enormous manly brute like him.

In the absence of anything better to do, and with nobody here able to report back on her comings and goings to her father, she fetched her measuring kit and set off again in the direction of his farm.

It was near six when she arrived there and exactly as he had claimed, Ned was in the near pasture with Falstaff, shepherding his flock of new lambs and their mothers towards their barn. He hid his initial surprise at the lateness of her visit behind a put-upon sigh.

'Haven't you tortured me enough for one day?'

She shrugged as she climbed over the gate and made a fuss of Falstaff, who made no secret of the fact he was delighted to see her again. 'I did warn you that you were going to take a lot of work, and if you are determined to be pedantic and not go to the tailor's, you are going to have to suffer me doing it in his stead. I cannot make you a dashing waistcoat without knowing your exact size, and then there will need to be fittings to ensure I have got the cut right.' Which would all go some way to filling some more of her empty hours. 'But alas for you, a bargain is a bargain, so it is too late to back out of ours now that we have a battle plan and I've bought brocade.'

To his credit he did not try to, but still shook his head in disgust as he went back to rounding up his lambs. 'You do know that you are giving your father more ammunition to fire at you next Sunday when his spy informs him that you are out so late unchaperoned.'

'Mondays are the day he granted Tess her day off because nothing ever happens on a Monday evening in the village. She rarely comes home till late on her days off—if at all.'

The latest maid-of-all-work-cum-housekeeper-cum-cook her father had hired to keep an eye on her had a penchant for gin and a fancy man in nearby Fobbing who was excellent at distracting her from her duties. So excellent, that Isobel had turned a blind eye to the increasing number of nights the woman spent away from the house she was supposed to be keeping. 'That is why I like her so much more than her predecessor, and that is why you are going to have to suffer my measuring you before I leave you in peace. The quicker we get these sheep to bed, the quicker you can be rid of me.'

'An excellent point.' He offered her a begrudging smile. 'So step lively.'

Chapter Seven

Although Isobel hadn't worked on this farm in almost the decade since Caleb had passed, chivvying the sheep alongside Ned felt familiar and came as naturally to her as breathing, so it did not take long for the pair of them to get the job done. The easiness between them was lovely too, just like the old days, but for some reason, things became a bit awkward the moment they went inside the house.

She put that down to the impending measuring because despite the fact that her being here alone with him was nothing new—it had happened at least once weekly nowadays and had done for years—the prospect of her manhandling him in the parlour most definitely was. The most physical contact they had had as adults was the odd nudge here and there or her taking his arm from time to time. That had all felt normal and…

almost impersonal. Whereas this—him standing in a thin shirt after she had instructed him
to remove the bulky waistcoat he wore around
the farm—felt intensely personal. Intimate, even,
and that was most disconcerting.

But she had made the decision to do this and
had several yards of pricey material awaiting her
attention that he had paid for, so no matter how
peculiar it felt to get so close to Ned's robust and
suddenly overwhelming body, she was just going
to have to get over it.

'We should probably start with the length required.' Because measuring the long distance
from his nape to the base of his spine from behind seemed a less daunting start to proceedings than wrapping her arms around his middle
and staring up at his face. 'So if you could just
turn around.'

He did, and when confronted by his ridiculously broad shoulders, she was instantly more
off-kilter than she had been before. Good heavens above but he was an impressive specimen
of manhood! And it wasn't only those shoulders
that her wayward eyes wanted to feast upon, the
strong muscular arms encased in nought but the
soft linen of his rolled-up shirtsleeves had a separate allure all of their own.

Isobel blew out a quiet breath in the hope that

would help calm her quickened pulse. Trying not to focus on Ned's disquieting arms and looming presence, she unravelled the measuring tape she had meticulously embroidered on a reel of ribbon in January for something to do when the house had been too empty and the nights had been too dark, cold and interminable. 'How do you feel about burgundy?' Idle conversation was the answer. It was always the answer when one's usual centre was off in some way.

'I can't say I've ever given it much thought.'

She had to stretch to place the top of the tape at his collar and then let the rest fall. Experience had taught her that a too taut tape made for an ill fit and this ribbon, like fabric, would find the most natural end point without much help from her. Except she would still need to anchor the end to take the measurement and that end, in the case of a waistcoat, was a scant few inches above his buttocks. She would be lying to pretend she hadn't noticed them before as they had distracted her from time to time while she had watched him working—especially when Ned bent over and the fabric of his breeches pulled tight across them. But she would not notice them now.

On that she was resolute.

'Does that mean that you do not care for it?' As she couldn't avoid her fingers grazing the small of his back while she used the tape to decide where his new waistcoat would end, she tried to focus on the question rather than the odd sensations happening in her body or the way the muscles of his back seemed to stiffen at the contact.

'It means I haven't given it any thought, Izzy.' His tone was impatient. 'Or do you think that I have the time while I am mucking out my stalls to contemplate the colours of the rainbow.'

'I'd have thought the one thing you would want to do while mucking out your animals was contemplate something less unpleasant.' Nerves made her forget the number the second she had settled upon it, forcing her to have to do it all again. 'I know I certainly would, but knowing you and your no-nonsense manner, I suppose you contemplate nothing beyond the dull task at hand.'

She yanked her tape away and picked up her notebook to jot the first measurement, supremely grateful for the distance between them so that she could give herself and her bouncing nerves a stern talking-to. Because honestly, she had touched a man's back before, and a semi-naked man's back at that, and it had never affected her in quite the way that Ned's currently was.

In all honesty, her prior experience had rendered her ambivalent as she had long acknowledged that she wasn't one of those women who revelled in the pleasures of the flesh. She had naively allowed two men into her body. She had naively assumed the first would marry her because she had gifted him her innocence, but instead he hightailed it out of Whittleston with the rest of the militia within days of her unforgivable stupidity, leaving her feeling dirty and used and thoroughly ashamed of herself. The second, less than a year later, had convinced her that he was going to put a ring on her finger and then cajoled her to into anticipating their vows. Vows which he then swiftly took with the fiancée who was awaiting his return to London and who he had neglected to tell her about before he had lifted her skirts.

Yet despite those two idiotic and hideous mistakes with two absolute wastrels, after the dire loss of her virtue and to her further shame, she had given several more unworthy, lusty wastrels carte blanche to take lesser liberties with her person over the years in the hope that one of them would be so desperate to consummate their union that he would march her down the aisle to do it. None had, of course, because even wastrels expected a chaste bride, but while she hadn't outright hated those hasty, furtive, almost sordid forays into passion she hadn't liked them either.

None of those opportunist disappointments had made her flesh awaken in the way it had now. Bizarrely, in the case of the two men who had been her only supposed *lovers*, she had been disconnected from the experience. There in the physical sense but almost a bewildered spectator as far as her emotions and body were concerned. Always contemplating what it was about that act that made the men completely lose their heads while wondering why hers remained entirely lucid and…underwhelmed.

Yet—and this frankly staggered her in view of the unpassionate nature of her body—her curious fingertips currently itched to learn what the rest of Ned felt like. And more staggering still, she was genuinely worried that the odd nervousness she was experiencing in the strangest places might actually be that elusive creature known as desire.

But of course it couldn't possibly be.

Because this was Ned.

Ned!

The boy who had tormented her with slippery worms and slimy snails because he knew she could not bear them. The youth who had teased her constantly about her fluffy curls and silly daydreams. The man who had barely tolerated her in almost a decade and who she wanted to smash over the head with a shovel.

Clearly, thanks to the increasingly unpredictable situation with her father and the fertile seeds of uncertainty that he had gone out of his way to sow, her mind was more addled and irrational than she had previously thought. It was playing tricks with her. Confusing the task of getting him in a presentable enough state to appeal to Rose, which by its very nature involved making him become more attractive, with something else.

It was probably best not to overthink what that something else was after yesterday, when her emotions were still not quite over the trauma of Silent Sunday, or even over the Blistering Sunday Lecture of the week before. Instead, she would enjoy the distractions which came from her new sense of purpose and she would make Rose fall in love with Ned, and vice versa, if it killed her because they were perfect for one another.

Utterly perfect.

Meant to be.

The next quiet breath that she blew out was one of relief and she managed to briskly measure the vast width of his shoulders without her mind wandering to them too much. She even managed to smile with unaffected nonchalance as she twisted those shoulders back around to face her. 'Waist next, so lift your arms a bit.'

He did and she looped her tape around his middle. As she brought the ends together, the flat muscles on his abdomen jumped slightly beneath her fingertips and she heard him swallow. And because she also had the sudden urge to gulp because scant inches now separated them and that was playing havoc with all five of her senses and not just her sense of touch, her fingers fumbled, and it seemed to take for ever to comprehend the number on the measure. In her panic, unchecked words tumbled out before she could stop them. 'While you already look impressive enough in your favoured muted tones, you will look more handsome in burgundy.'

Impressive!

More handsome!

Compliments that rather suggested she already thought him handsome—which she always had—but not in that way.

Surely not in that way?

'I shall take your word for it.' Poor Ned looked suddenly terrified and then supremely relieved when she stepped away to log the measurement.

'In your own scruffy, oafish, salt-of-the-earth way of course.' A comment that made him roll his eyes as well which put them both on a surer, more familiar footing. 'You do understand that even I cannot make a silk purse out of a sow's ear?'

'Of course.' His rare chuckle sounded a tad forced. 'You are making the best out of a bad job.'

'Exactly.' She forced a smile of her own, as the task at hand had now apparently reached the most awkward and unsettling part. The chest and the neck—two parts of his impressive body which she was mentally now dreading having to deal with. Although conversely, and much to her chagrin, her newly awakened wayward body was chomping at the bit for her to get started.

With the benefit of dratted hindsight, the one skill she had never had any talent for, she should have dug her heels in about the need to visit the tailors. Giving herself the added purpose of making him some clothes was all well and good in theory, but in practice it was proving to be hellish for all the wrong reasons.

When this was Ned.

Ned!

Isobel repeated that mantra as she tried to loop the tape around his ludicrously wide ribcage, and then wished she was anywhere but in the intimate confines of his parlour at twilight, when the only way it was possible to do that was to practically embrace him. Who knew that the intimate heat of a man's clothed body millimetres from hers could be so heady? Or that the whisper of his breath against her forehead could force a million goose bumps to erupt all over her skin?

Not her, that was for certain.

It took all her concentration to get the ribbon to sit in the right place, and more still to drag the ends together tight enough to get an accurate measurement. Beneath her hands, beneath the solid, alluring wall of his chest, she could feel the beat of his heart against her palms. She had no clue if the rhythmic thudding seemed to match hers because his was meant to beat that fast or if his was, worryingly, as erratic as hers in this odd moment. All that she did know was the air around them now felt charged. Unusual. Surreal.

Disconcerting.

Fraught enough that they both seemed to sag in relief as she left him to record it in her notebook. A task which Isobel had to take her time over simply to recalibrate.

'Please tell me that we are done.' There was a hint of panic in his voice too despite that comment being laced with his customary irritation and impatience. 'I've had a long day, Izzy, with too much of you in it and my armchair is calling.' His eyes darted to it as if he needed it more than air and it gave her the most splendid idea.

An idea which blessedly relieved her of the

uncomfortable chore of standing on tiptoes to measure his neck. Of looping her arms around that neck while she tried to focus on the tape. Of staring up at him as if they were about to kiss. Of even thinking about what it might be like to kiss him, because she did not trust her mind in its current wandering state not to wander where it really had no place wandering.

'Then for goodness' sake, go sit in your chair now as it will make it easier to measure that thick, annoying neck of yours.' She pushed him towards it, furious now at her palms for enjoying that pathetic excuse to touch him again, and keen to leave him to his evening so that she could finally escape him and rationalise what her mind thought it was playing at to be thinking about *him* in that way. 'Trust me, there is only so much of your scintillating company I can tolerate in a day too and I would remind you that I am helping *you*, Ned.' She jabbed her finger at him. 'Helping *you*! There is nothing in this for me except the sainthood I shall undoubtedly deserve if I ever manage to fix the sorry mess you have got yourself into.'

He went to say something undoubtedly sarcastic, then clamped his jaws shut. 'Then get on with it then.' He jerked his thumb at Falstaff, who was curled in a giant ball on the hearth rug and snoring. 'Because that is what my evening should already look like, and I've had about as much of your nonsense as I can cope with today.'

'Fine.' As them bickering felt more normal than whatever the hell had been going on mere moments ago, she snapped her tape like a whip. 'Hold still and keep your mouth closed, or I might just do something to put us both out of our misery, you ingrate.'

He glared in stony silence as she stepped forward to arrange the tape around his throat, and it was then that she realised that the armchair wasn't a better solution to her unfortunate predicament as him standing was. If anything, it was worse because she either had to lean precariously over him—thanks to his ludicrously long legs—or she had to stand between them. Neither option reduced the intimate proximity one jot. She tried the former, but after much faffing it was Ned who spread his thighs so she could step between them. He clearly instantly regretted that he had done that too, because her bosom was now level with his face, and he had no clue what to do with his eyes. With a wince, he decided it was safer to stare over her right shoulder, which twisted his neck at such and odd angle it stretched her tape out of shape.

'Oh, for goodness' sake!' For the sake of her sanity, she gripped his chin to bring it back front and centre and he tilted his face upwards, staring resolutely at hers rather than at her chest as if his life depended on it while she rearranged her measuring ribbon.

A new and painful awkwardness descended upon them like a shroud and she couldn't bear it, nor cope with the peculiar reaction her body was having to his. Like a drowning sailor in a storm lunging for some passing driftwood, she scrambled for some conversation to distract them both.

'What are your thoughts on stripes? Only I might have accidentally spent your money on two bolts of fabric and I've never seen you in stripes.' He fidgeted before she could gauge the correct number of inches and the tape slipped, so she caught his cheek while she arranged it for the third time.

'I suppose that depends on the stripes.'

As that was such a typical, difficult Ned thing to say, she rolled her eyes, or started to, but stopped the moment they locked with his and, mesmerised, she could not find the strength to tear them away.

If measuring his chest had felt like an intimate position for them to be in, this took that feeling and multiplied it exponentially.

Isobel was used to looking up at Ned, never down. She was used to seeing the powerful, gruff man who worked his fingers to the bone but still had strength to spare. The reliable, upright, stubborn, standoffish yet indomitable Ned who went out of his way to rebuff people. The Ned didn't need the another living soul because he was perfectly all right by himself, thank you very much.

But this incarnation of the man she couldn't remember not knowing was different.

This Ned had a vulnerability about him that Isobel had never witnessed before. A softness and gentleness, and even loneliness, that he was obviously able to hide with his height while he towered over everyone else, which he couldn't now. By the wariness of his expression, she suspected he knew that she had somehow found a chink in his impenetrable armour. That she suddenly saw more of the man he truly was rather than the one he wanted the world to see.

And seeing as it was obviously a moment for revelations, the biggest one of all was that this new knowledge had the power to shift something within her, although where it had shifted to yet, she didn't understand. The best way to describe it was akin to the world randomly tilting on its axis and then immediately righting itself—but in a different way. A better way. As if that was precisely how it was supposed to have been all along and was now all the better for it. And that was…

fascinating…but also unnerving. Making absolutely no sense yet perfect sense at the same time.

Conscious she was staring, she found the wherewithal from somewhere to grope for those stripes to tilt the earth back to where it had always been. 'The main colour of the fabric is blue.'

Except it didn't because she was smiling—but had no recollection of when that had started or why it was happening. Or why her fingers had gone from gripping his fidgeting chin to cupping his cheek and marvelling at how soft the whiskers beneath them felt. All very peculiar and not at the same time. 'What are your thoughts on blue, you joyless grouch? Or are you as ambivalent about blue as you are about burgundy?'

She had the urge to caress his face but didn't. That was a step too far into this new unknown and something niggled that it was much safer to hang back on the periphery.

'I've always adored blue.'

His mouth curved upwards too, the wariness in his dark eyes replaced by something else which appeared to be part confusion and a greater part unfathomable, but like her he seemed quite content to remain entranced by this strange moment while they both figured it out. Eyes locked. Searching. One palm still resting on his cheek.

The other still clasping the loose ends of the tape measure together around his neck.

Smiling.

Her lips tingling in anticipation when his gaze suddenly dropped to them and lingered.

Leaning.

Not caring if it was safe or not because in this charged and unexpected moment it simply did not matter.

Until the arrival of Falstaff's wet nose thrust between their perilously close bodies and snapped them both out of the spell.

As if she had been caught with her hand in the till, Isobel jumped back and blushed crimson. Thankfully Ned was too busy stalking into the kitchen to notice, loudly apologising to his dog for the lateness of his dinner and blaming her latest, stupid, fluff-for-brains nonsense for it.

Chapter Eight

'They are called Jezebel, Salome and Delilah and they are the three most spoiled pigs on the planet.' Izzy was having a high old time making fun of him at the rectory cake sale and all for Miss Healy's benefit after she had orchestrated a cosy table in the furthest corner of the garden for just the three of them, no doubt on purpose. 'They eat like queens despite never once earning their keep because the Parker farm has never produced so much as a single rasher of bacon, let alone a piglet.' There was a vivacity about her when she told a story. A certain something which made an audience lean forward and lap it all up. It was uniquely her and such an intrinsic part of her charm that it couldn't possibly be emulated, yet if she could bottle it and sell it she would make a fortune. 'The poor thing tried everything, of course, to make the venture a success and spent a fortune hiring out various male Tamworths to *holiday* with them over the years, but his fussy ladies would have none of it, would they, Ned?'

It was a rhetorical question because she was in full flow, and he knew better than to do anything but nod when she held court. So he nodded, enjoying the joke despite being the butt of it and wishing she was embellishing the sorry tale rather than speaking nothing but the truth. His ladies had been nothing but trouble since his father had brought them home and he was always a soft touch when it came to animals. He would never admit that aloud, of course, because it hardly fit with his gruff, no-nonsense character. But Izzy knew the truth of it and loved to tease him for his weaknesses. Yet she always brought treats for the belligerent, ragtag, no-hope collection of useless beasts who called his farm home. A gesture he appreciated despite teasing her in return for doing it.

'In fact, they became quite aggressive whenever a gentleman pig came to visit and bullied the poor things horrendously. It is quite the tragic sight to see a huge, rampant boar cowering in the corner of a pigsty squealing for mercy. The poor things left traumatised, and their owners refused to lend them afterwards, so that was the end of that. Now they are quite content living in the lap of porcine luxury in his yard and because they are as fussy about their diet as they are their gentlemen callers, they still cost him a fortune.'

'Which beggars the question of why you continue to keep the pigs, Mr Parker?' Miss Healy was as justifiably baffled by that complete waste of money as any sensible farmer's daughter would be.

'I'm fattening them up for my table.'

Izzy, of course, laughed aloud at that shocking lie. 'Or so he has claimed for the last five years. I personally think those girls stand about as much chance of being eaten as Falstaff does and am confident that they will all end up dying of old age just like his crotchety rescued billy goat did. He built Brutus his own little house too and the thing always hated him…'

Ned let his mind wander while she regaled another amusing tale about his inability to wash his hands of ungrateful animals who were past their prime and a constant drain on his resources. He was quite content to let Izzy have her fun at his expense because he was beyond relieved that she didn't seem the least bit perturbed about their awkward interlude of a few nights before.

He sincerely hoped that was because she was oblivious of the fact that, at least for him, there had been an awkward interlude. She had certainly

behaved as if nothing at all was amiss that night
after he had come to his senses and he thanked
his lucky stars that he had come to his senses before he had done something that they both would
have regretted for ever.

Thankfully, nothing *had* happened.

On the outside at least.

Unless she had the ability to read his mind,
he sincerely hoped she was none the wiser about
how close he had come to doing the unthinkable—of kissing the minx because she had bewitched him so.

He still had no clue how he had almost allowed
that to happen.

One minute he had been intensely uncomfortable at the prospect of being measured, the next
he had wanted to wrap his arms around her, haul
her into his lap and feast on her mouth until they
were both breathless. Worse, if Falstaff hadn't in-
tervened, he was convinced that he would have,
and goodness knew where that folly would have
left them.

Such an unwelcome travesty would have likely
killed their lifelong friendship stone dead, that
was for certain. But while that friendship, thankfully, remained unharmed and intact, the knowledge that he had been so close to ruining it still

left him stunned and, frankly, shaken by the madness which had temporarily possessed him.

Three sleepless nights later and he still couldn't fathom what the hell he had been thinking, beyond the fact that he clearly hadn't been thinking at all, which was odd in the extreme when he had long ago trained himself to never act on impulse. Ned always weighed a situation carefully and if it was too risky stepped back. However, he had been so caught up in the moment, so caught up in her, that he gave no thought to the outrageous risk he was taking and kissing her was not only the natural next step but as necessary as the air which filled his lungs.

He had tried blaming the out of the blue and wholly inappropriate compunction to fuse his lips with hers on all manner of potentially reasonable, albeit embarrassing, explanations ever since. The sublime sensation of being touched by an attractive woman after so many years without one. The intoxicating scent of her perfume and the seductive nature of the twilight. Even the peculiar intimacy the closeness of their bodies created. But while he knew that all those things had played a small part in his unconscious and unexpected reaction to her that night, it had been staring into Izzy's lovely eyes which had ultimately been his undoing. The intense connection he had foolishly thought he saw swirling in those deep, cerulean irises had blindsided him. They had simultaneously made his body want and his heart yearn in a way neither ever had before.

Then, and this mortified him almost as much, like a lovesick fool, he'd vocalised exactly what he was thinking as he'd gazed besotted into her eyes.

I've always adored blue.

Four stupid, blasted words he had regretted and flagellated himself for ever since. Just thinking about the way his hungry eyes had latched on to her lips straight after made his entire body cringe painfully with embarrassment.

Proof if proof were needed, he supposed, that maybe she was right and he did need a wife. It clearly wasn't natural for a man to deny all those base carnal needs and urges for so long if he was suddenly mapping all that need and all those urges onto her. And on the back of nothing more erotic than having his ungainly, thick neck measured for a blasted waistcoat too!

Rather than focus on Izzy and inwardly cringe again at what he had almost done, he slanted a glance at Miss Healy in the hope that he might feel some sort of similar stirring for her too and when he didn't, huffed.

So loud Miss Healy apparently heard him.

'It is quite all right, Mr Parker. I know several farmers who have formed attachments to unproductive and unreasonable old animals—my own father included. I do not judge you in the slightest for keeping an ungrateful goat who rewarded you for that kindness by kicking you at every available opportunity. It is a testament to your character that you still afforded him a decent dotage even after Brutus knocked you into the river.' Because of course Izzy would have ended that sorry tale with his dunking. 'Was it very cold?'

'It was every bit as bracing as you would expect for October, Miss Healy.'

'His lips were as blue as the air afterwards, Rose. I am just thankful I happened to be there to witness it as it truly was a spectacular tumble.' Izzy shot him a mischievous and unrepentant grin. 'The very definition of head over heels as I recall, which was no mean feat for the goat to achieve as Ned is the size of a mountain. I could barely breathe for laughing.'

She had laughed her pretty little head off from the second he had hit the water to the second she waved him goodbye several hours later as he recalled. After she had bundled him in a blanket in front of a roaring fire, and then fed him hot tea laced with brandy while he grumbled. She had visited daily for a week after too, in case he developed a chill on the back of it. For all the fun she had always got at his expense, she always made it up in other ways. A fact which made him smile back at her begrudgingly. 'She laughed so much she turned purple and then rewarded Brutus for his treachery for the rest of his days by bringing him carrots as a thank-you.'

'Food made the old curmudgeon happy—much as it does you. On that note, fear not…' The ever-present glimmer in her lovely eyes increased as it became more calculated. A sure sign she was about to do something mischievous. 'I shall personally fetch you some of the fruitcake you've been staring at longingly on for the last ten minutes.' Izzy took his plate even though she knew that he had been doing nothing of the sort and turned her sunny, innocent smile on Miss Healy. 'Ned is always at his most crotchety when he is hungry, so it is always best to keep his belly topped up.'

'The way to a man's heart is through is stomach.' Miss Healy gave Izzy an odd look over the rim of her teacup.

'Never a truer word was spoken.' Izzy stood with purpose. 'What can I fetch you from the cake stall while I am there, Rose?'

'The same if you do not mind, as I've always been particularly partial to fruitcake too.'

An apparent coincidence that made Izzy's meddling eyes light up. 'Yet another thing that you and Ned have in common.' And off she went, doing precisely what he had specifically warned her not to do by finding a flimsy excuse to leave him alone with the woman she was hell-bent he should marry.

Miss Healy watched her go and then also gave him a funny look as she put down her teacup. 'Now that I have you all to myself, can I ask you a question of a sensitive and personal nature, Mr Parker?' Not at all what he had expected her to say.

'Er… I suppose so.' Although thanks to the twin alarm bells ringing at the mention of sensitive and personal, he already dreaded agreeing.

She leaned close, her voice an octave above a whisper. 'Am I mistaken, or is Isobel trying her hardest to convince us both that we are a match made in heaven?'

'Er…' Good grief this was awkward. 'Well…' As he couldn't think of any way to answer that without saying yes, he winced as he nodded. 'She's never been particularly subtle.'

'I thought as much.' Miss Healy took a thoughtful sip of her tea. 'And can I ask why you are going along with it when it is as plain as the nose on your face that you aren't keen on the idea?'

'Er… Well… Um…'

She chuckled at his embarrassment. 'Please do not try to spare my feelings, Mr Parker, as I can assure you that the feeling is mutual. I am as unkeen on the idea of *us* as you are.'

'Right…' Well, that nipped Izzy's daft idea firmly in the bud. Although Ned was oddly more relieved than offended yet frowned anyway as some disappointment in her romantic disinterest seemed polite.

She grinned at his effort. 'If it is any consolation, I think that you are a *very* nice man and a handsome one too, so please do not take my frankness to heart.' So much for the word *very* being significant. 'However, I think it is best to be honest about it all now rather than build up Isobel's expectations that wedding bells are in our future, as you could honestly be the nicest and most handsome gentleman in the world, and I fear those attributes would be wasted on me at the moment.'

Miss Healy sighed and stared at her tea. 'You see…and I would hope that you would keep this horrid, humiliating reason for my reticence a secret from everyone including Isobel…' Her gaze lifted briefly to his for a moment and it was filled with sadness. 'Only I recently had my heart broken, I am afraid, and it is nowhere near mended enough for me to risk it again anytime soon.' Her smile was wry and yet tragic at the same time. The sadness in her eyes palpable.

'I am sorry to hear that.' And he was. Not because he had really held any hope that he might develop an attraction for her if he tried hard enough, but because he hated to see anyone in pain. There was suddenly no doubting Miss Healy was and the effort of hiding it so well was etched into her face.

She shrugged, determined to put a brave face on it. 'I am trying to convince myself that it happened for a reason, while still castigating myself for not seeing it sooner when nobody else in my village seemed particularly surprised that my fiancé eloped with my best friend.'

Ned sighed in genuine empathy because he knew how it felt to have everyone witness your pain and humiliation. 'That is both the blessing and the curse of village life.' As he hadn't been able to escape it like Miss Healy, the only way he had been able to cope with everyone's well-intentioned pity and charity was to shut them all out of his life and not welcome them back. The only one who had refused to be completely pushed away was Izzy, Lord love her, and although he had never admitted it to the minx, she had been his lifeline in that first two years when he had felt his life wasn't worth living. Especially in his darkest days during when scraping together enough food to survive the week had been near impossible. She still brought her welcome baskets of food even though he could well afford it nowadays, and it always touched his heart that she spent some of her pittance of an allowance at the baker's shop so that he always had a fresh loaf of bread.

'Isn't it just?' Miss Healy exhaled, momentarily allowing him to see what a toll it had all taken on her. 'I found it impossible to lick my wounds privately back home, so I came here to find some space to heal, free from all the pity and all the constant reminders. I did not come here to allow history to repeat itself—not that you strike me as the jilting type but...' Her eyes wandered to Izzy. 'Once bitten, twice shy.'

At a loss of what to say to that, he grasped an appropriate but empty platitude out of the air even though he knew it wasn't enough. 'Things like that take time to get over.' He offered her his most sympathetic smile and took an awkward sip of his own tea, silently willing Izzy to come back and save him from elaborating. He found his own turbulent inner emotions awkward enough to deal with so he was practically useless with those of others.

Except the minx was too busy giving them some space to have fetched any cake at all yet. Instead, she was serving it and appeared to be in the throes of convincing Mr Bunion he should pay double for the generous slice she was cutting, or perhaps treble for the sake of those less fortunate. He watched with amusement as the foppish fool hung on her every word because he was hypnotised by her charm and then happily piled coins in her outstretched palm. Ned wondered, not for the first time, why her father had always resisted putting her permanently behind the counter of his shop as he was convinced Izzy could sell milk to a cow.

'But enough about my misery, why on earth are you going along with Isobel's matchmaking when I am pretty certain your heart isn't in it either?'

'Urgh…' He huffed out a weary breath. 'Izzy has taken it upon herself to do it despite my expressly telling her not to, so I feel I must apologise to you for this.' He gestured to their solitary table miles away from the rest of the gathering. 'All I agreed to was allowing her to drag me kicking and screaming back into local society because she thinks it will be good for me.' He glanced towards Izzy again and almost groaned aloud when the minx winked at him across the garden. 'Apparently, as you also mentioned when we last collided, Miss Healy, all work and no play makes Ned a dull boy and it makes no difference that Ned is perfectly content to avoid tiresome tea parties and puerile parlour games. She has decreed that I must attend them and so here I am.'

'What a sad pair we are, Mr Parker. Should we tell her that she is fighting a losing battle or simply let her think that her cunning plan is working for the sake of a quiet life?'

Ned chuckled at her perceptiveness. 'There is no doubting that if she believes the latter, we shall both be spared the torture of her trying to match us with someone else instead. Izzy is famously relentless when she sets her intractable, nonsensical mind to something.'

'Then let us play along as at least we are wise to her machinations. I can feign a frisson if you can.'

A frisson was the perfect description for what was missing at this table. It said so much more than Izzy's daft ideas about thunderbolts. He liked Miss Healy a great deal—but nothing more than that simmered between them when surely something would if they were meant to be? Not even Izzy, with all her enthusiasm for the cause, could manufacture that. However, being the eternal optimist, she was still convinced of it. The confident, smug smile she was currently bestowing on Mr Bunion, as Ned sipped his tea, was that of a woman thoroughly pleased with herself.

'And it will make her happy.' He could already see how much she was enjoying things. She was still surreptitiously spying on the pair of them behind the cake table while doing a very poor job of pretending that she wasn't.

'I wonder…' Miss Healy rested her chin in her palm as she stared up at him. 'Does Isobel realise yet that you are hopelessly in love with her?'

The sip of tea shot out of Ned's mouth in an ungraceful splutter. 'Um… *No.* I mean no!' He swiped the liquid from his chin and forced out a laugh while his heart raced in panic. 'Izzy and I are friends, is all. Nothing more.'

'That would be why you cannot take your eyes of her.'

Couldn't he? *Oh, dear.*

'It's because we've known each other since we were small—' he held out his finger and thumb an inch apart to emphasise the longevity of their connection '—that I know it is never wise to take your eyes off her in a social situation as that is when she is likely to make the most mischief.

Like her nonsensical matchmaking today, for example…'

His voice trailed off, leaving just the sound of his suddenly hammering heart echoing into the void he had no clue how to fill without digging himself a bigger hole. 'I mean look at her.' Ned gestured towards the minx who was now working her unique magic on the local constable as she wielded the cake slice, then instantly cringing that he was proving Miss Healy's point about his eyes in the process. To make him panic some more, Izzy sensed him staring and her answering smile warmed his heart in a way that no friend's smile should.

Oh, dear!

So much for knowing his place and not reaching for the stars.

'The menace is always interfering in something.' He choked back some more tea in the vain hope that it made him appear nonplussed and amused by the accusation, when he couldn't have been further from that if he tried. His heart was pounding. His collar felt too tight and something untoward was going on with his gut. 'She can't help herself from poking her nose in where it's not wanted or doing what she thinks is best, so you have to keep your wits about you in her presence.'

That was his sorry excuse for his wandering gaze, nothing more, and he decided there and then that it was a hill he was prepared to die upon if necessary. Being hopelessly in love with Izzy was not where he wanted to be.

That was the ultimate hiding to nothing. Too risky a wager.

A disaster waiting to happen when the quickest way to lose the minx for ever would be to clip her wings. 'The only emotion I feel for her is exasperation.'

He was certainly exasperated right now, albeit with his own blasted stupidity. As if his heart really believed that Izzy—*Izzy for goodness' sake*—would want to stay in dreary Whittleston with him! Clearly it had gone stark staring mad.

'Ah…' Miss Healy patted his hand across the table with all the suppressed insincerity of a disbeliever. 'My mistake. My sincere apologies for bringing it up, Mr Parker. I did not mean to embarrass you with my wild and obviously unfounded speculations.'

'I can assure you that am more amused than embarrassed, Miss Healy.' His chuckle felt as brittle as glass because there was no denying that she had planted a seed that had already taken unwelcome root in his whirring mind. As she was the second person to have brought it up in a week—and worse, within the same week as a thoroughly seduced Ned had almost kissed the menace his eyes kept wandering to—Miss Healy might well have a point.

Even so, and now more than anything, he still wanted to argue that point. Deny that he harboured anything beyond friendly feelings for Izzy because friendly feelings were safe and anything else was too dangerous to contemplate. But he knew that if he did, he would likely only make a horrendous situation worse. With his clumsy way with words, he probably ending up digging more of a trench than a hole for himself, so he clamped his jaws shut.

For the simple truth of the matter was that if he did harbour futile romantic feelings for Izzy— *if he did*—then he needed to get over them fast as they weren't reciprocated and nor were they ever likely to be. Furthermore, even if some miracle occurred and she did happen to glance his way with feminine interest, then there was no way that would last. Izzy wanted to escape Whittleston-on-the-Water and Ned now owned deeds that shackled him here for eternity. Deeds he had worked his fingers to the bone to buy and a promising future which he could not sell for what was tantamount to little more than a pipe dream.

Like his father and his mother, oil and water never mixed—even if they tried their hardest to.

As if she would want to the further shackles tying her to this village she wanted out of? As if he and Izzy could ever really go from being friends to…

Conscious that his eyes had wandered to her again and that Miss Healy was watching him watch her with interest, Ned pasted on a concerned expression and put down his cup. 'If I might share a confidence with you, Miss Healy, as in truth I am really here solely at the express behest of Sophie.' These suspicions needed to be nipped in the bud. For his pride's sake if nothing else. Because the whole of Whittleston would have a field day if any gossip about his futile feelings leaked out of this garden and went Mrs Outhwaite's way. 'She is convinced Izzy is out of sorts and needs a distraction, so I reluctantly agreed to allow myself to be that distraction so that I could keep a close eye on the minx. For Sophie's sake, obviously. Because she is the one who is worried.'

Miss Healy leaned forward, intrigued. 'In true village fashion, the plot thickens. What is Sophie worried about? It must be something serious for you to willingly endure tiresome tea parties, puerile parlour games and her unsolicited efforts to find you a bride.'

'Sophie suspects it might have something to do with her father.' Was it disloyal to admit that? A betrayal of Izzy's trust. Probably, but desperate times called for desperate measures, and he wouldn't be having this awkward conversation in the first place if Izzy hadn't reneged on their agreement and betrayed his trust in the process. Sharing a confidence gave his so far unconvincing explanation some gravitas. 'Because it usually is to do with him. George Cartwright is not a nice man and treats her abominably.'

'Really? Yet my aunt speaks so highly of him, and he seemed nice enough when I met him at church last Sunday—but then—well…' She raised her brows with a shrug. 'As I have bitter first-hand experience, few of us ever really know what goes on between people behind closed doors.' Miss Healy glanced towards Izzy, giving him the handy excuse to do the same as keeping them off her was suddenly impossible. 'Poor Isobel. How awful for her. She puts on such a brave, cheerful face in front of everyone that I never would have known that she was out of sorts.'

'That is but another of her many frustrating characteristics. She is the consummate actress and always has been, so you never truly know what is going on inside her irritating head or what she really thinks about anything.' Like what she really thought about him, for instance, after the odd moment they had undoubtedly shared in his parlour. Had she genuinely been oblivious? Or had she felt the strange pull between them too? Or was that his wishful thinking?

Quite possibly and that realisation frankly scared the hell out of him.

First Sophie and now Miss Healy had given him some serious food for thought which he wasn't sure how he felt about beyond terrified. 'I suspect her entire world could be falling apart and nobody would know it.' Just like him. Izzy had always been too proud to allow anyone to see her falter. Although there appeared to be little bothering the smug, smiling meddler as she undulated back towards them carrying what appeared to be half a fruitcake.

'If you will excuse me from wildly speculating again, it appears that it isn't just Sophie who is worried about your mutual *friend*.' Miss Healy's voice reminded him that his eyes had wandered of their own accord to Izzy again, but he did not dare respond to her loaded comment or her more loaded look as the subject of both was now too close for comfort. So instead, he pretended he remained nonplussed by the blatant insinuation and sipped his tea and almost spat it out again with what she said next. 'Who looks thoroughly jealous of us too, by the way.'

'What scandalous gossip were you two discussing so intently while I was being hounded by that dreadful Mr Bunion?' Izzy beamed at them as she handed out that cake as if he and Miss Healy had been engaged in something far more scandalous than a conversation. 'Or is it none of my business?'

Was it his imagination or was her smile a tad strained?

'Potatoes. We discussed nothing more scandalous than growing potatoes, Isobel. But it was nonetheless a pleasant and *enlightening* experience for the both of us.' Miss Healy shot him a mischievous glance before she reached out and squeezed his hand like a consummate flirt who could give Izzy a proper run for her money. 'Wasn't it—*Ned*? It is so lovely and so rare to chat to a gentleman I have *so* much in common with.'

As her hand lingered on his proprietorially, Izzy's eyes latched on to it and stared making Ned's foolish, glutton-for-punishment heart hope that Miss Healy might be right.

Chapter Nine

⟨decorative flourish⟩

'I think that went well, don't you?' Isobel nudged him because Ned had been practically mute most of the mile walk back to his farm. 'You and *Rose* certainly appeared to be getting along like a house on fire. Even you cannot have failed to have noticed that she was flirting with you today.' He harrumphed at that in dismissal. 'Why, she even *caressed* your hand, Ned, so there is no mistaking that she is interested in you.'

Isobel had to work hard to banish the snippiness which wanted to leak into her tone by reminding herself that this was all going as she had intended. Thrusting Ned with Rose was all going swimmingly. She seemed very keen. He had seemed a little less so to begin with but had risen to the occasion as the rest of the afternoon had unfolded, and they both deserved to be happy.

Ned might be a trifle annoyed with her for

breaking her promise not to find excuses to leave the pair of them alone, but as it had all clearly worked out for the best, she doubted his present irritation with her would last long.

Any more than her irrational and unjustified current irritation with him would last either.

And it was irrational and unjustified to be feeling so uncharitable towards him when she certainly did not want Ned in that way, no matter how much the one, single peculiar moment they had shared suggested she might feel otherwise. Therefore, there was absolutely no reason to be envious of his deepening relationship with Rose or personally insulted by it. However, there was no denying that her initial reaction to witnessing her new friend openly flirting with him was outright jealously. A response that was both visceral because it had, momentarily at least, felt like the worst sort of betrayal. As if Ned had somehow been unfaithful to her of been yet another man to reject, which was utter madness in the extreme when they had never been a couple.

Laughable even, except every laugh she had mustered since the incident had felt as fake as the smile she had pasted on as she had sat back down with them, pretending to be delighted that things were moving forward when her fingers had begged to be allowed to scratch Rose's beguiling eyes out.

'I was heartened to see that you made arrangements to see each other at church this Sunday.' So heartened the fingernails of the clenched fist behind her back had left four red indented moons in her palm, which she had gratefully covered with her gloves the second she and Ned had said their goodbyes.

'They were hardly arrangements, Izzy. We merely noted that we might see each other at the service.'

'But you are going to church especially to see her, Ned. *You*—' She prodded him in his much too solid bicep. '—are going to church when you *never* go to church. That says everything.' She made a great show of sniffing the air. 'Do you smell that? Because I still smell rose petals in your future, Edward James Parker. Rose petals and wedding cake. Rose petals for you and the lovely *Rose*.' Whose thorns scratched her throat as she made that galling joke.

'I am going to church because *you*—' he prodded her right back '—said that I had to. It's underlined on your damn battle plan and pinned up on my pantry door. If you want to read more into it than that, there's not much I can do to stop you. You've always leaned towards the fanciful in your thinking.' By the angry set of his dark eyebrows and the curtness in his tone, it was apparent that he was indeed peeved that she hadn't kept her word about meddling. 'And I'm all done with it for today, so be off with you.' He stopped dead and made a shooing motion with his big hands. 'I'm all done with your help too, so I'll finish my own chores by myself if you don't mind. In blessed silence!'

'Well, that smacks of the ungrateful.'

He glared back blandly then set off again shaking his head. 'No doubt you'll get over it soon enough.' Without turning around, he executed a lacklustre wave. 'I'm sure I'll see you too at Sunday's service. Lucky, *lucky* me.'

Isobel watched him leave for all of ten seconds before she remembered the depressing, empty house awaiting her with nothing else to do and scurried after him to avoid it.

'A bargain is a bargain, Ned Parker, and I refuse to give you the satisfaction of telling everyone that Isobel Cartwright welched on one.' He groaned aloud without breaking his stride. 'I agreed to assist you with the feeding and lambs in return for your attendance at the cake sale, and as you held up your half, I fully intend to hold up mine. My word has always been my bond.'

'Like it was when you exploited the first available chance to leave me alone with Rose! Your word is your bond all right! I wouldn't trust it as far as I could throw you.'

As the insufferable man's long strides forced her to scurry behind and he was forcing her to talk to his back, she picked up her skirts and ran in front of him to block his path into his own yard. 'And thank goodness I did for she is now *Rose* to you and not Miss Healy, so instead of being furious at my little nudge, you should be thanking me for it! I even martyred through ten full minutes of Mr Bunion so that the pair of you could have a moment, and trust me, that was the ultimate sacrifice, you ungrateful wretch!' That reprimand issued, she opened the gate and marched in as if she owned the place. 'You go feed your precious pigs and I'll see to the chickens, then I'll meet you in the pasture in fifteen minutes.'

He stomped past her muttering under his breath but without arguing and snatched up a bucket while she stripped off her gloves and bonnet and left them with her basket on the wall outside his house. While he marched west towards his pigsty, she headed east towards the barn where he kept all the feed, castigating herself as to why she even bothered with him when he never failed to let her know what an unwelcome and royal pain in his backside she was.

Clearly, she was a glutton for punishment.

A needy, pathetic glutton for punishment who hankered so much for the past that she couldn't bring herself to let go of it. Or maybe it was some sort of affection she sought, close kinship with another human, as that had always been woefully missing from her life? Which was doubly pathetic if she was expecting that from Ned, who only saw her as one great inconvenience.

Dratted m—

As she flung open the barn door, something enormous flew out of it in a blur of white feathers and knocked her to the ground.

Isobel screamed as the thing came at her, shielding her face with her hands as best as she could while scrambling backwards on her bottom as it attacked her arms, then pecked furiously in his quest to do the same to her ankles.

She heard the thunder of Ned's boots as he charged towards the bird, shouting at the thing in an attempt to make it stop, but she did not dare drop her guard for a moment until the swan turned its attention to him, in case she lost an eye. Wide wings spread to intimidate; one flapping. The other—which for some ungodly reason had been lashed between what appeared to be batons of wood—jabbed the air like a weapon. The swan's pointed tongue vibrating like a serpent's as it hissed menacingly.

From somewhere, Ned had procured a loose gate which served as both a shield for his body and a cage to corral the furious bird into his barn. Even with it, it still took him several minutes to wrestle the thing back to whence it came, and it took Ned's full weight pressed against the door to close it enough to shoot the bolt back in place.

He was significantly dishevelled and wide-eyed when he finally rushed towards her, but probably nowhere near as dishevelled and stunned as she was.

'Are you all right?' He reached down for her hand, enveloping it in his comforting strength as he hauled her up, frowning at her arms. 'You're bleeding, Izzy.'

'Well of course I am bleeding!' She slapped his hand away, more because it had such an odd effect on hers than because she blamed him for what had just happened. Although there was no denying that she did blame him for what had happened. 'A stupid oaf shut a deranged swan in his barn and neglected to warn me of that fact!'

He shrugged, sheepish, obviously riddled with guilt at that mistake. 'I clean forgot about Old Nick. Sorry.'

'Since when have you owned a swan?' She rubbed ineffectually at the dirt stuck to her backside while she tried to ignore the way her nerves in her fingers still fizzed after encountering his. 'And why in God's name has he got a wooden wing?'

'I found him in a right old state on the riverbank a couple of weeks ago. I think he was hit by a boat and that's how he broke his wing.'

'Don't tell me, you couldn't bear to see it suffer so you decided to save it rather than let it die as is nature's way?' How typical of him, and how sweet. Instantly her annoyance abated. For all his gruff surliness, the oaf had always had an enormous, soft heart. If she had found the poor thing, she would have done the same. Or at least she would have brought it to Ned to work his magic on. He had always had a canny way with invalided creatures. 'Splinting that wing must have been...*fun*.'

They had both been pecked to pieces as children when they had rescued a mallard with a similar injury. That bird had repaid the favour by nesting on the field by the river every year until the flood.

'Not quite the adjective I would use for the unenviable ordeal but...' The ghost of a smile played at the corners of his mouth. '...you know me. I've never been one to shy away from a challenge. Not that the feathered maniac is grateful for my efforts, of course. Every time I go in to feed him, the blighter goes in for the kill.'

'Only you would nurse a maniacal swan back to health.' Sometimes she just wanted to cuddle him for his innate kindness, but as that was something they had never done she resorted to teasing him instead. 'You're so sweet, Ned. So *very* nice.'

He scowled at her soppy expression even though they both knew that she had read the situation correctly. 'It's a swan, Izzy. A *swan*. As all the swans belong to the King, no matter how much I wanted to, I could hardly eat it, now, could I? Men have been locked in the Tower for less. There's a law about protecting swans. It's an actual crime enshrined in the statute to wilfully let one die without trying to save it.'

She laughed at that blatant balderdash. 'While I *obviously* believe you, Ned, thousands wouldn't. Enshrined in the statute indeed! Do I look like I was born yesterday?' She pointed in the direction of the hissing as the rampaging swan attacked the door of his prison. 'You've even named it. You always name the animals you've adopted as pets.' He set his jaw affronted and she laughed at that too. 'Will Old Nick be getting his own bespoke swan house if that wing doesn't heal, like the one you built the dearly departed but bad-tempered Brutus or the porcine mansion you lovingly crafted for your barren, boar-hating pigs?'

'Have you gone soft in the head!' He was always at his surliest when confronted by the indisputable evidence of his benevolent character. 'For the record, before you decide to tell your own nonsensical, over-embellished version of this event to anyone daft enough to listen to you, I simply call him Old Nick because he's clearly the devil incarnate.'

He jerked his thumb back at the rattling barn door still battling against its hinges as proof. 'He'd have pecked your eyes out if I hadn't have stopped him. He's not a fan of people—as I've learned to my cost.' Feeling daft but still clearly amused that he had been rumbled, he lifted his shirtsleeve to show her the deep beak mark he now sported above his left elbow. 'He took that chunk out of me last week when I turned my back on him for a second. This is his barn now and woe betide anyone who enters his domain unarmed.' His bad mood now gone, he winced at the trickle of blood making its way down her forearm. 'I feel awful that I forgot to warn you. I've got some bandages back at the house.'

She walked beside him towards it. 'Will the wing heal enough for him to fly again?'

Ned shrugged. 'The splints were Dr Able's idea, but the wing is supposed to be bandaged tight against Old Nick's side, but he won't have it. No matter how secure I bind the blighter, he keeps gnawing his way through them, so who knows?'

'If it doesn't, we both know you'll be building that swan house and digging Old Nick his own personal pond.'

'Not a chance!' He chuckled at his own unconvincing attempt at lying as he opened the kitchen door for her. 'I shall enjoy roasting the thing for my dinner and to hell with what the King has to say about it.'

He gathered a bowl of water, some salve and the bandages while Isobel made a fuss of Falstaff, then pulled at chair out from the kitchen table. 'Sit. Let me clean up those cuts.'

'They are more nicks than cuts.' Suddenly nervous at the prospect of his potent touch, she giggled as she did as she was told. 'You really don't need to fuss over Old Nick's nicks, Ned.'

He rolled his eyes at her silly attempt at humour. 'Old Nick's nicks might still turn nasty if they are not tended properly, Izzy, and I don't want you getting gangrene on my conscience too.' His gaze flicked pointedly towards the bloody puncture marks on her skin as he squeezed the excess water from the clean cloth he had brought and waited for her to dutifully hold out her arm. 'Thankfully these look shallower than the bite he gave to me.'

With surprising tenderness for a man so big, Ned dabbed carefully at her wounds.

'Perhaps that is Old Nick's way of being gentlemanly?' His touch unnerved her and yet felt sublime at the same time. 'Or perhaps he simply liked me more than you? Let's face it, I am easier to like.'

His dark gaze locked with hers, amused. 'And you are so modest about it too.'

There was something about the way he looked at her, as if he could see past all her defences to the inner workings of her mind, which rattled her more than the way her nerve endings rejoiced at his gentle ministrations. Enough that she needed to distract herself from the seductive pull of his eyes. 'But at least Rose likes you, although there is no accounting for taste, so I suppose you should be grateful for small mercies.'

'I suppose so.' The warmth in his dark irises disappeared as they shuttered for a moment before Ned broke the hypnotic contact to reach for the salve. He focussed on opening the jar yet seemed to be deep in thought. When he finally spoke again, his tone was casual. Almost a little too casual. 'Are you pleased that your machinations are working?'

Isobel wanted to be.

Would pretend to be no matter what.

But the truth was she was inexplicably worried about him and Rose and annoyed at the same time. Annoyed at him for some reason, for making such a concerted effort to get along so well with another woman but knew that made absolutely no sense when him getting along with Rose had been her intention. 'I am delighted.' Her answering smile pulled taut and fit ill on her face. 'I knew that you two would be perfect for one another. You have so much in common, it is uncanny.' And she was feeling most uncharitable towards Rose for each and every one of those similarities.

And for flirting with him.

Isobel was irrationally still put out about that too.

He applied some salve to her forearm with a gentle caress from the tip of his index finger, sending all sorts of inappropriate longings ricocheting around her body. 'But aren't opposites supposed to attract?' His gaze lifted briefly to hers, questioning, before it flicked back to the task in hand. 'Isn't the path to true love never supposed to run smooth? This all feels too neat and tidy for me.'

'There is nothing wrong with neatness where the heart is concerned, especially if it avoids messiness—which I can attest is painful and never seems to end well.' She hadn't so much ever had her heart broken, because she couldn't honestly say she had ever been even halfway in love with any of the let-downs she had set her desperate cap to, but she had repeatedly had her dreams crushed and been made a fool of in the process. All, shamefully, things Ned knew only too well because he had shaken his silent head at all of them. 'At least for me it hasn't at any rate, so if I were you, I'd be thankful that everything is only going in the right direction.' Even though an annoying voice in her head was currently screaming that this was all wrong she still persisted to encourage him.

Because she was a good friend.

Because he was still her best friend even if she was no longer his.

Because she wanted this for him.

Because Ned deserved to find happiness with someone who understood him.

Four excellent reasons to add to the undeniable fact that he and Rose *were* perfect for one another.

'It strikes me that Shakespeare got it all wrong when he claimed that, as the path of true love *is* usually meant to run smooth. The proof is that the world is stuffed to the rafters with happy matches who have never encountered a single bump in the road, and therefore surely they are the luckiest ones to be able to skip towards the unblighted sunset together unhindered, secure in the knowledge that they are doing it with the right one.' The image of her and him watching all those sunsets as children suddenly sprang to mind, alongside them watching it rise only the other week, and that instantly made her mourn the loss of him even though he wasn't yet gone.

Until that moment, she hadn't given much thought to things ever changing between them, but if he married the perfect-for-him-in-every-way Rose and she miraculously found a man who would rescue her from Whittleston and the bad reputation she had earned here, then she realised they would have to. Even if she failed to find a man—as it increasingly looked likely she might —the chasm between them would widen further as it should with such a monumental change in his marital circumstances. Especially if he and Rose had a family, and the past she had never been strong enough to let go of would shift further out of her reach. Which she supposed made her selflessness now the real supreme act of martyrdom.

Something to be proud of facilitating, not jealous for blossoming.

'When something is right it is right, Ned. It is as plain to me as that scruffy beard on your face that you and Rose are perfect for one another. Surely you can see that?'

He did not seem convinced and pulled a face as he dipped his finger in the salve again. 'I like her—but I don't *like* her, if you know what I mean.'

Why was that a huge relief?

'So I'm not keen to rush headlong into something that doesn't feel right to me, no matter how right it might seem to you. That was never in our agreement, Izzy, and you know it.'

She offered him her best reassuring smile, which was as much for her benefit as it was for his. 'It is always unsettling to sail in unfamiliar waters, and it is perfectly understandable that you are experiencing cold feet after dipping your inaugural toe in them, Ned. The first step is being open to the idea of romance, that was all I wanted. Now that we have cleared that hurdle with a light nudge from me, I am quite content to leave you both to it and let nature takes its course. You cannot surrender to irrational fear after your first

foray and if nothing is ventured, nothing potentially wonderful will be gained. All I am asking
you to try to do is to continue to be open to the
idea. Surely that isn't too much to ask after things
went so well today?'

'Maybe...' His finger paused on her skin
and as she watched it mesmerised, she heard
him swallow. 'But this feels like more than cold
feet.' His free hand touched his chest briefly as
if he was speaking from the heart and the subsequent shrug was boyish and uncertain because
he wasn't usually one to ever admit to feeling
anything at all beyond irritation. 'I know that I
agreed to go along with your nonsense, Izzy, but
already after just the one *foray* I can't help thinking—*hoping*—that maybe fate has other plans
for me that aren't so neat and tidy.' His thumb
caressed the sensitive skin under her arm as his
eyes seemed to stare into her soul. 'That it has
always had a master plan and it's just biding its
time for the right moment to reveal it to us.'

Us?

Surely her foolish, suddenly soaring heart was
reading far too much into that one tiny throw-
away word than it warranted. As if her and Ned...

As if Ned wanted her.

Her! The irritating bane of his life. The tar-
nished, fallen disappointment he barely tolerated

nowadays. Good heavens she really was in a desperate, addled state if she was hoping that he could put all that he knew about her unfortunate past to one side to want to have a future with her!

'Now which of us is talking nonsense?' She tugged her arm away out of necessity as his touch and his gaze were working together to thoroughly scramble her wits. 'I haven't got the time to waste waiting for fate to intervene. If I do that, I could be long gone from weary Whittleston before that miracle happens and without my interference you will likely be doomed for ever to your lonely life of bachelorhood.'

She jumped up and made a fuss of Falstaff in case her expression accidentally informed him that she wasn't quite as keen on being his matchmaker now that she understood the stakes. 'Why don't we make a start on warming your cold feet up by rounding up your sheep while we discuss how to build on today's success as best as we can? Especially in view of the sparseness of the coming week's scintillating social calendar.'

Chapter Ten

'Has the world gone mad or do mine eyes deceive me?' Mrs Fitzherbert delighted in lifting her quizzing glass so that she could look him up and down. 'For surely Mr Edward Parker hasn't actually come to church?' As she practically shouted that, all the worshippers queuing to get into the church turned around to stare at him. One of them was Izzy who beamed at him and the worrying effect of her smile on his insides confirmed all of his worst fears. He did have feelings for the minx and many of them weren't the least bit friendly. 'For nine and a half years you have only turned up for hatches, matches and despatches, so to what do we owe this unique honour today?'

'Last time I checked, all were welcome in the house of God.' Politeness made him stop and answer, but Ned made no secret of the fact that he wasn't amused by her sarcasm, any more than he was pleased to be here at all.

He almost hadn't come because he was still furious with Izzy for thrusting him at Miss Healy at the cake sale, and more furious at her for her enthusiasm that the pair of them were perfect for one another when he had as good as admitted that his heart might well already lay at her door. He blamed Miss Healy for putting all that nonsense about Izzy being jealous in his head in the first place, when she had never glanced his way like that ever, and still cringed at the way he had been desperate to believe it with no further proof whatsoever. Desperate enough to make a veiled suggestion, at least, that he would be willing if she would.

But of course, Izzy had shot that daft, fanciful and impractical idea dead in the paddock when she hadn't shown one speck of regret that he and Miss Healy had apparently been getting on so well. She had also been quick to reiterate that she was still hell-bent on leaving. If anything, she had been over the moon about the swift progress she had witnessed and was so self-congratulatory about the success of her 'little nudge' while she had helped him round up his lambs that he had almost thrown a tantrum and told her the truth.

He still wasn't sure why he hadn't. Any more

than he could explain, even to himself, why he was here to once again be the sacrificial pawn to her self-appointed queen in a game he had no desire to play. Not when he knew, without any shadow of doubt, that he did not want Miss Healy in the romantic, hearts and flowers sense and Miss Healy had made it plain that she didn't want him either. Which all rather suggested the joke was well and truly on him seeing that he was indeed here and only because the irritating minx had commanded it.

Because he, like his father before him, apparently could not say no to her. Because like his father, his stupid heart wanted what it couldn't have. A woman would leave him the first chance she got—and that was if she would even have him in the first place!

Hell, he was pathetic! Especially if he thought history wouldn't repeat itself when the writing had always been on the wall.

'All *are* welcome in the house of God.' Mrs Fitzherbert turned up her nose. 'But the last time *I* checked you were still furious at the Almighty for sending a pox to your house and have remained consistently determined to snub him on the back of it.' That was because he hadn't sent a pox, he'd sent almost all ten of the Biblical plagues of Egypt and Ned still bore a grudge about the glut of death, flood and famine he had had to endure as a result. 'So I shall ask you again, young man, what—or perhaps who—has precipitated this abrupt change of mind?' She turned her quizzing glass pointedly towards Izzy who was now chatting to Miss Healy.

'Unlike the rest of the population, we farmers do not have the luxury of resting on the Sabbath—but miraculously I found some time today, hence I am here.' And that, frankly, was all he was prepared to say on the subject.

'A convenient excuse and you know it. If your father was still alive, he'd have your guts for garters for your wilful neglect of your spiritual health, Ned. As I daresay the Parker pew is shrouded in dust after so many years without any sign of your bottom, I shall allow you to share mine.' Mrs Fitzherbert thrust her cane at him then leaned heavily on his arm, too proud and stubborn to admit she had worn herself out by her continued insistence of walking everywhere still despite her age, that she desperately needed the support.

As frustrating as that was, he empathised with the sentiment even if pride always did come before a fall. He was irritated enough with himself to know that his pride had had a big hand in him turning up here this morning. In fact, it had seemed necessary in case he had been too overt with Izzy the other evening when he'd waffled on nonsensically about fate and opposites attracting when his own parents' experience of that begged to differ. Coming here, he had reasoned after another sleepless night disturbed my too much thinking about her, let the hellion know that if she had any notion whatsoever that he had been hinting about them, as he plainly had been, then this suggested she had read him entirely wrong. He hoped she would think that he was here because he was interested in Miss Healy and, more importantly, she would witness him embellishing that falsehood some more today. He was even prepared to attempt to flirt if it convinced Izzy that he wasn't the least bit interested in her.

Despite the unsettling fact that he now very much was!

Seeing as he was clearly a suggestable idiot who went all peculiar at something as commonplace as an Isobel Cartwright smile, Ned was so angry at the futile stupidity of his misguided affections he could barely stand to look at himself in the mirror. Or look at her either, as looking at her only seemed to give him more inappropriate ideas which were as pointless as this convoluted charade involving Miss Healy was.

With impeccable timing and all for Izzy's sake, Miss Healy turned around, pasted a flirtatious smile on her face which had no effect on him whatsoever, and wiggled her fingers in coquettish greeting. Izzy, of course, was so buoyed by that apparent display of intent she shot him a knowing look and Mrs Fitzherbert cackled uncontrollably.

'And now, your sudden appearance here today all makes perfect sense—and yet still doesn't at all.' She looked him up and down, then stared at the disappearing backs of the two young ladies as they entered the church. 'Intriguing though, as now I find myself on tenterhooks wondering how this will all pan out. You and, *apparently*, Mrs Outhwaite's niece.' She cackled some more. 'Who would have seen *that* implausible twist coming in the ongoing romantic drama between you and Isobel?'

Rather than dig himself another hole in front of the wiliest woman of the village, Ned feigned confusion. 'As usual, I have no clue what you are talking about, Mrs Fitzherbert.'

She slapped his arm as she laughed. 'You remind me so much of dear Caleb. Your father, God rest him, was a dreadful liar too—yet still persisted regardless.' She nudged him as she gestured towards Miss Jemima Gilbert, Sophie's aunt and the real love of his father's life. 'He denied there was anything going on between them until his dying day rather than paint her as a married man's mistress, when we all knew different, didn't we? Yet for nineteen years he maintained that useless lie even though nobody had seen hid nor hair of your mother for all of them. And good riddance to the feckless strumpet too as she was never good enough for either you or your father.' She used the handle of her cane to tap his nose. 'But it's all the eyes, dear boy. The Parker eyes have always been windows into the Parker soul. Yours certainly say so much more than that belligerent mouth of yours ever has.'

He rolled his offending eyes as if her ludicrous comment was all water off a duck's back as they shuffled towards the door together, but inside he was starting to panic that his blasted eyes were indeed letting him down if Sophie, Miss Healy and now Mrs Fitzherbert had all commented upon them in such quick succession. Thankfully, Reverend Spears distracted them from having to continue with that awkward conversation when he greeted Ned like the prodigal son, pumping his hand enthusiastically and welcoming him back to the fold as if they hadn't collided at least twice a week all his life while they went about their daily business.

From her seat near the front, Izzy smiled at

him as he settled Mrs Fitzherbert into hers across the aisle, but as he took his place beside her, he watched her face fall and just knew that was because old Cartwright had arrived. Her body stiffened as her father took his pew beside her and they greeted one another with the distant formality of occasional acquaintances rather than a father and daughter who had probably not seen each other for a week. Her expression was bland, ostensibly unbothered. While Ned knew that was as much of an act as it had always been, her cold sire's was unmistakably one of disdain.

Noticing his scrutiny with undisguised interest, Mrs Fitzherbert leaned towards Ned's ear. 'I am not surprised that she is cross with him. I heard a rumour just yesterday that that pompous fool's business is doing so well in Chelmsford he intends to cut all his remaining ties with Whittleston quick sharp. The jumped-up nitwit is apparently buying himself a fancy house in Chelmsford.'

'Says who?' Instant panic gripped him at the prospect. Unlike most idle village gossip, which relied predominantly on hearsay and speculation, Mrs Fitzherbert's was always as accurate as the village clock—as her recent comment about his eyes was testament.

'I was visited by an old friend who lives there,

and she has it on the highest authority that he has put an offer in on a residence in Moulsham Street, within walking distance of his fancy emporium. Obviously, we shan't miss him, but I cannot deny I shall miss his daughter terribly. Isobel will be a great loss to the village and to me personally. Probably because she reminds me of…well…me so much. But do not tell her that. We don't do sentiment, either of us. It's far too revealing.'

The thought of Izzy leaving made the acid churn in his gut. He had always known that she would leave eventually, because she had reminded him weekly of her plans since girlhood, but he was still nowhere near ready to wave her off. 'Surely, she won't be going with him? They loathe one another.'

'By all accounts, it is quite a substantial family house and as she is still an unmarried daughter, I think it unlikely she wouldn't be going with him, don't you? Him leaving her in the lurch these last few months was unorthodox enough. To abandon her completely goes entirely against what is morally right.'

As subtle as the vexing young woman who she plainly adored, Mrs Fitzherbert wagged a wizened finger in her direction. 'I haven't had chance to ask Isobel about it yet because I did not see her at all yesterday after my visitor left, but I also cannot imagine he would continue pay rent on his house here now that he is uprooting completely. Maintaining a house here might make sense while he has been staying at his son's, but such an unnecessary extravagance once he has his own place, even for Isobel's sake, is unlikely in the extreme. George Cartwright has always been tight with his money and hasn't ever once considered her happiness in all the years she has been alive, so I sincerely doubt he will start now. Besides, with no shop tying him here any more and even less friends, there is no other incentive for him to keep the lease going.'

Was that why she had lost her sparkle? Was that also why she was in such a hurry to see him settled before she left for good? Had she known for a while that her time here was finite and that she had no choice but to move to Chelmsford?

Maybe—but surely she would have mentioned that? If not to him, then she would have confided in Sophie as the pair of them were as thick as thieves. Izzy had never been very good at keeping secrets and it made no sense that she wouldn't have told her two closest friends that the end of an era was nigh.

Which all rather suggested that she didn't yet know of her father's plans...

That was a more likely scenario. She would

be the last person her father considered consulting in any decision, let alone a life-changing one.

While the congregation chattered as they awaited the Reverend to take his place at the altar, Izzy and her father sat in stony silence. While the sourpuss stared straight ahead, she thumbed idly though her prayer book rather than attempt to make any conversation with a man who clearly had no intentions of making any in return. Once or twice, Ned noticed him glance at the scarlet silk flowers pinned to one side of his daughter's pale pink bonnet with open disapproval, but apart from that she might as well have not been there for all he cared. The sorry state of their relationship was emphasised further by the foot of space between them on the narrow pew they were forced to share. A foot of space which they managed to maintain even after the sermon started and they repeatedly stood to sing the hymns or knelt for the prayers.

At the end of the service, she dutifully filed out beside her father, although they might as well have been complete strangers as neither so much as acknowledged the other's presence on their journey down the aisle. It was all very strange and very sad. All so at odds with Izzy's naturally friendly and sociable character.

The pair of them had separated by the time

Ned emerged into the churchyard with Mrs Fitzherbert. Cartwright had placed himself next to the vicar, no doubt so that everyone who left the church had no choice but to glad hand him no matter how much they would have preferred to avoid the chore. Those who believed his convincingly charming demeanour, including Mrs Outhwaite, happily stopped to chat with him. Rather than watch that, Izzy was milling with some of the local ladies, smiling as was her way, but only on the outside. Like his, it was her eyes which let her down. There was no mistaking the sadness currently swirling within those bewitching cornflower depths.

Ned deposited his elderly charge with her usual gaggle of matrons and then headed Izzy's way.

'I need to talk to you urgently—but not here.' He paused only long enough to convey that message. Then sailed on by hoping she would follow him along the path which circumvented the church on its way onto the graveyard, without giving Mrs Fitzherbert more cause to be suspicious.

Even so, it took Izzy several minutes to extract herself and join him and in unspoken tacit agreement, they strolled towards his father's headstone before she spoke. 'Surely it is Rose you should be sneaking away for a private moment, not me? Or are your big cold feet bothering you again, coward? And why on earth are you still sporting that scruffy bush of a beard when I have begged you to shave it off repeatedly for poor Rose's sake? No young lady wishes to be kissed by a shrub.'

'Did you know that your father is buying a house in Chelmsford.'

'What?' By her stunned expression, this indeed was the first she was hearing about it, exactly as he had suspected.

'Mrs Fitzherbert heard it from friend who lives there. The house is apparently on Moulsham Street, I think she said, and he is awaiting acceptance of his offer.'

She shrugged despite being obviously bothered by the news. 'Why am I not surprised that Mrs Fitzherbert knows more about my dear papa's plans than I do? I've always been a begrudging afterthought to everything, and largely superfluous to all of his plans, so good luck to him.'

'But he is going to expect you to move there with him.'

She scoffed at that. 'He really isn't. He has already made it quite plain that me, and my shocking reputation, are unwelcome in Chelmsford as he cannot afford to have the hallowed Cartwright good name there sullied. I cannot imagine the purchase of a house will change that opinion.'

'Then you assume you will be staying here?' Relief washed over him at the prospect. 'He'll still maintain your house in the village?'

'Unless he decides to disown me or evict me first.' She grinned with dismissive confidence, but as mischievous as it was, it still did not quite reach her sad eyes. 'In which case you might have to suffer a lodger, Ned.'

'Perish the thought.' Although, to his great surprise, his heart leapt at the idea. 'But if I have to, I am sure I can make some space for you in the barn with Old Nick—seeing as he likes you more than I do.'

She shrugged, almost all sign of her disquiet at the unexpected news buried under a thick layer of typical Izzy bravado. 'That suits me just fine as I like Old Nick far more than I do you, too.'

Her father's ostentatious yellow curricle was sat outside the house by the time she returned a short while later. That he was leaving on a Sunday was no surprise, but that he was leaving so early in the day was. He usually meticulously went through the household accounts straight after church to ensure that she wasn't squandering the increasingly small allowance he gave her to run it. This deviation from his routine on top of the news he was purchasing a house only served to unsettle her further, but she would not give him the satisfaction of seeing that.

'At what point were you going to tell me that you had purchased a house on Moulsham Street? Or was it your intention to never tell me in case I darkened its door, Papa? Which of course, I would rather die than ever do.' When the wind had been knocked out of your sails, it was always best to come back fighting, so Isobel asked that with the breezy nonchalance of one who did not care one whit about the hurtful oversight. Or, more importantly, was not the slightest bit worried by what it meant.

'Who told you?' He did not bother denying it and was obviously aggrieved that she knew.

She offered him one of the tinkling laughs he found so annoying. 'Chelmsford is barely fifty miles away and shares the same road to London as we do, so it was hardly going to remain a secret for ever now, was it?' She peeled off her gloves and placed them inside her bonnet but continued to hold it in full view as her father glared at her over the top of his copy of yesterday's *South Essex Gazette* simply because she knew that he disapproved of it.

She knew that irrefutably because he had vehemently disapproved of the smaller sprig of harlot's scarlet silk roses which it had sported two weeks ago. Hence she had added a few more red petals as a quiet act of continued defiance. It was those tiny little flashes of rebellion which always got his dander up the most despite them doing little to make her feel better about her lot.

With hindsight, which she had never been good at pre-empting, this latest petty revolt had probably not been wise. 'As I am sure you can imagine, that juicy titbit is already doing the rounds about the village. Everyone so far seems delighted that you have no plans to return here permanently.' She would be one of them if only she could be assured that her place here was still secured. 'Dare I ask what that means for this place?' She gestured around the drawing room which so often felt like a prison, but which suddenly seemed like the last sanctuary she had left.

'There is six months left on the lease.'

Fear made bile rise in her throat, but she smiled regardless. 'And when those six months are up?'

'I am rather hoping that six months is all the incentive you need to finally find a man foolish enough to relinquish me of the burden of your tiresome upkeep.'

'And if it isn't?'

Rather than answer with something tangible and honest, he did what he always had since time immemorial and sowed more seeds of uncertainty. Simply because he enjoyed toying with her mind and leaving her unsettled. He smiled smugly as he flipped open his watch and then stood as he snapped it back closed. 'I shall leave that conundrum with you as I must get back.'

'What? Without bestowing your customary blistering lecture because I denied you that pleasure over breakfast?' She had instead watched the sunrise again alone on a riverbank nowhere near Ned's stretch which had called to her. An act born more out of cowardice than rebellion as her deteriorating relationship with her father was rattling her more than she wanted to admit. As she refused to admit it now, too, Isobel threw herself onto the sofa, because he had always hated such unladylike displays of wilfulness, and picked up her embroidery as if this whole topic bored her. 'I shall look forward to receiving double the usual vitriol next Sunday instead.'

'I shan't be coming next Sunday. Nor at all for the next month as I have a new house to organise after I head to the coast for a little holiday with your brother and his family. Now that my daughter-in-law is expecting again—' He glanced with disgust at the vicinity of her unused womb. '—Richard thinks some sea air will do his wife good.'

'What fun for you all.' She tried not to be bitter that she had never once been included on any of the family sojourns to fashionable Brighton. 'And how fortuitous for me to be spared the arduous chore of your company for the rest of the spring.' At least she wouldn't have to dread Sundays, so she would find some joy from his unexpected house purchase, albeit only temporarily.

'I trust you will use the time wisely to do what you should have done years ago, and I should hope that I do not need to warn you to behave with the utmost propriety as you do it.'

'I am sure that your spy Tess will keep you informed of any infringements.' Not that there was any chance of any infringements. Nor any chance of her being stupid enough to do anything potentially that disastrous, which would give her father the excuse he so desperately needed to prematurely sever their flimsy familial bond altogether.

'I mean it, Isobel. I cannot afford to tolerate any more of your scandals. Chelmsford society is less forgiving of a bad reputation than common folk here in Whittleston are, and I have a fledgling business to think of.'

'Thank goodness it is fifty miles away then.' She forced a sunny smile as she jabbed an unperturbed needle into her embroidery.

'Yet as you said yourself, what is fifty miles when Chelmsford shares the same road to London as Whittleston does? Bad news always travels the fastest.' That veiled threat issued, he stalked out the door without bothering to pause to say goodbye.

Chapter Eleven

When Ned arrived home the next evening, he found a parcel wrapped in paper and ribbon alongside a handwritten invitation and a hastily scribbled note on his kitchen table.

The invite was from Sophie for an impromptu dinner at her house tonight. The note from Izzy instructed him to arrive fashionably late, to dress to impress and to shave off his dratted beard or risk actual harm to his person. The parcel contained the most Izzy-like waistcoat he had ever seen.

As promised, it was burgundy, and surprisingly sedate in its simple but impeccable cut despite the bold colour of the luxurious fabric. That she had made it expressly for him made it special. That it fit like a glove after just one set of measurements staggered him. But fit it did and he looked quite distinguished in it too, even if he did say so himself.

That did little to make him feel less self-conscious, however, when he arrived at Hockley Hall precisely fifteen minutes after the stipulated time of eight. All eyes swivelled to Ned as the butler showed him into the drawing room. All bar one pair widened with surprise to see him looking so smart. The beguiling cornflower-blue ones, of course narrowed, because he had kept the beard to spite the interfering menace and to prove to himself that he bloody well could resist her if he put his mind to it.

'Sorry I am late.' Why the blazes had he obeyed that royal command when he hated being late—especially for a good friend like Sophie. 'I had to herd up a few ewes who refused to be herded.' He made sure to send his apologetic smile the way of each of the other guests after their hosts. While Izzy still glared at his beard, Miss Jemima, Mrs Fitzherbert, Archie and the local physician Dr Able all smiled back. 'I hope you haven't delayed your dinner for me.'

'Not at all. We are still awaiting Rose, so you are not the last to arrive.' As her husband, Rafe, pressed a brandy into Ned's hand, Sophie winked at him. 'Unfortunately, it will be just Miss Healy tonight from that household as her uncle is away on business and her aunt is under the weather. Obviously, I would have postponed tonight if I had known that she was indisposed.'

'What utter rot.' Izzy typically said what they were all thinking.

'What can I say?' Sophie delighted in looking as guilty as sin as she passed her aunt a glass of sherry. 'Other than it is obviously a complete coincidence that Mrs Outhwaite's unfortunate bout of sickness coincided with my decision to christen my newly decorated dining room with a spur-of-the-moment dinner party. As proof of my obliviousness, I even sent her an invitation which she understandably had to decline—the *poor thing.*'

Izzy laughed out loud at that. 'Then you fervently deny all the rumours that Mrs Fitzherbert tipped you off that she was ill this morning an hour before those hastily written invitations were sent?'

'How dare you,' said Mrs Fitzherbert with more convincing aplomb than Sophie managed. 'As if I would be party to such underhand and ungracious shenanigans.' She snatched her own glass from the proffered tray and then turned her nose up at it before she put it back and snapped her fingers at their host. 'I vowed never to touch another drop of sherry after my third husband's wake. It's a vile drink which is foisted on the ladies only so that the gentlemen get to keep the good stuff for themselves. As I gave up behaving like a lady after my second husband's funeral, you can pour me a brandy, Rafe. And please don't be stingy with it like you were the last time. We both know that no matter what dear Dr Able here has to say on the subject, I am going to get tipsy and behave outrageously tonight because, in the first instance, I enjoy it and in the second, at ninety-five I have earned the right to do as I jolly well please! So let us work together on the endeavour rather than be at odds. We all have to die of something, and I would much prefer to go with a cognac-inspired smile on my face than frowning from the foul taste of one of his supposed health-giving potions.'

'As if you even bother to take them,' said the doctor with such an exaggerated roll of his eyes it made everyone chuckle.

'You might well be five and ninety, but I'll wager you could still drink me under the table, Mrs Fitzherbert.' While the doctor glared unconvincingly at his oldest patient, the new Lord Hockley poured her a generous snifter which he then delivered personally along with the decanter. 'I'll also wager it would take more than brandy to kill you.'

'Can I have a brandy?' This came from Archie, who despite his smart coat and intricately tied cravat was sat in the middle of the rug tickling Fred the dog's upturned belly. 'I'm old enough.' Perhaps in age and body he was, but sadly, Mother Nature has given Rafe's sweet brother the mind of a child.

'Absolutely not!' Rafe nipped that request in the bud. 'The last time somebody gave you alcohol you disgraced yourself all over the floor of the village hall in the middle of the assembly.' He pointed an accusing finger at Mrs Fitzherbert. 'And ninety-five or not, you slip him any tonight and it will be you who cleans the mess up.'

'It was waltzing so vigorously with Sophie that upset Archie's stomach that fateful night, not the miniscule nip of brandy I allowed him to sip.'

'As your complaint about my stingy pouring is testament, your definition of a nip and mine, Mrs Fitzherbert, are vastly different. Furthermore…' Rafe's lecture was stopped mid-sentence by the polite cough of Hockley Hall's butler who arrived with Miss Healy in tow.

Except she wasn't alone. Beside her was a dashing soldier in smart regimentals. A man so effortlessly handsome, Ned hated him on sight because he just knew that he was the exact sort to turn Izzy's flighty head.

'Miss Healy, my lord…and her brother, Lieutenant Healy.'

Instantly intrigued, Izzy dazzled the newcomer with her most attractive smile while Miss Healy apologised to their hosts.

'I do hope that it is all right that I brought along Daniel—he only just arrived this evening, out of the blue as is his usual wont, and I did not want to cancel on you nor leave him alone for the evening with my sick aunt when we haven't seen one another for months. Obviously if that isn't convenient, we shan't importune you beyond this introduction, but I wanted you all to meet him.'

'It is perfectly convenient.' Unfazed and unintimidated by the arrival of the stranger, Sophie welcomed him with open arms while her husband had a discreet word with the butler to set another place at the table. 'Welcome to Whittleston-on-the-Water, Lieutenant.' She commandeered him from his sister to walk him around the room to make the introductions.

'Well, he's as fine a looking specimen as ever I saw one,' said Mrs Fitzherbert in what was supposedly a casual aside to Ned as she peered through her eyeglass, but which carried much further. 'He has the shoulders to display that uniform with pleasing aplomb and an excellent jawline.' Two unmistakable details which infuriated

Ned but seemed to please Izzy immensely. She was a huge fan of a whisker-free chiselled jaw. Stick a fetching dimple in the centre of an annoyingly square chin and the interloper's was about as perfect as it was possible for a jaw to be.

'And this is Miss Isobel Cartwright.' Sophie and the Lieutenant had made it as far as the sofa.

'Miss?' To thoroughly ruin Ned's evening completely, his latest rival's expression managed to be flirty, mischievous and charming all at the same time. Just like her. So like her in every conceivable way that it was galling.

They were both too handsome.

Both golden-haired and blue-eyed.

Both didn't so much wear their clothes like all lesser mortals had to, more the way they wore theirs made all the lesser mortals' sartorial efforts pale into insignificance. Even a good six inches taller than the smarmy new soldier in his scarlet regimentals and bedecked in ridiculously expensive, striking burgundy himself, Ned had had never felt so invisible in his life.

'If I might be impertinent, that strikes me as an utter travesty, *Miss* Cartwright. How foolish are the fine fellows here in Essex to have not swept such a prized gem off the marriage mart?'

Izzy, of course, lapped that old flannel up like a cat did cream because she had always had a particular soft spot for a man in uniform. 'Alas, Lieutenant, fine fellows are few and far between in this part of the county.'

'Then, thank goodness I arrived, Miss Cartwright. Where Essex woefully fails to do its duty, the Suffolk contingent are only too keen to step into the breach.' Of course, the silver-tongued charmer then placed a lingering kiss on the back of her gloved hand while his hooded eyes ate her for breakfast. 'I look forward to furthering our acquaintance in the coming weeks.'

It took all Ned had not to groan aloud or glare or growl at that. But as Sophie tugged the randy lieutenant away to meet her Aunt Jemima, Miss Healy headed towards him. 'My, don't you look handsome tonight, Ned Parker?' Like her vile brother, she had a mischievous twinkle in her eyes too. One that willed him to play along.

While he struggled with how best to do that with words, which had never been his forte, Mrs Fitzherbert thankfully filled the void.

'Not as handsome as you look, Miss Rose, isn't that right, Ned?' A bony, ninety-plus elbow jabbed him firmly in the ribs while the end of her cane pressed down hard on his big toe to encourage him to agree.

'You look quite beautiful tonight... Rose.' Which to be fair to her she did. If his wayward eyes hadn't apparently been ruined for all other women by the eyelash-batting, officer-loving menace a few feet to his right, Miss Healy had all the enticements necessary to turn his head.

'You exaggerate with such convincing assurance, Ned, that I shall take that lovely compliment and treasure it even though I do not fully believe it.'

'Oh, believe it, Rose.' Was it his imagination or did Izzy's tone suddenly sound off? 'Ned is a man of few words and even fewer compliments, so that fact that he offered you one is a rare miracle indeed.'

'Both facts are true,' said Mrs Fitzherbert with a wicked twinkle in her eye. 'In all the years that I have known Ned, I have never once heard him resort to idle flattery. For the record, he is right, young lady.' She turned her wily smile towards Miss Healy. 'You are quite the beauty.' The gnarled elbow jabbed his ribs again. 'Move over, Ned. I am sure Miss Healy can squeeze in between us.'

He was pretty sure that she wouldn't without a very tight squeeze indeed, but did as he was ordered regardless, and was proved correct when Miss Healy squashed herself in the insubstantial gap. To say that the end result left the pair of them cosy was an understatement, as the side of her body was now plastered to his from shoulder to ankle, and just in time for him to be introduced to her brother.

'It is good to meet you, Mr Parker. My sister speaks *very* highly of you.' At her mock, chastising stare, Smug Chiselled Chin winked at him as if they were already friends, which Ned sincerely doubted would ever be the case. 'In fact, Rosie waxed lyrical about you and your "pretty, riverside farm" all the way here.' He stuck out his hand, forcing Ned to execute an awkward handshake made more difficult by his tight proximity to Miss Healy's person.

'Lieutenant.' Ned nodded and left it at that because he had never been any good at small talk and certainly not with an over-confident upstart whom he was sorely tempted to punch just for breathing the same air as him.

'Like Papa, Ned is an experimental farmer, Daniel. Always on the lookout for a way to do things better.' For reasons best known to herself, Miss Healy had woven her arm through his. 'I suspect that he and Papa would discuss farming for hours if we put them in the same room together.'

'The apple did not fall far from that tree, Mr Parker.' Lieutenant Healy gestured towards his sister with a flick of his eyes. 'Unlike myself,

Rosie has inherited our father's love of the land and will use any excuse to stick her oar in about how best to use it. Be mindful of that if she ever wanders down your riverbank again as before you know it, she'll have taken it upon herself to roll up her sleeves and tell you how to do it better. She is annoyingly practical and has always been my father's right arm as a result.' His wistful smile was perfectly symmetrical and emphasised the dimple in the centre of his smug, square chin. 'Whereas I've always been more the adventuring type than the sort with roots planted firmly in the soil.'

'It's true,' added Miss Healy with a wistful smile of her own. 'With all his big dreams and untamed wild spirit, Daniel was never destined to stay in Suffolk.' Yet more that the bastard had in common with Izzy.

'Dinner is served.' The butler saved him from having to hear any more depressing similarities, but to compound Ned's misery further, Sophie had placed their unexpected guest practically opposite him at table. A position which gave him absolutely no choice but to watch Izzy flirt with the interloper throughout the meal while he did a very poor job of pretending to do the same with his sister.

Chapter Twelve

Isobel used the protracted game of whist going on between Rafe, Dr Able, Lieutenant Healy and Rose as an excuse to slip out of the drawing room unnoticed. In case one of the servants spied her, or Archie followed as he was prone to do, she darted down the hallway and into the partially decorated ballroom on purpose, and once inside, headed straight to the French doors and the cool fresh air beyond.

Five minutes alone in the garden with her troubled thoughts might help put some of them to rest. If it didn't, at least those five minutes would give her some respite from pretending to enjoy herself. Her cheeks ached from smiling and her heart was heavier here at Hockley Hall than it had been at home.

There, the only things she had to worry about were potential destitution and her entire world crashing around her ears. Here, she had all that still but also had to watch Ned, bit by bit, fall head over heels in love with the woman of his dreams too. An onerous task which, it turned out, was akin to torture in her current turbulent state of mind. Torture of her own making, to boot, so the irony of the situation wasn't lost on her despite the fact she now felt little satisfaction in her phenomenal success as a matchmaker.

Was it wrong to feel so ungracious that Ned might finally find some happiness after all that he had been through?

Of course it was!

Which meant that Isobel now had to add shame into the current, tangled mix of emotions plaguing her and sucking all of the joy out of her usually joyful soul. That shame, combined with the rampant jealousy which had reared its ugly head at the rectory cake sale and refused to go away, certainly left a bitter taste in her mouth. Worse, since her father's ultimatum, a niggling voice in her head told her that Ned would be the perfect solution to that problem—if she married him. An errant thought that, once it had taken root, had grown with the speed of a bramble bush because she was convinced wouldn't actually mind marrying him. Despite his gruff exterior, he was generous and kind. Clever. Resourceful. Hard-

working. Loyal. All those marvellous character traits were combined with a handsome face
and an impressive physique which she suddenly
found appealing in the feminine sense, which all
suggested that doing her wifely duty with Ned
wouldn't be the chore she feared it would be with
another man.

Yet if she discounted her newly awakened desire and her rampant jealousy at his blossoming
affinity with Rose, because she knew both of
those things were dreadfully selfish, she knew
too that it was unfair and unreasonable to want
him for herself when she hadn't taken a moment
to consider it until her world threatened to implode.

Ned was her friend first and foremost. Her oldest friend. A good friend she had loved all her life
in a friendly manner, and her strange new feelings for him were likely as transient as all her
feminine feelings for a man always were. She had
always been flighty in that way, and despite all
her romantic failures and disappointments, she
was honest enough with herself to know it was
only ever her pride and her self-esteem that had
been seriously wounded by all those rejections.
Her fickle heart, like her usually disinterested
body, had been left unaffected. Which all rather
suggested that her current and sudden attraction

to him was only heightened because her world seemed likely to implode now that her father had as good as threatened eviction.

Ned had always been her constant and her confidant, so it made perfect sense to her that she would instinctively gravitate towards him in a time of trouble. That was nothing new and had happened time and time again until things improved, and she did not need him quite so much. And bless him, no matter how much he feigned tolerance or claimed to be sick of the sight of her, he had never castigated her for her poor choices or shameful mistakes, as if he knew nobody could punish her for them more than she did herself. As if he knew that she had nobody else in the world who cared that she was out of sorts and needed a best friend so very badly.

But he had never so much as hinted that he could ever be any more than that.

Had never flirted her or glanced upon her covetously, and he had certainly never had as much in common with her as he had with Rose. Watching him with her tonight had been so painful because there was something about Ned and Rose that was just right. They were birds of a feather and quite a different species to Isobel. As perfect a pairing as anyone could ever wish for.

Therefore, as much as she feared for her future, it wasn't right to ruin his too by foisting herself upon him further by attempting to shift the dynamics of their relationship from friendly to so much more. Especially when he had suffered quite enough in the last decade and thoroughly deserved some proper happiness. The sort that only came alongside a woman of his choosing. A woman he had heaps in common with. A woman who wasn't a constant source of gossip when he preferred to keep himself to himself. A woman free from scandal and shame, who didn't disappoint him in any way. Who wanted him for him and not because he was the convenient solution to a problem that was not of his making.

Ned was her best friend, and she would treasure and honour that by ignoring her inappropriate new feelings and continuing to do what was right for him. To encourage him to dip more than his toe in the choppy waters of *l'amour* until he felt confident enough to dive headfirst into them and then swim unaided.

Something she was mindful she needed to do again herself, especially since her father's bombshell yesterday. Because if she didn't find some fool willing to marry her before the lease on the house ran out, she had no idea what was going to happen or what to do about it if it did.

She had no money of her own. No savings

or nest egg to help her weather the threatening storm. She had no skills to support herself either beyond her talent with a needle or behind a shop's counter, and while the creative dreamer within would probably adore the challenge of owning her own haberdashers-cum-drapers or even chancing her arm as a modiste on the side and creating clothes, common sense told her that you needed the means to set yourself up in business before you could start one. Which she very much did not.

That left only one pragmatic solution to the gathering threat of homelessness—marriage.

But thanks to her shocking reputation, the only way she could manage that as rapidly as she now needed to, was to marry someone who was oblivious of her history and had no plans to linger here any longer than he had to so that it didn't matter. Then basically lie to him for all eternity that she had one at all, while constantly hoping what had happened in Whittleston stayed in Whittleston. Or she married a stupid and desperate man like Mr Bunion and spent the rest of her life regretting it.

Neither option particularly appealed. But as her father was so fond of saying, you reap what you sow, so she supposed she had to find someone willing fast.

She wandered deeper into the garden until she found a bench, trying hard to feel positive about Lieutenant Healy's timely arrival as she stared up at the stars with the weight of the world on her shoulders. The eternal optimist inside her wanted to believe that him turning up at her most desperate moment was a sign. Call it fate—to use Ned's uncharacteristically romantic descriptor— but surely it had to be a good thing that she now had another potentially marriageable candidate hovering on the horizon who wasn't the awful Mr Bunion? Especially as she couldn't quite bring herself to see that lacklustre sycophant as a candidate at all despite her current dire straits and distinct lack of options. The thought of kissing him gave her the shivers—and not in a good way. Whereas she probably wouldn't mind kissing Lieutenant Healy.

He was certainly handsome enough.

He was fun too and an interesting conversationalist.

And while there was no disputing that he was clearly a shocking ladies' man and an outrageous flirt, he and she appeared to have much in common. He also seemed the sort to act in a hasty and rash manner, like her, and not give too much thought to the consequences, which conversely made him perfect in view of her current precarious situation. And he already seemed keen, more than keen in fact judging by his constant flirting this evening, so why was she so unenthused about the prospect of flirting back? Of going out of her way to seduce him into whisking her away from Whittleston? Why was she out here wandering in somebody else's garden and not inside their house continuing to use her wiles to entice him when the clock was so loudly ticking?

Sadly, she knew the answer to that already and it was the enormous oaf who was now enamoured with very woman she had thrust him at.

It was proving impossible to concentrate on her own flirting when her gaze kept being drawn to Ned and Rose. The sight of them enjoying each other's company so much now bothered her more than her father's thinly veiled threats had. She could compartmentalise that problem in her mind in the same way as she had always locked everything to do with her dismal family situation in a box which she only opened if she had to. She had always much preferred to bury her head in the sand while her optimistic soul hoped something would come up. After all, six months felt like a long enough distance away not to immediately panic about it.

A lot could happen in six months.

Sophie could have had the baby she was still

determined to keep a secret from everyone, Rose and Ned could still go their separate ways despite the promising start to their relationship, and her father's threats could still be empty ones.

Such blatant denial was undoubtedly false hope, but it was at least something to cling to. Ego, she had spent the last day doing what she always did where her problems were concerned, by doing whatever it took to distract herself from them.

Like spend every waking hour since her father's bombshell making Ned a waistcoat that, if she said so herself, he looked magnificent in. Magnificent enough that Lieutenant Healy's dashing, scarlet regimentals had rather blended into Hockley Hall's panelling.

As if she had conjured the brute, she saw his unmistakable huge silhouette striding up the path towards her, so strapped on her blithest smile and straightened her shoulders in case he noticed that she was lost.

'Don't tell me that you are taking a wander beneath the moonlight on your way to a tryst, Ned?' In case her smiled slipped as it wanted to, she nailed it in place. 'I should probably disappear elsewhere if you have made plans to meet the *beautiful* Rose here.' His pretty compliment of earlier stuck in her throat as she had never heard Ned be so effusive in his praise before. He had certainly never complimented her on her looks. Probably hadn't ever given them a passing thought either. Why would he when they had grown up together and he only tolerated her?

'Er...no...sorry...' He ran an agitated hand through his dark hair as he checked behind him. 'Am I interrupting you...um...and...' He jerked his thumb back towards the house and winced, looking every ridiculously long inch a man ready to run. 'It never occurred to me that you had snuck out here for a tryst, Izzy.'

'I did not—so you can stop hopping awkwardly from foot to foot. I have no interest in cards or Mrs Fitzherbert's tipsy wander down memory lane, so came out for some air.' She shuffled to one side and patted the bench beside her. 'Is that your excuse for being antisocial too?'

'No.' He sat with relieved heaviness, seeming awkward still. 'You looked occupied just before you snuck out and I came to see if you were all right... Only we haven't spoken since Sunday morning, and I wondered what happened with your father after church.'

How to describe that hornets' nest without sounding as if her sky was falling down?

'Oh, well, he is buying a house and putting down permanent roots in Chelmsford as you said, so Mrs Fitzherbert was as well informed as usual. I shan't be living in it, of course, because he doesn't want my dubious reputation to sully his or my sainted brother's pristine ones in any way, so I cannot help thinking that it's a positive turn of events in the long run.'

The optimist in her wanted to view this as a blessing in disguise. The push she needed to step out from her father's suffocating shadow and live her life her own way for ever after. The problem with that was, for all her talk of being an adventurer, she lacked the confidence in herself to truly be one on her own. As much as she chafed against her father's constant disappointment in her and his copious criticism, he had made some valid points. She wasn't much more than a pretty face who could act as if she was more than she was but lacked the ability to actually be it. She would have achieved something by now otherwise.

'Then you are staying here?'

For the time being at least. 'I am indeed. So you are stuck with me until my knight in shining armour gallops in and carries me away from this dull place.'

She wanted to believe that his answering smile meant more than it did. 'You never know, Izzy, you might change your mind about Whittleston with no remnants of your father in it. It might feel more like home without his oppressive control over you and constant admonishments. Maybe you might even decide to plant your roots here permanently…'

'Perish the thought!' She brushed that away in case her desperate melancholy showed. 'All that waits for me in dull Whittleston is a boring life of spinsterhood. No indeed, I will *never* settle here permanently.' She had no desire to be pitied or gossiped about for ever, for all her poor choices. Had no wish to be the depressing moral to the tale as the years crept by and all her shame and secrets eventually leaked out to all and sundry as such things had an annoying habit of doing in such a small community.

Here lies Miss Isobel Cartwright
A fallen woman of this parish
Whom nobody wanted to marry because she
was thoroughly soiled goods

That deserved but tragic epitaph notwithstanding, she most especially could not bear to stay here if Ned did fall in love with Rose and marry her. Watching that would likely kill her. 'Let us not waste another moment discussing my irksome father or this dreary place.' Her tears hovered too close to the surface to stop them from leaking in despair. 'How does your new waistcoat fit?' She had been a scrawny ten-year-old the last time she had grizzled in front of Ned and he had teased her mercilessly on the back of it. Nobody else had seen her shed a tear since and allowing anyone to now would feel like her father was winning. 'I intended to fit it to you properly before I finished it, but used the drab one I stole from your wardrobe in the end, as soon as Sophie mentioned her dinner party plans, and hoped for the best.'

Without thinking she opened his unbuttoned coat to peer at her handiwork herself before she considered how inappropriate and intimate that was and sat back holding her errant hands in her lap. 'Is it too tight anywhere?'

'Not at all. You did an excellent job.' To prove it, he shrugged halfway out of his coat and spun on the bench to show her his broad back. The damask moulded to his body, emphasising its strength and impressive masculine shape as if inviting her to touch. 'Thank you.'

Before she could stop herself, her fingers smoothed over his shoulders to check the fabric sat right with the lining, and then instantly regretted it when his shoulders gave her them ideas.

Years of manual labour had laid proper, hard muscle over his enormous frame and they tensed some more beneath her touch. Very probably because she was making him uncomfortable with her unwelcome and inappropriate ogling.

She tugged the hem to pretend she was double checking the length rather than his shoulders before she sat back. 'I knew this bold colour would suit you. Rose has been shooting you covetous glances all evening despite your stubborn refusal to get rid of that horrid beard.'

He shrugged as he put his coat back to rights, smiling a little rather than pull his usual belligerent frown at her admonishment. 'It's too damn dark, Izzy. That's the problem. And grows faster than weeds. So if I shave it off it'll be back again in no time, and I don't have the time to scrape my chin in front of a mirror daily like one of those dandified fellows with nothing better to do.' He jerked his thumb back in the direction of the house as if one of those dandies resided there.

'Perhaps…but for a special occasion you could make the effort, Ned.'

And there was the belligerent frown she usually got, accompanied by folded arms that made the muscles in them strain against his smart sleeves. 'I came out here to be a good friend, not get nagged again, Izzy.'

A gesture she appreciated too much to spoil. 'Then allow me to be a good friend in return.' The true measure of a best of friends was how selflessly they worked for their friend's happiness. Isobel would not be selfish, no matter how much she wanted to be, because he deserved better. 'Seeing as we are both here, why don't we take advantage of this brief moment of quiet to start our lessons?'

'I beg your pardon?' He stared at her as if she had gone mad.

'When we struck our bargain, Ned, I promised to help you to navigate all social situations properly.' This was true martyrdom for a cause. The selfless, brave and righteous thing to do.

'Is this your unsubtle way of trying to tell me that my manners need work then you can—'

She stayed him with an imperious raised palm. 'Obviously, your manners *could* use some polishing, but we have bigger fish to fry this evening.' She wiggled her eyebrows to cover the uncertainty of what she was about to offer. 'Especially with things between you and Rose progressing so rapidly.'

'Oh, good grief!' He stared heavenward then shook his dark head. 'How many times do I have to tell you that I do not require your intrusive services as a matchmaker? That wasn't what I agreed to, Izzy, and you know it!'

Rather than get into that circular argument again, she decided it was best to ignore it seeing as it was ultimately for his own good. 'When an opportunity presents itself, Ned Parker, one must seize it, and your fickle friend fate has afforded you a splendid one tonight.' She wiggled her brows again and when he stared back blankly, she huffed. 'Oh, for goodness' sake, Ned! There is a woman back there doing her utmost to tell you that she is interested in you, and only a fool wouldn't use that to his courting advantage. Fortunately for you, I have an idea.'

His expression had shuttered at the word *courting*. 'One that I am pretty sure I have no interest hearing.'

'When we head back into the house, I shall have a quiet word with Mrs Fitzherbert to tell her that I do not require her carriage to take me home this evening because *you* are going to.'

'But I don't have a carriage, Izzy.' He slapped his hard thighs, drawing her gaze to how the soft fabric of his breeches pulled taut over them. 'I came on Shank's pony.'

Good Lord, but he was exasperating! 'That is the whole point, Ned. Do try to follow along.' She whacked his belligerently folded arms. '*We* shall be walking because Rose and the Lieutenant will *also* be walking back to the village.'

'And?'

She painted an arc in the air with her palm.

'And the stars are twinkling and the moon is full and we shall have the lane all to ourselves.'

'And?'

Clearly he did not possess one romantic bone in his big body. 'And while I find some ruse to distract her brother somewhere en route—'

'How convenient!' The beefy arms unfolded and slapped hard against his thighs once more. 'I might have known this nonsense was more about you than it was about me! Stick a uniform in front of you and you completely lose all sense of reason!' Like a child, he showed her his back again, his stubborn chin jutting as he looked away. 'You can arrange your own *trysts*, Izzy, and without my help!'

That accusation stung, because it genuinely hadn't been her intention at all until he had mentioned it. 'Actually—it was *your* tryst I was planning!' She tried to push the intractable wretch off the bench onto his backside and only managed to shift the big brute an inch. 'Because if you had let me finish my sentence before you rudely interrupted, I was going to suggest you used those few moments alone to steal a first kiss from Rose!'

'Of course you were.' In view of her benevolence, he was being disproportionately disgruntled and twisted back to snarl at her. 'Never mind that it gives you the perfect opportunity to lock lips with Smug Chiselled Chin in there.'

She supposed it did. Two birds killed neatly with one stone. Except...

Except... '*Smug Chiselled Chin*?' His bizarre comment finally permeated her brain. 'Smug—*Chiselled*—Chin. What sort of nickname is that to give to your future brother-in-law?'

Ned shot up from the bench like a firework. 'That's it! I'm going back inside where the people are sane!' And off he went, his long legs eating up the ground while he muttered, big arms waving, until she caught up with him and managed to grab his flailing sleeve.

'Before you disappear, all self-righteous and affronted, at least allow me to give you a few pointers on stealing the perfect kiss.'

'I don't need any blasted *pointers* on that score, thank you very much!' He tugged his sleeve from her grasp and stalked onwards, forcing her to scurry to keep up.

'You have been hiding away on your farm for almost a decade, Ned! Where the only company you have kept is your sheep, so of course you need a few pointers, and better they come from a good friend like me, who will not judge you for your lack of experience, than make a hash of it with Rose.'

He refused to either turn around or slow down. 'I know how to blasted kiss, Izzy!'

'I am not suggesting that you don't, Ned.' Bless him. He was ashamed of his inexperience but she was right. It was better to tackle that issue with her than mess it all up with the woman of his dreams. But if he was going to listen to her advice, she needed to tread carefully. Not be judgemental and to keep the mood light. Airy but matter-of-fact. That was always the best way to broach a difficult subject. 'I'm merely saying that, as far as us ladies are concerned, there are nice kisses and not so nice kisses, Ned. The nice ones make a girl's heart melt and the not so nice are, frankly, a lot like being licked by Falstaff.'

'I know how to kiss, Izzy!' He was furious, she could tell, and no doubt hideously embarrassed. But this had to be done.

For his own stubborn good.

She kept her tone breezy despite practically having to jog alongside him now. 'I want yours to fall in the melting hearts category, Ned, and that is a dark art which will require some practice. But once you have mastered the basic rules it is very simple and, luckily for you, I am no stranger to the sport. Therefore, I can categorically state that the most important thing to remember about a first kiss is that it will set out your stall. You want to show Rose the sort of lover she can expect in you.'

'Stop, woman! For the love of God, stop!'

'The first thing you need to do once you get Rose alone later is—' Isobel couldn't finish that sentence because she slammed into his back as he had stopped dead.

His back was still to her, but his raised finger was in the air like a fire and brimstone preacher about to launch into a sermon about eternal damnation. 'I'm warning you, Izzy, say one more thing and—'

'Go slowly, Ned. Don't rush, whatever you do. When the moment is right lean in and—' She couldn't finish that sentence either, because he suddenly spun around, dipped his head and pressed his mouth to hers.

Instantly, hers blossomed into life.

To his credit, Ned did not fall into the Falstaff category.

Nor did he fall especially into the melting hearts category either, although hers still did in the most thorough and overwhelming fashion when his lips gently whispered over hers and promised so much more. As his other hand snaked around her waist and tugged her closer, he also deepened the kiss and that was when she quite forgot where she was or what she was supposed to be doing.

That was when she discovered that Ned Parker's kisses fell into a special category all of their own.

The out-of-body, floaty-headed, heart-melting, knee-weakening, wit-scrambling, take-me-I'm-yours category which had thus far eluded her despite all of her experience with kissing.

In fact, his was such a revelation, she quite forgot that she was supposed to be a selfless martyr and could have happily stood beneath the stars being kissed by him all night, and probably would have if he hadn't stopped it as abruptly as he had started it. Then marched off toward the house still clearly furious after tossing one parting salvo over his distractingly broad shoulders.

'I know how to bloody well kiss, Izzy!'

And, heaven help her, he was so right. She had to stagger back to her bench and take several stunned minutes just to get over it.

Chapter Thirteen

Isobel ended up scrambling into Mrs Fitzherbert's carriage that night after all. So fast her petticoats might have been on fire. Before she ran away like a woman chased by a pillaging Viking, she hadn't been able to look at him after he had kissed her, and she barely managed to utter more than two words when she finally made it back to Sophie's drawing room.

Not even when her chiselled chin redcoat had tried to flirt with her.

Ned hadn't seen her since. Even after four days of flagellating himself, he had no idea what to say to the menace if he did, so it was just as well.

He had always been useless at apologising. Could never quite find the right words at the best of times to do proper justice to any remorse he felt for putting his clumsy big foot in it, but he had no earthly idea what the correct way was to beg for forgiveness for manhandling a woman, plundering her mouth and doubtless scaring her witless in the process. It wasn't as if he'd ever done such a monstrous thing before, and he sincerely doubted he would ever do something so hideous again. His father had brought him up to respect women. To treat them with gentleness and protect them—not ravage them in a jealous temper!

And all to prove a point!

Or at least that had been his warped thinking at the time. With hindsight, he had probably proven hers better and that he really had no idea how to act with any finesse or charm or clue around women.

Because he was an idiot.

And a ham-fisted one at that!

So much of one he'd been avoiding the village like the plague since too, an inconvenient act of pathetic cowardice he wasn't proud of either when he had run out of bread, cheese and sugar. His pantry was bare thanks to the distinct lack of Izzy's visits, and aside from his rumbling belly there was an ache in his heart. For it turned out he wasn't an island after all and never had been because she had always been the one person he reliably had in his life. Through thick and thin and all his belligerence, she had always visited him at least twice a week for as long as he could

remember. Even in his darkest days when he had
shut out the rest of the world, she hadn't let him
exclude her. Yet now, thanks to his stupidity, he
missed the menace.

He missed talking to her. Missed her teasing
and her nagging and her interfering. Missed her
precisely sliced sandwiches and perfectly brewed
tea. More than anything he missed her cheery
smile. Her face. Seeing her in his empty house
or coming down the lane swinging her basket.
He hadn't realised just how much she had always
been his sunshine too. Often the one bright part
of the dull drudgery of his day.

If all that was gone for good now thanks to
one ill-considered, impulsive kiss, he genuinely
didn't know how he was going to cope.

Annoyed at both his reckless behaviour and his
continued reluctance to face her and atone for it,
Ned attached halters to Flotsam and Jetsam, the
two sturdy black Lincolnshire work horses he had
rescued from a drunkard upriver. It might well be
the entirely wrong time to do it, and wholly pointless in the grand scheme of things, but ploughing his most useless field now that there was no
chance of any potatoes seemed like the right sort
of miserable penance to punish himself for what
he had done. He also hoped that a morning of
hard labour before he tackled all his other chores

might wear him out enough that he'd be too tired to ponder his idiocy for the rest of the day.

As he led them out to his yard, Flotsam had the unmistakable wonky gait of a horse who had lost its shoe.

Ned groaned aloud while flagellating himself some more for his lack of tools and the farrier skills necessary to fix his horse. This ill-timed irritation now necessitated a trip to the village whether he liked it or not. Ned was happy to suffer drinking his tea un-sugared and to practically starve because he deserved to suffer for what he had done, but he couldn't let an innocent animal suffer unnecessarily too. That really would be beyond the pale.

With a weary sigh he removed the remnants of the broken shoe from Flotsam's hoof, then took a deep breath before he walked both horses up the lane, praying he wouldn't see her on the way. At least it wasn't market day, then he really would be doomed, as Izzy always seemed to be there from the crack of dawn until the traders' carts left when she invariably wandered here to bother him. But there was no reason for her to be in the square on a Friday morning this early, so with any luck he could nip in and out of the blacksmith's without them crossing paths before she ventured to the weekly sewing circle this afternoon.

Like the mortified coward he was, rather than continue on the lane to the smithy's as was fastest, he circumvented the village completely by using the fields surrounding it. He had an excuse ready in case anyone questioned him, and a believable one too as it stood to reason that the last thing any farmer would want to do was damage a work horse's hooves on the compacted road. Thankfully, he saw no one and that lulled him into enough of a false sense of security that when he emerged from the narrow alleyway between the blacksmith's and the postmaster's office, the absolute last person he expected to run into was her.

She spotted him at the same moment as he spied her, and her step faltered. Then, and this was pure agony, he watched her rearrange her horrified features into a mask of nonchalance.

'Good morning.' Her smile was too strained and her pretty eyes were blinking too rapidly for a woman who didn't wish she was meeting anyone but him. 'What brings you here?'

'Flotsam.' Ned tried his best to act nonchalant too as he patted his horse rather than meet her eyes. It did nothing to stop every muscle and organ he owned tensing in abject mortification. 'He's thrown a shoe.' And because some sort of polite conversation seemed appropriate, although he was buggered if he knew why, when he should probably just drop to his knees instead and grovel for all it was worth. 'You?'

Izzy glanced sideways at the post office. 'Mrs Fitzherbert's letters. I always pick them up for her on post days.'

'Oh.' And that was that.

Ned had nothing else.

For once neither did she as she smiled as they both shuffled awkwardly until she glanced to the post office again.

'Well, I suppose we'd both best get on with things then.' She spun on her heel, strode with purpose to her destination and the coward inside him wanted to let her go. But he knew that wouldn't fix things, just as he knew that not apologising wasn't right.

'I'm sorry about the other night.'

She paused mid-step and he watched her slim shoulders visibly steel before she turned around and waved that away as no matter. 'There is nothing to apologise for.' Blushing for all she was worth, she offered him a dire approximation of a smile that melted almost immediately. She chewed her bottom lip—which he now knew tasted of sunshine and strawberries and sin incarnate. 'In fact…it is I who should probably be apologising to you. I went too far. Much too far and made insulting assumptions that I had no right making and you simply put me in my place.'

She was letting him off lightly, bless her, and the coward within desperately wanted to leave it at that. Let her take the blame, because his ears were already crimson and he suspected his rapidly heating face would soon match. Yet he couldn't.

Wouldn't.

Her friendship was just too important.

'I could have put you in your "place," as you put it, in a much better and a less forceful manner than I did, Izzy, and I feel awful for it. In temper, I took advantage and...'

She laughed.

Genuinely laughed. 'I've been taken advantage of more times than I care to remember, and I can assure you, that you very much didn't.' The light in her lovely eyes dimmed momentarily before she banished it with a flick of her hand. 'You proved a point, is all, and nothing more, while I learned not to judge a book by its supposed cover. No harm was done, Ned. Honestly.' She started to turn, to go about her business seemingly unperturbed, and yet he still couldn't leave it there.

'If that's the case then why have you been avoiding me?' She usually visited him at least twice between Monday and Friday.

She inhaled deeply before she shrugged, wincing. 'I was dreading the inevitable awkwardness because I had no earthly idea how to play the cringy, awful first conversation afterwards. You?'

'The same.' There was no point denying it, so he chuckled while kicking a stone with his foot. 'It wasn't my finest hour.'

She brushed that away too.

'It's not as if it meant anything, Ned, now did it?'

'No.' The ready lie came as quick as it was necessary. Maybe for her that foolish kiss hadn't mattered, but for him it had been profound. Profound enough for him to now be in no doubt whatsoever that Miss Healy and the rest of them had been right. He did harbour feelings for Izzy that went way beyond the bounds of friendship. He wasn't convinced, or more likely was in complete denial, that he was hopelessly in love with the menace, but he knew that he wanted her. Wanted her body and soul and everything in between. In his house. In his arms. In his bed.

In his life.

But he also knew that only one of those wants was likely possible and he would gladly sacrifice all the other things just to keep her as his friend. The thought of a life without Izzy in it depressed the hell out of him too much to risk pushing for more than she wanted to offer him. She'd be gone from his life soon enough anyway without pushing her out of it. She would leave Whittleston when her prince came, and he was already dreading having to grieve for that loss without expediating it.

'Good.' She seemed relieved, so he knew he had handled this right. Hares weren't meant for tortoises and vice versa, no matter how much he wished they were. 'Then let us put it behind us and never speak of it again.'

Ned did let her go then. Had to, truth be told, as he didn't trust his expression or the blasted wandering 'windows of his soul' to give the game away. He then used all the time it took for the blacksmith to fix Flotsam's foot to reconcile himself to it all. The irony of finally realising how much she meant to him when his father had likely known it all along. Encouraged it. Pushed for it. Harder and harder the older she and Ned had got. He wished now that he had listened to him sooner because if he had, if he had plighted his troth to Izzy when Caleb Parker had still been alive to see it, before Ned had learned not to act on impulse or take foolish risks, before her father hadn't put her off Whittleston for ever. Before she hadn't had her head turned elsewhere when his had been too occupied with surviving...

Futile regrets which wouldn't change the now. More was the pity.

'I bought us all breakfast.' He wasn't expecting her to be waiting for him outside the smithy when he stepped out, but the sight of her beaming with basket filled with baked goods and waving a carrot for his horse fair took his breath away. 'I figured we should take our time eating it seeing as we have a battle plan to revisit.'

He groaned as was expected and rolled his eyes after Flotsam devoured his gift and she fell into step beside him, part relieved that he hadn't lost her yet and a greater part devastated that he could never have her. Or even risk trying. 'Not this again.'

'Yes, Ned. This.' She nudged him with her elbow. 'We've a critical week coming up and will need to do much plotting to ensure it goes well.' He had never really noticed how she talked as much with her hands as she did her mouth before, yet now seemed to notice everything about her. Almost as if he was consigning every tiny to memory to keep the essence of her with him for eternity in case her chiselled chin lieutenant stole her away before Ned was ready to let her go.

Which he would never be, he now acknowledged, because the meddling menace was his everything.

'And why, pray tell, is next week suddenly more critical than the last was?'

'Because we have the twin beacons of the May Fair and the monthly assembly to look forward to, and both on the same day. And because both offer perfect opportunities for you to impress your *beautiful* Rose to ensure all those rose petals and wedding cake I smell in your future.'

As he rolled his eyes, she threaded her arm through his as she had a thousand times before, and he marvelled at how perfect it felt for it to be there. Like all his recent revelations, again far too late to do anything about beyond mourn it.

She gently tugged him towards the big oak tree on the green where they had eaten their bakery delights since childhood. 'Obviously, you will need to be at the fair the moment that it opens for the jam making contest as Mrs Outhwaite is determined to keep her crown for the fifth year running, so Rose is bound to be there with her.'

'Impossible. Some of us have to work for a living, remember, and some of us have a farm to run. Daily jobs to do. Animals to feed. I can't neglect a whole day of chores for blasted jam…' She shoved a bun in his mouth giggling.

'Do stop your incessant moaning, Ned. Why do you always see the negatives and never the positives when nothing is insurmountable if you want it hard enough?' He would have argued that because him wanting her was about as insurmountable a problem as it was possible to have when she didn't want him back, but he instead took a hefty bite out of the bun and pretended to be bored with the sight of her. 'I said I would help you with all that beforehand and I will. I shall be your willing farmhand all week, so shut up and sit, you big oaf, and listen as I have already planned your May Day meticulously.'

'Heaven help me.'

He sat and allowed her to wax lyrical about the next stage of her plan. It was all typical Izzy nonsense involving casual collisions and idiotic opportunities for him to subtly impress, but he let it all wash over him because it made her happy. His only responses to any of it were the expected huffs, groans and eye rolls he always bestowed upon her. Eventually, after repeating it all twice to make sure that he knew it all, she sat back against the tree trunk and they ate the welcome feast packed in her cavernous basket in mostly companionable silence.

'I knew you'd be hungry.' She chuckled as he devoured the last pork pie. 'Your bread at home stale, was it?'

'I ran out of stale bread two days ago.' Along with almost everything else. 'I've subsisted on mostly apples since and that's given me a dreadful belly ache.' Not enough of one to distract him from the ache in his heart though. That pain superseded everything.

'What a daft pair we are, Ned.' She shook her head, wistful. 'Let's not do that again.'

'I thought we'd already agreed not to do *that* again.'

'I wasn't talking about the kiss, silly.' She gave him a playful slap while her cheeks pinkened. 'I was talking about avoiding one another on the back of it when you and I have surely known each long enough to be able to have an honest and frank conversation about anything if one is required. It is always better to clear the air, yet instead we allowed it to fester. *That* is what we shouldn't do again.'

'Agreed. I need my daily bread and it turns out it doesn't magically appear unless you turn up at my door like a bad penny with it.'

She acknowledged that with one of her Lord-give-me-strength looks, which reminded him how much he had missed those too and would mourn them in the future. Izzy was always so determined to make him a better person, he dreaded to think what sort of a curmudgeon he would be without her constant reminders over the years.

'We *have* known each other long enough that we should be able to discuss anything, Ned.'

'We should, Izzy. Within reason. Although I still think conversations like the one you forced me to have in Sophie's garden should remain out of bounds. Some things should remain private.' For the sake of his own sanity at least.

'Also agreed.' They both chuckled but she stopped first. 'It's a shame, though, as since the hitherto unmentionable incident in Sophie's garden I have the most burning question about it.'

His heart leapt. Dared to hope. 'Then I'll give you permission on just this one occasion to ask it.'

'All right then...' Her expression turned quizzical. 'Who on earth taught you to kiss like that, Ned? Because I have always assumed, clearly erroneously, that there haven't been any women in your life. Unless...' She suddenly looked a bit uncomfortable. 'I shouldn't really ask where you get your...um...relief.'

Splendid.

First, she assumed he was so unappealing to the opposite sex he had no experience with them and now she thought the only way he had got some was because he frequented brothels.

'There's been precious little *relief*, as you put it, for quite some time.' Nine years and one hundred and twelve days to be precise, as he had done a proper tally the other night after awakening hot and hard after another fevered dream about her. He'd had several variations of the same dream since that fateful night in Sophie's garden, and all of them picked up proceedings just before the real kiss had ended and his imagination had conjured a much more pleasing alternative version of events. 'But if you must know…' He sighed because he could not bear her thinking her alternative. 'Do you remember Colonel Fielding's wife, Lavinia?'

'No!' He winced as she threw her head back and laughed. 'Lusty Lavinia with the bawdy sense of humour?'

'It wasn't only her sense of humour that was bawdy, it was her appetite.' Ned shrugged, his own cheeks pinkening. 'She took me under her wing at sixteen and I remained there until the militia left Whittleston two years later. It was an enlightening time.'

'I'll just bet it was.' She was still highly amused by his revelation but was clearly as unaccustomed to this sort of discussion as he was, so she stared at her hands. 'She taught you well.' Was that an admission that she had enjoyed it? Although her enjoyment was a moot point in the grand scheme of things, it still warmed him that she hadn't been as repulsed as he had convinced himself that she was. 'The earthy Lavinia was—what? Twenty years your senior? Practically old enough to be your mother.'

'Four and twenty to be precise but to be fair to her, she didn't look like a woman past her prime.' Of their own accord, his hands flapped around his chest and his toes curled inside his boots at the unbelievable frankness of what they were sharing. Before his face spontaneously combusted, or she asked him something franker, he turned the tables. 'You?'

She seemed momentarily shocked that he had asked and stiffened, instantly defensive and wary. 'I was sixteen too the first time that I…'

Ned held up his palm. 'I figured as much when I saw the pair of you…' From the horrified expression on her lovely face, she feared his judgement and did not need any reminders that he had been the one to witness her and her smarmy officer looking the worse for wear at the back of St Hildeth's that awful night. 'But I wasn't actually asking about that. More who introduced you to the *dark art* of kissing.'

'Ah… Well…' Her shoulders slumped with relief then immediately shrugged in apology. 'Sadly, they are one and the same. Lieutenant Toby Nugent.'

Of course the blighter would have been a damned lieutenant!

'My first and greatest ever mistake, though sadly not my last as I repeated it less than twelve months later with another silver-tongued liar.' She toyed with an embroidered flower on her skirt, trying to put a brave face on it and failing and he felt for her. 'I was convinced the wretch would feel obligated to marry me and whisk me away from Whittleston-on-the-Water and my awful father for ever. More fool me, though, for assuming that's what all his hints meant rather than clarifying, as it soon became apparent that our motives were not aligned.' The shame and misery in her expression broke Ned's heart. 'Instead, he always had different plans which did not include me, so used me then tossed me aside with the same disregard as a worn-out shoe.'

'I'm sorry Izzy.' Because he was. He remembered that time with an element of shame. She had been so young and so alone in the world, her self-esteem constantly eroded with criticisms and coldness from both her father and, at that time, her foul elder brother too who was a chip off the old block. Ned and his father had always been her anchor, and while she undoubtedly grieved the loss of Caleb Parker too, instead of them supporting one another while they mourned him to-

gether, Ned had left her to flounder. All alone on
the troublesome brink of adulthood while he had
languished at the bottom of his own, personal
dark pit of despair.

He had vehemently pushed her away then, especially after he had witnessed her shame, yet he
had always known that charming soldier was a
wolf in sheep's clothing. Known about his reputation and all the women he chased. Known of
his many transient dalliances with young ladies
who did not have the experience with men to
spot a wrong 'un at fifty paces and neglected
to counsel her against him. But with his father
barely cold in the ground, Ned so wrapped up in
his own misery and drowning in debt, and her
father his usual callous, nit-picking, soul-destroying self, it did not take a genius to work out that
Izzy had been an easy target for the predator. 'I
should have been there for you.' At the very least
he should have given her father a warning before
the cruel bastard drove her into getting her kind
heart broken. He regretted not putting that sour
bastard in his place when it might have mattered
most of all. Still did when she had only had him
left to rescue her.

'To do what, Ned?' She smiled without humour. 'To save me from myself? We both know I
have always been too stubborn and too desperate

to escape to have heeded any of your warnings. Let us face it, I still am. I am a hopeless case, so do not feel a moment's guilt for any of my missteps, for I made them all with my dreamer's eyes wide open and likely will again because that is the way that I am made.'

She stared into the middle distance, her cornflower-blue eyes dulled by shame and regret. 'You and my father are right—I am flighty, I act too much on impulse, behave with scant regard for decorum and I do lack common sense—but *c'est la vie*.' He hated that he had ever done or said anything to her that mirrored that bastard's behaviour. Added to her lack of self-worth and sense of self-loathing. Hated more that she felt that she deserved it all because she flapped it away as if it was no matter when it very much was. 'None of us can turn back time.'

'I am so sorry, Izzy. I should never have—'

'Don't be.' She lifted her chin, as proud and stoic as she always was, determined not to hear any apology. Determined to pretend that she was, to her core, unbothered. 'A leopard does not change its spots and I dare say I've earned every last bit of my shocking reputation, so it doesn't really surprise me, any more than it surprises anyone else, that I'm still on the shelf.' Then she smiled with all the feigned mischief of a woman who had inadvertently bared too much of her soul and wished that she hadn't, stood and dusted off her skirts. 'And talking of shocking reputations, I had best go as Mrs Fitzherbert will be awaiting her letters and you know how crotchety she gets if anything arrives late.'

'Izzy, I…' It was on the tip of his tongue to tell her that he would happily rescue her from that shelf if she would deign to have him, but she stayed him with her hand before he could find all the right words such a frank and honest declaration warranted.

'It is all right, Ned. I am all right.' She beamed as if she was and began to walk backwards away. 'Something will come up. Something always does and I have long been of the opinion that what I need is a fresh start, somewhere new. Then my shocking reputation and all my bad memories can stay here where they belong.' She spun a slow circle, taking in the village as if looking at it wistfully for the last time, then pulled a disgusted face. 'Trust me, that day cannot come soon enough as I loathe this dreary place and almost everyone in it.' Her wistful smile returned as she directed it at him. 'And I am so glad that we are back to being all right again. For reasons I cannot fathom when you are one of the people I loathe, I missed seeing your cantankerous, much too hairy face.' She glared at his beard and sighed. 'For the love of God, shave that monstrosity off, Ned. If not for me, please do it for Rose.'

Chapter Fourteen

Thanks to a begrudging compromise, Ned hadn't attended this morning's church service so that he could begin getting ahead of himself for Saturday's May Fair. Without her father's presence to ruin the day, and with nothing better to do to pass the time, Isobel had invested all her energy into making the striped waistcoat for him to wear to the assembly that night. She was determined that to make sure he looked as dashing in it as was possible, then it needed to not only be bold but to conform to the latest fashion.

To that end, she had tried to copy one of the new styles Rafe had had made in London which had a wide collar which went all the way down the deep V in the front that emphasised his fine physique. As Ned's was finer, he would look magnificent in it. But the style required a much closer fit than the one she had stolen from his

wardrobe to make the burgundy, and then kept
for reasons she had decided not to fathom for the
sake of her own sanity. However, and as much as
it bothered her, there was no getting away from
the fact that the only way she was going to get
that precise fit was altering it properly on him
before she sewed in the lining.

That meant no matter how much she wanted
to avoid it, Isobel was going to have to suffer a
repeat performance of *The Measuring*.

Heaven help her!

'If there's nothing else, Miss Cartwright, I
might retire for the night.' Tess, the maid-of-all-
work and her father's latest inept spy, executed
an exaggerated yawn despite it being only six.
'I also thought that I should remind you that it
is my day off tomorrow—as usual—so I'll be
leaving extra early in the morning.' Which of
course meant that she was sneaking off tonight
to her fancy man in Fobbing and would come
back on Tuesday still smelling of gin and with
whisker burns all over her cheeks from all the
vigorous congress the pair of them would doubtless be indulging in. Because Tess, according to
Mrs Fitzherbert, had quite the reputation of her
own in Fobbing where she hailed from, and had
earned most of it on her back. It was so bad that
the good houses there would no longer employ

her, which no doubt explained why she was prepared to accept the paltry wagers Isobel's father had offered her to do his dirty work. Perhaps Isobel had that future to look forward to when her father evicted her?

Now, there was a depressing thought she would absolutely not allow to fester for a moment longer when she already had more than enough to worry about!

'Of course. Good night, Tess. Sleep tight and don't let the bedbugs bite.' Which of course they wouldn't have a chance to, because her buxom maid and her fancy man would have rolled all over them and squashed them before the poor bedbugs could retaliate. 'I shall see you Tuesday. Bright and early, if you please, as I have a busy day.' She said that purely to spite the maid for spying on her as, thanks to her fondness for gin, Tess wasn't a fan of early mornings. Or mornings in general lately, which all suited Isobel just fine. The less she saw of Tipsy Tess the Turncoat the better, and the less gossip her father got to hear from her.

The maid left and ten minutes later, she pretended not to hear her slip out of the back door. The idiocy of the woman made her chuckle, as the more Isobel turned a purposefully blind eye to her dereliction of her duties, the more liberties she took. A state of affairs which would, no doubt, only get worse—or in Isobel's case better—the longer her father stayed away. By default, that meant a huge chunk of freedom beckoned where she could breathe, continue to bury her head in the sand and largely do as she jolly well pleased.

She picked up the waistcoat again to ponder rather than ponder her potential and depressing future as a servant, then tossed it back down when she realised that with Tess gone, there was nothing to stop her fitting it to Ned this evening while it was still daylight so she could work on it properly again till bedtime.

That decision made, she rushed around like a whirlwind to collect everything she needed, raided the pantry for some treats for his eclectic menagerie of pets, then escaped out of the back door herself and across the fields to avoid causing any further undue gossip herself. Because if ever there was a time to err on the side of caution, it was now.

It was a lovely, balmy evening thanks to the early spring sunshine the village had basked in for weeks and she revelled in it. It had made such a difference to her not to have to dread a Sunday, that her shoulders and her heart felt lighter and she refused to allow all her others worries spoil these precious few moments of sheer bliss.

On a whim, she picked every late daffodil she saw poking out of his hedgerows. Not only would they make a cheery arrangement in the centre of Ned's big kitchen table, but such an overtly feminine frippery would also irritate the big brute so she would get twice the joy out of them. Thrice if she attached one to some ribbon and tied it in a jaunty bow around Falstaff's neck. He'd had a conniption when she had decorated his dog thus for Christmas and claimed that the poor thing was so ashamed of himself he had hid in the corner and refused to come out when they had both known the opposite was true. Falstaff loved a fuss and he had adored the additional attention of a costume to attain that.

As if she had summoned him, the dog appeared and bounded towards her. Isobel allowed him to lick her as she petted him, then sat beside him on the ground while she made his floral collar, all the while laughing in anticipation as she gazed towards his cottage and wondering what Ned's explosive reaction would be.

She was pleased things between them were back on their even footing again now that they had cleared the air. Not coming here for just a few days had been an awful wrench. Several times her feet had brought her this way, and each time she had forced them to turn around because she had no earthly idea what to say to him after he had blindsided her with that kiss.

A kiss so perfect she hadn't been able to stop thinking about it—even now that the air was cleared, and he had reassured her that it had meant nothing.

Maybe it hadn't to him, but she had decided to treasure its memory anyway, and use it as a benchmark for all the kisses she hoped were still in her future, as no kiss had ever unravelled her so far in the way that his had. If she couldn't have Ned, then she was now resolute that she would at least have a man who made her nerves fizz and her knees weak in the way he had.

Or as resolute as she could be when the sands of time were running out and her choices were limited to the stinky, fawning Mr Bunion and a handsome lieutenant who was, by his sister's own admission, a shocking ladies' man like all the others she had fallen foul of in the past.

Annoyed that her father's ultimatum had reared its ugly head again on this glorious evening when she had promised herself it wouldn't, she ran the rest of the way with Falstaff bounding along behind her to banish those unwelcome cobwebs from her mind. It mostly did the trick too, because she was breathless and smiling when she stepped through Ned's open doorway, but that turned to gaping shock when she realised what was going on inside.

Ned was sound asleep in his bath. His long body was semi-reclined in the steaming water, his wet head propped on the raised back of his specially built tub but tilted slightly. One of his powerful arms dangled over the side displaying every contour and sinew, the other was resting on his flat belly and was gently rising and falling in time with his slow, shallow breathing. His big feet were relaxed and crossed at the ankles and propped up at the opposite end, only the barest few inches of his muscular calves visible.

Propriety and politeness dictated that she should look away, but she couldn't. Instead, because the high sides of the bathtub hid everything interesting, she crept forward a few steps while she marvelled at the obvious strength in his broad shoulders. The sun-kissed golden hue of the skin stretched across them that suggested that sometimes he worked without a shirt. How vulnerable, yet powerful he looked cradled in the arms of Morpheus. How intriguing the dark dusting of hair on his chest became when it narrowed and arrowed beneath the water. How irritating it was that whatever mysteries lay beneath that soap-clouded water were too hazy and blurry to discern properly. The hint of secret flesh amongst the shadowy patch of dark enough to make that region of her own body come over all...unnecessary...as her improper mind wondered if that part of Ned too was in proportion to the rest of him. And if it was, what it would feel like inside her.

All the way inside her...

Falstaff barked and Ned started, and in case he turned and caught her ogling him, she shrieked as she spun around, hoping it looked as if she had just that moment walked in and disturbed his dog. 'Oh, my goodness! I am so sorry!' She wasn't. She was irritated that she had been so rudely disturbed from her wayward and shockingly carnal musings. 'Why the blazes didn't you shut and lock your door if you are in the altogether?' She grabbed that door now and pulled it closed behind her, then lent her back against it while she fought to calm her erratic breathing. 'Come and find me in the yard when you are decent!' By which time she hoped that she would be in a decent state too.

She heard him mutter an obscenity, then heard water slosh onto his flagstone floor as he heaved himself out of it and her libidinous mind tried to picture exactly what that looked like.

Ned.

All wet.

Water drizzling down his body.

Droplets falling from his hair, over his broad

shoulders and puckered nipples. Down that intriguing arrow of dark hair and dripping off what she presumed was his impressive manhood, and she came over even more unnecessary.

Unnecessary enough that she picked up her skirts and ran towards the Thames as that was as far away from him and his overwhelming nakedness as it was possible to be without fleeing his farm entirely.

'I thought you said the yard.' Fifteen minutes later a sheepish, but blessedly dressed Ned found her sat on their stump by the river ostensibly staring at the boats. She couldn't see them, of course, because her mind refused to relinquish the sinful images of him that were now seared onto it, but at least it would appear to him that she could. 'In my defence, nobody ever bothers me in the evenings, Izzy—not even you—and it was so hot today and I wanted the air.'

'That is as maybe, Ned, but there are some things that simply cannot be unseen.' Good heavens above her cheeks were heating again as another vivid memory of his impressive physique assaulted her. 'Look at me.' If she was blushing, she would own it. 'I am horrified. Shocked. *Scandalised!*'

'Are we going to pretend you haven't seen a naked man before, Izzy?' He had the nerve to chuckle. 'You saw a bit of skin, is all, so there is no need to be so missish about it.'

'I saw those by choice!' Although she hadn't seen either of the duds she had stupidly allowed to take the ultimate liberty completely naked, nor them her. The haste, the locations and clandestine nature of those uninspiring couplings had necessitated that only the most essential body parts were uncovered in case they were caught. But even if she had seen them both completely naked, she knew without a shadow of a doubt that neither man would have looked as impressive in his birthday suit as the vexing one currently teasing her. Lieutenant Nugent had been quite slight of frame and the humiliating other let-down had sloping shoulders and skin as pale as milk. 'Yours was sprung on me!' And she hadn't been the least bit prepared for it.

'Well, you did rather spring yourself on me too, so I suppose that makes us even. You scared the hell out of me, woman! And you've covered my poor dog in daffodils.' He flicked his head towards Falstaff, who seemed delighted by his floral halo. 'He won't be able to show his face in the village ever again if one of the other dogs sees him dressed like that.'

He sat beside her, smelling of fresh soap, the damp, dark ends of his hair curling slightly on the breeze coming off the water. Much to her continued chagrin, her wayward and suddenly wanton body also found that alluring. That hadn't happened with the other two either. She had faked her initial desire. Pretended that their kisses stoked those flames and then acted as though her body was enjoying theirs when it was too late to do otherwise. Yet Ned's had given it all manner of outrageous ideas without even trying to. Enough that there was a strange, new ache between her thighs which refused to go away. That hadn't ever happened before!

'Has it occurred to you that you might not get so hot if you scraped that thick pelt from your face?' Perhaps more anger was the answer to distract her from her current, inappropriate bodily predicament?

He smiled as he rubbed his chin. 'I trim it weekly with the scissors, Izzy, and just did it especially for you, so it's not as thick today as it was yesterday. Look—' He pulled on a whisker. 'It's not even a quarter of an inch long. Its more stubble than beard.'

'Let's not split hairs.'

'Don't you mean trim them?' The wretch still found her obvious discomfort amusing before he feigned chagrin at her narrowed eyes. 'But all that is by the by and I am sorry you saw me in the buff. What dire emergency dragged you all the way here this late in the day?'

Oh, good grief! The waistcoat.

'I need you to try something on so that I can pin the darts properly.'

He eyed the basket which she had practically thrown on the floor nearby, the blue and gold striped brocade spilled half out. 'I presume that's going to be waistcoat number two?'

Relieved that she had something to do to take her mind off the distracting throb in her nether regions, Isobel retrieved the basket, placed it on their stump and stood while she unfolded the unfinished garment. As it was here and so was he, it made perfect sense to get the job done now away from the intimate confines of his house and the reminder of the bathtub which was likely still sat in the centre of the floor. 'Slip this on and once I've adjusted the fit, I can leave you to the rest of your evening.'

He did as she asked and stared at the sky while she pinned the still-buttonless front closed. 'I take it this is my outfit for the dreadful assembly you are forcing me to go to next week.'

'It is. Wear it with your black coat and your smartest pair of buff breeches. If your boots don't have a mirror shine, I want it noted that I will not be responsible for my actions and because I do not trust you to do it, I am going to personally starch a cravat for you. There is nothing worse than a limp cravat and I've noticed yours could use some turgidity.'

'Have I ever told you that you are bossy, Izzy, as well as maddening?'

'Somebody has to take you in hand, you big oaf.' She brusquely turned him by the shoulders and set about pinning the seams along the curve of his back, convinced that the more matter-of-factly she approached this unavoidable process, the less unsettled it would make her. 'But thankfully, if all my cunning plans work, you will be Rose's problem to deal with in the future.' She was pleased with the nonchalance she managed to inject into her tone. 'Then I can refocus all my energies back into escaping this awful place.'

'Ah—your fresh lieutenant.' Even though she hadn't even considered him in days. 'I suppose the May Fair and the assembly also give you an opportunity to entice that handsome knight and convince him to whisk you away from Whittleston on his charger. Do you have a battle plan for that too?'

She probably should have, but she didn't. She had been too busy thinking about Ned and burying her head in the sand about everything else. 'When you have as much experience of flirting as I do, you don't need a battle plan. I have always excelled at thinking on my feet and using my wiles, so I have no concerns on that score. He'll be putty in my hands—just you wait and see.' She popped the last pin in the back dart. 'Turn please.'

He did and seemed content to let her get on with what she was doing while he stared out towards the river and as Isobel only had to make a few minor adjustments to the front of the waistcoat, it was all done in less than a minute. While she unpinned the front, she asked a question to fill the prolonged silence. 'Do you want gold buttons to match the thinner stripe or blue to match the thicker?'

'Whichever makes you the happiest.'

'Gold then.' She held out her palm rather than help him ease the garment off his shoulders, and then neatly folded it back in her basket. 'And I shall wish you a good night.'

Instead of wishing her the same back, he sat on their stump and smiled. 'Aren't you going to stay and watch the sunset with me?'

With everything else going on she hadn't noticed it, but as he used his folded arms to signal towards the river her gaze followed, and the sight of the burnt orange and crimson sky fair took her breath away.

'Mother Nature has put on a good one for us today, Izzy.' He smiled and patted the stump beside him. 'Red sky at night, shepherd's delight and all that.'

'Shouldn't that be sailor's delight?' She sat smiling in wonder at it herself.

'I suppose that depends on who you are and what you are doing when you witness it. As I have sheep, I am technically a shepherd, so I'm claiming that saying as my own.'

Side by side they watched the sun creep ever closer towards the horizon and despite the black silhouettes of the passing boats and ships on the busy waterway, it felt like they were the only two people on the planet.

'How long has it been since we did this, Ned?'

'Too long. Since before my father died, I reckon, which is a shame when we used to do this every night, didn't we?' He sighed as if he too missed those halcyon days. 'Don't let this go to your head, but every single time I've sat here and watched it since without you, I always think of you and wish you were here.' A touching admission that brought the prickle of tears to her eyes. 'Apparently sunsets just aren't the same without my best friend here to share them with.'

Like him, she stared resolutely at the horizon, too touched by his admission that she was his best friend too not to feel a little overcome, but too proud to let him see that that declaration meant the world. Instead, she leaned a little closer so she could nudge him with her elbow. 'That is officially the nicest thing you have ever said to me.' It was also, depressingly, the nicest thing anyone had ever said to her.

'Ah…well…' She felt him shrug and could sense his embarrassment at his uncharacteristic compliment. 'It seemed appropriate now that we are suddenly being all honest and frank with one another. I still think you're a royal pain in the backside though, before you get all soppy about it.' He leaned sideways and nudged her with his shoulder. 'But even so, I shall miss you when you've gone.'

If the first admission brought tears to her eyes, that one choked her, but she disguised it as a snort. 'I've got to convince a man to run away with me first, and we both know my success at that has been appalling. I fear I am destined to be one of those women who nobody wants to risk everything for.'

He was quiet for several moments before he sighed again. 'Seeing as we are being frank and honest, can I give *you* some courting advice?' He didn't wait for her to scoff. 'Stop throwing yourself at men, Izzy. I know you're desperate to get away from here, but that desperation shows, then that gives all those idiots a chance to exploit you and take advantage. This time around, try letting Smug Chiselled Chin do all the running. Because he *should* do all the running. You're a prize catch, Izzy Cartwright—so stop believing all your father's nonsense that you aren't worth it and thinking that they are the ones doing you the favour. Not when the opposite is true and always has been. You are kind and clever and witty and more beautiful than this here sunset, and you have the biggest heart of anyone I know. So don't you dare give it to someone who doesn't fully deserve it, or I promise you that I'll not be responsible for *my* actions.'

She had no words.

Even if she did, she would not have been able to push them past the huge lump in her throat. So instead, she rested her head on his shoulder and stared straight ahead into the emerging darkness, grateful that he was indeed her best friend too and always had been, and that with the sun blinking into the night, he couldn't see the soppy tears that were now streaming unbidden down her cheeks.

Chapter Fifteen

It had been an odd week.

Tortuous in fact, because Izzy had made good on every single one of her promises to help him out on the farm so that he could spend most of tomorrow at the May Fair. However, as tortuous as that all was undoubtedly going to be, Ned suspected that this morning's shenanigans were going to be the most unpleasant ordeal he would have to suffer this week—but there was no putting it off any longer. For the sake of his sanity, this had to be done.

'Are you ready?'

'As I've ever been.' By the steely look of determination in her eyes she was braced for the onslaught. Swaddled in several thick layers of sacking wrapped around her arms and legs, her skirts knotted around her knees like makeshift trousers, an empty sack in one hand and wielding the lid to his ancient butter churn like a shield in the other, she had the air of a warrior about her.

'And are you ready, Archie?'

Similarly attired but armed with the broken gate Ned had been using to corral the beast these past few weeks, their sturdy press-ganged but unexpected helper nodded.

They had a plan, and thanks to Archie's timely dog walk across Ned's fields they had an extra pair of hands, but now that the time was nigh it was likely worth repeating just in case. 'You two herd him, I'll catch him, and the good doctor here will do the necessary before we're all pecked to death.' Dr Able was already poised with a handful of the medical tools necessary to remove the splint from Old Nick's wing. 'After three.' Ned sucked in a fortifying breath and braced himself against the barn door as his fingers hovered over the bolt. 'One…two…' Everyone crouched ready to fight. 'Three!'

Ned flung open the door exactly as Izzy had suggested. She figured it would be best to use the element of surprise as the mad bird would only get madder if he had to ram himself against the door. The customary hissing began straightaway and a few moments later the swan appeared from behind a bale of hay, his wings spread menacingly despite one of them being splinted, so that they filled the doorway.

As they probably only had one clean shot at this before the bird went berserk, Ned swallowed his fear and lunged as per their battle plan, and as he had hoped, the sight of a six-foot-six man flying through the air towards him shocked Old Nick enough that he was indeed surprised and unprepared. The second his fingers touched feather, he wrapped his arms around the swine then hugged him tight while he rolled onto his backside and hoisted the thing into the air.

With impressive stealth, Izzy managed to get her empty flour sack over the swan's snapping head before it attacked her, and then she flung her body over the front of it to sandwich it between them. It wasn't enough to stop the wooden wing from whacking her, but she endured the flailing blows stoically in the moment it took for the doctor to take over and catch it.

With Archie now behind the injured wing and gently supporting it despite Old Nick's violent protestations, the former military sawbones worked fast to cut through the strapping and to remove the splint. Then it was his turn to count them down for the planned dismount. 'I am letting go in three...two... *one*!'

Ned watched Archie and Dr Able dart sideways to take cover, but he did not let go of his charge until he saw Izzy roll into a tight ball out of harm's way a split second later. That's when he did the same, ensuring that he put himself between the hissing devil and the fearless woman who had insisted on helping despite all his gentlemanly attempts to stop her.

Old Nick hopped away at speed lopsided, with his good wing still flexed and the now splint-free one folded close to his body. Only when he was several yards away did he carefully unfurl it to test it.

'Is it fixed?' Izzy's hand came out of nowhere to help him up.

'Not unless he can fly.' The physician had warned them already not to hope, seeing as the swan hadn't followed doctor's orders to keep the wing immobile. 'Even if the bone has healed, the muscles surrounding it will have wasted, so it might take him a few days to attempt to get airborne, and even then it's in the lap of the gods whether that happens.' Ned couldn't resist smiling at her because he could read her mind. 'Before you ask, I've already started planning for that contingency. There's a nice spot behind the barn to dig a pond and build a swan house—but you'll be the one digging the pond.'

'Not only will I dig it, but I'll do a better job

than you ever could. I'll even plant it with colourful reeds and pretty water lilies just to spite you.'

'You cannot tame a wild swan.' Dr Able looked at them both as if they had gone mad. 'We should probably just let nature take its course if the wing hasn't healed. I know that sounds cruel but its nature's way.'

'He looks fixed to me,' said Archie as if he alone knew better than all of them. To encourage the bird, he chased it down the path flapping his own arms. 'Go on, Nick. Fly like the wind.'

Threatened, the bird turned again and hissed with such aggression, Poor Archie's eyes widened as he stopped dead, but then to everyone's surprise, Old Nick decided to take heed and copied. Flapping both his wings as he ran in the direction of the river. As he gathered momentum, he had two mis-starts where he went up and came straight back down. Then, he bounced in the air a third time and just kept rising.

'I told you he was fixed!' Archie danced a little celebration jig as he waved the swan off until he disappeared out of sight. Then frowned at them all. 'He'll come back to visit, won't he?'

'I hope not!' Ned slapped the dust from his hands as if metaphorically washing them of the troublesome bird. 'If I never see that feathered lunatic again, it will be too soon.'

'He's a wild animal, Archie, not a pet,' said Dr Able in matter-of-fact agreement. 'You must prepare yourself to never see him again but be happy that he will now have a long and happy life thanks to our interventions.'

More mindful of Archie's tender feelings than they were, Izzy hugged him. 'I am sure he'll come back to visit the two of us because he likes us, Archie.' She skewered first the doctor and then Ned with her glare. 'But I doubt he'll waste his time with Whittleston's resident curmudgeon again and who can blame him? Ned is an acquired taste, and a bitter one at that. And a scruffy, hairy one to boot.'

'I'll have you know that I trimmed this last night in honour of tomorrow.' He rubbed his stubbly chin proudly to vex her. 'I've even polished my boots exactly as you asked me to.'

Her pretty, blue, still-narrowed eyes latched on to his beard in disgust. 'I also asked you to shave but I see that has been ignored.'

'To remind you that I'm my own man, Izzy, and to frustrate the hell out of you.'

Smiling, he strode towards the water pump to wash his hands and pretended not to notice her legs as she untangled her skirts and removed the sacking armour padding from her shapely ankles.

Ten minutes later and he caught a glimpse of

them again as he helped her up into the doctor's curricle before he waved them away, leaving him with a very chatty and excited Archie.

'I've been asked to judge the cake contest tomorrow afternoon.' From the huge smile splitting the young man's face, he might as well have just been given the moon. 'The Reverend's wife picked me because she said I'm the local expert on cake because I eat so much of it. She said I'm to choose the one that is the most delicious as the winner, but Mrs Outhwaite said she'll give me a sixpence if I pick hers.'

'You're not thinking of taking that bribe are you, Archie, as that wouldn't be right.'

'Of course not.' He giggled as if Ned had gone soft in the head. 'Especially as Mrs Fitzherbert's offered me a shilling to put Mrs Outhwaite's last. I'm going to buy Fred a bone with it at the butcher's because cake upsets his tummy too much, so I've been banned from giving him any.'

'Does Sophie know all this?' Because Ned decided he should probably tell her before her brother-in-law caused a war in the cake tent.

Archie shrugged, his attention already wandering elsewhere. 'Did you know there is going to be a juggler at the fair too? And a puppet show in the afternoon.' He bounced on the spot with glee. 'I love Punch and Judy. I hope I don't miss them while I'm judging the cakes.' He seemed perturbed at the thought.

'If you do, there'll be a repeat of the show, so don't worry. Mr Punch and the long-suffering Judy perform on the hour, every hour from noon.' At least until the drunken puppeteer from nearby Romford could perform no more and got poured back into his cart. Taking bets on how soon that would be was one of the May Fair's greatest traditions and he was bought several tankards of ale by those vested enough in the outcome that they would like to sway it. All was fair in war here in Whittleston, so cheating was always rife, as Mrs Outhwaite's promised sixpence was testament. There was always some daft wager going on somewhere hereabouts, and even Ned, who wasn't usually the sort to waste his hard-earned money on a reckless gamble, had two shillings on the puppeteer being pie-eyed by four as that was a sure bet. So sure, that with the odds at five to one for so early in the day, he would make a tidy profit. 'There will be Morris dancers too and some acrobats. Although between you and me, they are a bit long in the tooth nowadays and not worth watching, so take your time with the cake judging but be sure to send a few slices my way.'

'Oh, I will. Then we'll both go and get our fortunes told.'

'I'll give that nonsense a miss, if you don't mind.' The absolute last thing he needed was a fortune-teller telling him that there was nothing better in his future than more of the same. 'Those people are charlatans.'

'What's a charlatan?'

'A person who tells lies for money.'

Archie frowned as he followed Ned to where they had tied up the dogs. 'Why would anyone do that?'

'Because the lure of a sixpence or a shilling sometimes convinces people to be dishonest.' He untied Falstaff first to give him a fighting chance against his boisterous son, then freed Fred, who bounded after him, tongue lolling. 'That's why you need to be honest at the cake contest and ignore both Mrs Outhwaite's and Mrs Fitzherbert's offers of money. Lying would make you a charlatan and you should always remember that a man is nothing without honour.'

'Daniel said something similar about soldiers and I don't want to be a charlatan.'

'Who is Daniel?'

'Lieutenant Healy, silly, Rose's brother.'

'Oh.' Ned's least favourite person in the world. 'Has he given you leave to call him by his Christian name?'

'Of course he has! Because he's my friend and friends call each other by their first names.'

'Right.' Ned decided that if he was going to have to listen to Archie extolling the virtues of his new nemesis, then he might as well muck out Flotsam and Jetsam's stalls while he was about it, so he headed to his barn to fetch some fresh hay while Archie trailed along.

'Daniel's nice and tells funny jokes.'

'Does he indeed.' Never had Ned wanted to wring a man's neck more.

'He does. Very funny jokes.' He was coming to loathe the blasted word *very* almost as much as he hated the name Daniel. 'They are funnier than Isobel's even, but don't tell her I said that in case it upsets her.'

'We wouldn't want that now would we.'

'He's got his eye on her you know.' Archie jogged beside him. 'Daniel told Rafe yesterday that he's enamelled by her.'

'I think you mean enamoured.' Which was a huge worry. Even though Ned had told himself that he would let her find the happiness she deserved with Smug Chiselled Chin if that was who she wanted, that he would be noble and gracious and honourable about her desire to escape the village as a good friend should, the potential reality made jealous bile rise in his throat and his fists clench by his sides. Yet like so much of what he had learned about himself in the last few weeks, it turned out that thinking you could be noble as you stepped aside and actually doing it without hating yourself for it were two very different things entirely.

'It was definitely enamelled,' said Archie, oblivious of Ned's visceral reaction to this news, 'because he picked her a flower yesterday afternoon when they were chatting in our garden and Rafe said that was a sure sign he fancied her. Daniel picked it and tucked it in her hair.' He twirled his finger above his ear. 'It made her look very pretty.'

The opportunistic bastard!

'Izzy and that soldier were in your garden yesterday?' That was the first Ned had heard about it, and more acid churned now that he realised that explained why she hadn't dropped by to bother him yesterday afternoon like she usually did on a market day.

'He and Isobel stopped by for tea after the market.'

'And what, pray tell, were they doing at the blasted market together?' More importantly, why hadn't she mentioned it this morning? And why hadn't he had the foresight to go to the market himself yesterday to chaperone them both?

'Daniel was with his sister, and I was with Isobel and then Sophie found us altogether and suggested some tea on the lawn seeing as the sun was shining. I played hide-and-seek with Rose, Isobel and Daniel. Then Mrs Fitzherbert taught me how to make a daisy chain while Daniel and Isobel went to stretch their legs.' Ned was in no doubt that the flimsy excuse of leg-stretching was a shameless ploy on the slimy *Daniel's* part to get her alone.

Pick her a blasted flower.

Steal a spectacular kiss from the menace the second they were out of sight.

His gut clenched at the thought.

'We had a high old time. You should have come, Ned, then you could have played hide-and-seek too.'

'I wasn't invited.' A slight he would have been relieved about a few weeks ago but which now felt like a betrayal. No matter how off-the-cuff the invitation had been, Sophie of all people should have included him seeing as she knew that his eyes liked to wander Izzy's way. She'd even called him on it, so aiding and abetting The Chin felt like outright treachery. As surely Sophie should be on his side after all the years they had been both friends and neighbours?

Except he'd outright denied having any such feelings to Sophie when she'd asked. Just as he had vehemently denied it to Miss Healy and Mrs Fitzherbert too, so he supposed he only had himself to blame now that they were unwittingly—or perhaps wittingly—assisting *Daniel* in his quest to court Izzy.

'Daniel's promised to teach me archery tomorrow.' Archie's pace quickened as he followed Ned back to the barn. 'He's a crack shot according to Rose.' Because of course he was. Smug Chiselled Chin would obviously over-achieve in everything as he was the sort. 'He's entered the archery competition and Isobel has promised to put shilling on Daniel to win. My money's on Rafe, of course, because he's my brother, but if he wasn't shooting I'd be backing Daniel too because he's my friend.'

Ned's hatred doubled with every passing second.

'Can you shoot an arrow, Ned?'

'Archery strikes me as a great waste of a man's time.' Never mind that he couldn't hit a cow's behind with a plank as he'd never had the time to learn any sport beyond sheep-wrangling and swan-wrestling. 'So I shan't be entering such a daft contest.' Instead, he would doubtless silently seethe on the side while Izzy cheered on Whittleston's new hero *Daniel*. His natural aversion to reckless gambles aside, he'd lay good money that the blasted flower that he gave her was already pressed between the pages of a book on her nightstand, which meant the wretch had already inched one of his over-polished military boot inside her bedchamber and soon the rest would follow.

The charming, conniving, chiselled chin rascal!

'That's a shame,' said Archie as he watched Ned hoist a hay bale and carry it back to the door. 'If you change your mind, Daniel is meeting us extra early at the fairground to give us both our first lesson. Eight sharp, before the fair opens, so the three of us have the field to ourselves.'

The three of us! 'He's teaching Izzy too?' The mere thought of that practised seducer getting intimate with her person under the pretence of adjusting her grip on the bow or to oh-so-helpfully assist her with sighting the arrow made his eyeballs bulge. 'Since when has she had any interest in archery?'

'Since Daniel, Rose and Sophie talked her into it yesterday.'

'At eight sharp, you say?' So much for Izzy helping him feed the animals first thing tomorrow as she promised then. Which meant that while he'd be doing that all alone, Izzy would be all alone with a man who was too handsome for his own good. And a uniformed one at that. 'The Lieutenant must be very *enamelled* indeed to want to get up that early. He will need to be up before the larks to get his ostentatious brass buttons polished to perfection and his dashing dimple properly shaved beforehand.'

'Daniel doesn't like to waste the day and says that the early bird always catches the worm.'

'And obviously Izzy is the worm!' In temper Ned threw the hay bale into the stable with more force than he intended, and watched it explode every which way except where it was needed.

Archie looked at the mess then looked at Ned as if he had grown two heads, which he supposed he had seeing as jealousy had suddenly reared its ugly one again at the slightest provocation. 'Why would you call Isobel a worm? That's not the way to speak about a lady, Ned. Especially not one that you love.'

'I don't love Izzy Cartwright and I'm sick and tired of everyone saying that I do!' The denial was as swift and visceral as his pride dictated, but clearly as unconvincing to Archie as it was to Ned because the young man squared his shoulders, his outraged expression calling him a liar, a cad and a pathetic coward all in one go.

'Well, Rafe says that you do! And he also says that he thinks you're a big, bumbling and cowardly idiot to let her go simply because you are too scared to fight for her!'

Chapter Sixteen

The first Isobel realised that Tess was nowhere to be found was when someone knocked repeatedly on the door at the crack of dawn while she was still brushing her hair and the lazy gin-swilling spy failed to answer it.

'I'm coming!' She tossed down her brush and stomped down the stairs with her hair still a tangle, then stared bewildered when the person at the door was Ned. When Ned had only once visited her at home in all the years that she had known him thanks to her father's irrational hatred of anyone with the surname Parker.

'What are you doing here when I'm supposed to be coming to you?' Unlike Isobel in her tatty work dress and sturdiest old boots, he was in his Sunday best. His hair was combed, his newest pair of boots were shining, and he had even donned one of the cravats she had starched for him expressly for today to pair with one of his smart but muted waistcoats and dark brown coat. 'Surely you are not wearing that to feed the animals?' She looked him up and down, incredulous. 'It'll be ruined before we even get to the fair and you'll stink like your sheep for the rest of the day.'

'I've already seen to all the animals, so I thought I'd save you the trouble of trudging to the farm on a wasted journey.' He shuffled from foot to foot, uncomfortable in his skin. 'And thought perhaps I'd buy you breakfast at the bakery and then escort you to the fair instead.'

Had the world gone mad?

First he was here, when he never came here, and then he was being purposefully thoughtful and gentlemanly when he was usually gruff and surly. Not that he wasn't thoughtful, considerate and kind deep down, because he was all those things to his core, but he always tried to hide it. Even from her.

'Are you unwell Ned?' To lighten the strange, tense atmosphere, she leaned out of the door to look behind him. 'Or are you not Ned at all but an imposter, for the Ned I know doesn't escort a lady anywhere.'

'I've walked you home a hundred times when its dark.' He had. He always insisted on guarding her person when night fell.

'And moaned about the great inconvenience I've caused you for every step of it.'

'Maybe I am trying to turn over a new leaf.' He stared at his feet and kicked a stone from the hearth. 'Maybe I'm trying to be a more sociable version of Ned in all aspects of my life—even the most irritating parts of it.' He managed a half smile as his gaze raised to hers, then scanned her patched frock with amusement. 'You aren't wearing that today, are you?'

'Clearly not any more, now that my pig-feeding services are no longer required.' She beckoned him over the threshold, miffed that he was so keen to begin his day with Rose that he had spoiled her plans for the morning. She had been looking forward to feeding the animals beside him. Those purposeful hours spent helping him so that he was free for the fair had been the highlight of her week so far. She had even got up earlier than usual so that she could catch the last of the sunrise on his land. 'I'll go change while you make us both some tea.'

'Right.' He stepped in warily, looking this way and that, before he whispered, 'But what about the maid? Your father will hit the roof if he learns I've been here.'

The only time Ned had ventured in, he had been eleven and she had been nine and her father should have been behind the counter of his shop for the whole morning. Except he had forgotten his pocket watch and had picked Ned up and thrown him, bodily, out onto the street bellowing that it would be a cold day in hell that he ever allowed a Parker to darken his door.

Isobel had been banned from playing with him then. That had been the first of her father's unreasonable dictates that she had purposefully ignored and her first proper act of rebellion.

'Tess is either not here, which wouldn't surprise me as she's a work-shy strumpet, or lying face down drunk in her room thanks to her fondness for gin. Either way, I wouldn't worry about her. If she has been on the mother's ruin, a marching band wouldn't wake her, and if she's gone off to see her fancy man then she's likely face down in Fobbing somewhere pickled in the stuff and two marching bands wouldn't wake her.'

'Right then…' He ventured a little further in. 'And I'd find the kitchen…?'

'At the end of this hall. If you find yourself in the yard, then you've gone too far.'

As it felt peculiar having him here, and it felt unsettling that he was here while her hair resembled a bird's nest, she left him to find it himself and went back to her toilette.

She toed off her battered boots the second her

feet hit her bedchamber and made sure to close the door before she quickly stripped off her dress and swapped it for another. Yet for some reason, undoubtedly the rare fact that Ned had volunteered, without duress, to escort her somewhere, the striped muslin she had laid out the night before specifically to wear to the fair didn't feel pretty enough. Especially when the man downstairs wore his smart coat and tight breeches too well. On a whim she changed it for another dress, then another, and was still in two minds about that one when he called up to tell her that the tea was ready.

That, inexplicably, then made her skittish. As nervous as she had been at sixteen on the evening of her first assembly, which was daft but no less disconcerting. Thanks to the three changes of frock, she had to do her hair in a rush and because she made a hash of it, she ripped the pins out as she descended the stairs and decided to do it all again when she had the calming weight of some tea and toast in her oddly fluttering stomach. She regretted that hasty decision when she skidded into the kitchen and he stared intently at her wild tangle of hair for several stunned seconds before he spun around to grab the teapot amused.

'I solved the mystery of the missing maid.' He handed her a note. 'I found this on the dresser.

Tess the Tippler apparently has a family emergency and won't be back till Tuesday.' He smiled sheepishly. 'It wasn't sealed, nor folded, so I read it. Sorry.'

'Family emergency.' Isobel huffed as she scanned the missive, so self-conscious of the state of her hair that she tried to tame it with her fingers. 'Does she think that I was born yesterday? She doesn't have any family—not any that will still speak to her at any rate—and she's taking advantage of my being out all day at the May Fair as an excuse to escape for her Monday off early. She did that on Sunday last week and now it's Saturday, so I suppose she'll disappear next Friday too!' She sat in the chair he solicitously pulled out for her. 'Honestly, she is the worst maid my feckless father has ever under-paid, and has got worse since he announced he's disappearing for most of the summer. The lazy good-for-nothing is doubtless banking on me not telling tales on her, which is rich when she's been telling them on me for months.'

'You are not going to tell him yet though, surely?' He plonked an empty cup in front of her without a saucer and filled it with tea so strong she could stand a spoon in it. 'If you need some help around the house, I suppose I could…' She stayed him with a raised palm before he offered to fit more work into his already work-stuffed week, touched that he would even offer.

'I can manage perfectly well on my own and I'm not daft, Ned. I couldn't be more thrilled that she is absent without leave for it means that I can misbehave to my heart's content all today and to-night safe in the knowledge that Tess cannot tattle any of it to my father.' She toasted him with her tea and then slammed it down when he immediately frowned his disapproval.

'I'm not actually planning on misbehaving, Ned. In fact, quite the opposite so stop being so prudish and judgemental. If you must know...' It seemed appropriate to give him some credit despite her uncharitable feelings about his obvious growing attraction towards Rose. 'I've been taking your advance and treating Daniel with the same polite disinterest as I've always treated Mr Bunion, and it has worked. I didn't think it would—but I was wrong because he now seems thoroughly besotted with me.'

As she was now staring at Ned's rigid back while he hunted for the saucer he had forgotten in the dresser, she allowed her triumphant expression to slip because the feeling wasn't mutual.

She had tried to feel some interest in in the dashing lieutenant, because he was a much better option to save her from destitution than the stinky Mr Bunion, but try as she might none was forthcoming. She wanted to explain away her indifference with the excuse that she was becoming more discerning in her dotage, but she knew it was because of Ned. Since she had started seeing him as a man instead of just her friend, he had ruined her for all other men.

'It's annoying really—' It was all so annoying. '—as if you'd deigned to give me your sage courting advice years ago, I'd probably be married already and long gone from this cloying village by now.'

'So I'm to blame for you still being here?' He slipped the saucer under her cup and sat opposite her. 'Is that what you're saying? I've inadvertently ruined your life.' He seemed bothered by that when he would usually scoff and tell her that she was talking nonsense.

'No. Of course not.' She pasted back her sunny smile to make him feel better and sipped her tea, working hard not to wince at the bitter, stewed taste of it. Good heavens above but if this is what he choked back when she didn't stop by to fix it for him, then it reaffirmed her belief that he was in desperate want of a wife—even if she was no longer happy about the perfect candidate she had chosen for him or his enthusiasm for her. 'I just wish we had been franker with each other sooner than last week. It would have saved a lot of my mistakes and practically all of my regrets... Maybe.' It wasn't fair to make him feel bad when all he had done of late is precisely what she had asked. It wasn't as if he was aware of the peculiar inner workings of her mind or the outrageous new reactions in her body since her eyes had noticed his. 'But knowing me, I wouldn't have listened so it's probably a moot point. I've never blamed you for my depressing lack of a husband. That's undoubtedly my fault.'

He loaded his tea with sugar, no doubt to disguise the awful taste. 'What depresses you more—the lack of husband or being stuck here in Whittleston?'

As it was an honest question, she supposed it deserved a frank answer. 'This depresses me more.' She used her cup to encompass the room. 'Being trapped in my father's house when I've never wanted to be here, and he's always resented having me here. I hate this place. Hate it with every fibre of my being.' She had never admitted that to anyone but saying it aloud at least felt a little rebellious and cathartic.

Ned slowly glanced around the careworn kitchen and down the dark, narrow hallway. 'I can't say that I blame you. When I think of you,

I instantly think of colour and light and this place is more him—dark and oppressive.'

She shrugged, touched by that uncharacteristic compliment too. 'Obviously, I have been forbidden to redecorate. Not that the old skinflint would ever pay for paint, of course, but any of the cheerful cushions and throws that I've made or little knick-knacks I've collected have always been removed. To spite him they are all in my bedchamber.' She flicked her gaze to the ceiling. 'Brightening up that room while they await a new home somewhere better. I can barely move for them all.'

'You can store them all at mine if you are tripping over them.' He watched his finger trace a dent in the table rather than look at her. 'My place could certainly do with some cheering up.'

'Be careful what you wish for, Ned, as I might make your farmhouse my next project after I've got you wed.'

His eyes lifted and locked with hers. '*If* you get me wed, I'd be somebody else's project.'

As that felt like a reprimand as well as being doused with cold water, she covered it with a shrug. 'An excellent point. You'll be Rose's problem. Thank goodness.'

'*If* Rose is the one.'

If?

It shamed her that that one tiny word buoyed her.

He suddenly pushed his cup to one side frowning at it. 'As this nasty brew is as oppressive as your father's house, shall we go eat before the rest of the village has the same idea? There are always queues on Fair day and I'm starving.'

'Give me five minutes to do my hair first.'

She did not expect him to follow her to the drawing room or to have to see him leaning with his arms folded against the door jamb, watching her with interest in the big mirror that hung over the fireplace as she attempted to fix it. 'I know that it is a disaster presently, Ned, but it won't be once I've pinned it into submission. Honest.'

'I'd forgotten how curly your hair is unbound.' He seemed disproportionally fascinated with it all of a sudden. 'Probably because you stopped leaving it loose at sixteen and I got used to it up. But it's still the same, isn't it? A riot of curls exactly as it was when you were a girl.' His baffled eyes locked with hers in the reflection. 'It's staggering really that a few tiny pins can hold that much hair, Izzy.'

'As you are about to witness, it takes a lot more than a few, Ned. I usually walk around with half an ironmonger's on my head just to look half-way decent.'

'Well, they do say it hurts to be beautiful.' He likely had meant it as a flippant comment, but her heart stuttered anyway and hoped that he meant it. 'Who knew that being a woman involved that much faff?'

'If we didn't faff, we'd all look like you.' She had hoped a teasing insult like the sort they usually traded might make her feel easier, but it didn't because his silky chuckle unnerved her further. So she twisted her hair into the fashionable shape that had eluded her upstairs and tried to ignore him to focus on the task at hand, but that proved impossible too. It was strange doing something so personal but mundane in front of him. Oddly intimate. As intimate as measuring him had been but in an entirely different way, almost husband and wife getting ready together in the morning sort of way, and her fingers fumbled yet again over a simple task she had done thousands of times as a result because she liked how that felt. So much she scared herself as her mind suddenly conjured an idyllic picture of them together in his cottage surrounded by her things intermingled with his. Falstaff nestled at her feet. Her boots stood warming next to his on the hearth. Enjoying a quiet moment eating breakfast at the table together as the sun rose before he went to feed his barren pigs and she made their rumpled bed...

By the time she poked in the last pin, her fluttering stomach was practically doing somersaults because he was still staring in the most disconcerting manner and continued to do so when she grabbed her bonnet and walked towards him.

Instead of stepping out of the way of the door, he remained a human barricade blocking her path while he bent to inspect her head. 'Intriguing.' His finger prodded the thick bun secured neatly to her scalp. 'I counted at least fifteen pins going in and yet I cannot see one of them now.'

'As you rightly pointed out, that's because I have a lot of hair to hide them in.'

'You do, so that confection is a feat of engineering, to be sure.' And then he did something else he had never done. He twirled a finger in one of the loose curls she had left framing her face. 'It's very pretty feat of engineering too, Izzy.' His eyes told her that he meant that too and something peculiar happened to her jaded heart. 'Just not as lovely as you were when your hair was indecent five minutes ago.'

When she blinked at him because she had no clue how to respond to that uncharacteristic and almost flirty compliment, he took his sweet time unravelling his finger from the tendril before he rearranged it neatly against her cheek and he stepped back awkward again. As if he couldn't quite believe what he had just done either. Then, because this was clearly the morning for venturing into uncharted territory with her oldest and dearest friend, he did something else he had never done before to unsettle her further—he offered her his arm. 'Shall we away then to this interminable day of unmitigated sociable torture that you are dragging me to?'

She nodded as she took it, and came over all unnecessary yet again when his big hand came to rest over hers in the crook of his elbow—almost as if he liked it there as much as she did—and wanted it there for ever.

Chapter Seventeen

'His nags know the way home.' The juggler pointed to the two thick-set horses munching grass close to the Punch and Judy man's cart behind the main tent. 'So well they don't need a pair of hands on the reins.' With that, he happily abandoned Ned and Dr Able to it.

The puppeteer was practically unconscious and hung like a dead weight between them, the only clue that he still lived the odd grunt as they dragged his inebriated carcass across the field. With perfect timing, the bells of St Hildeth's chimed four and the good doctor groaned aloud.

'Well, there's five shillings I'll never see again! Would it have killed this idiot to last till five?' His eyes narrowed at Ned over the puppeteer's lolling head. 'You must be feeling pretty smug though, seeing as you are the only one who predicted the correct time on the nose.'

'*Smug* is such an ugly word.' Ned chuckled as he mentally counted his winnings, silently praying that his good luck would last the day. 'I much prefer *righteous* to describe how I'm feeling.' Although that righteousness would soon evaporate and be replaced by sheer terror again, as that had been his constant companion since he had flung himself out of bed and decided enough was enough.

Since then, Ned had been Isobel's shadow all day.

A charming and attentive one.

Occasionally, he attempted to even be a flirty one although he wasn't confident in his success at that.

It had all felt odd.

Alien. Frequently awkward and petrifying but he had persevered because he knew that Archie was right. As unlikely as it was that a dazzling hare would want to spend eternity with a curmudgeonly tortoise, he would never forgive himself if he let her go without a fight. He had to throw his hat into the ring before Izzy ran away with her chiselled chin lieutenant, and he had to be honest to her about how he felt, even if it did have the potential to ruin their lifelong friendship.

If it did, she'd be leaving eventually anyway,

so what the hell! For once he was going to throw all caution to the wind and let fate decide the rest.

He was taking her advice, after all, and seizing what he prayed with all his lovesick heart was an opportunity and, in the unlikely event that Izzy was prepared to take a punt on him too, then he would live day to day and hope for the best.

Or at least that was how he had reasoned his rashness in the small hours when sleep had eluded him. He just had to accept that some things were in the lap of the gods and even with all the contingencies in the world you couldn't mitigate for them. Not when he really only had two choices in this protracted debacle anyway. He either risked having his heart broken by Izzy, or it would shatter anyway when she left Whittleston without him.

If push came to shove, there was also a third option. It meant leaving everything he had worked so hard for behind and leaving Whittleston with her. He was doing his best not to think about that as wilfully throwing away his guaranteed income gave him palpitations, but he would rather toss away his entire livelihood and all of his land than lose her. That was the true crux of what was at stake and the true measure of what he was prepared to risk.

Everything for her.

Everything and more.

As terrifying as that prospect was, his heart and his head screamed that the menace was worth it. That they were worth it.

'How many tankards of ale did you buy him?' The competitive Dr Able had never been good at losing.

'Just the one, unlike you who bought him two.' They reached the cart and both heaved the puppeteer into the back of it. 'However, if you want to call foul, I suggest you have a word with Mrs Fitzherbert, who had her maid deliver him every half an hour in the hope he'd be done by three.'

'That bloody woman!' In unison, they fetched a carthorse each. 'She'll stop at nothing to win.'

'But she didn't, did she?' Ned couldn't resist a grin. 'Because I did.'

'I'd rather you took my money that she did.' The doctor's brow furrowed. 'However, I would like to know why you joined in the wager in the first place when wagering is not your style, and then how you managed to win it—to the second.'

Ned tapped his nose. 'A sensible man plays his cards close to his chest.'

'Hmmm… I'll concede you're good at that.' He set about fastening the buckles around his horse's belly. 'So good you currently have the whole village speculating…' One buckle done and he moved to the next. '…as to whether you are going to make an honest woman of Miss Healy. Are you?' It was said with far too much nonchalance for it not to matter and Ned stifled a smile.

Ever since the dinner party at Sophie's he'd noticed the way Dr Able's eyes wandered to Rose, and how hers, despite all her protestations about being heartbroken, had a habit of wandering back.

'Why? Do you fancy her for yourself?'

The much too ready shake of the head was insincere. 'I've been married, Ned, and trust me, I shan't be doing it again.'

'Very wise.' Ned pretended to focus on his own buckles while he had a bit of fun. 'And probably just as well seeing as Rose is already taken.' Izzy wasn't the only one who enjoyed a bit of matchmaking, except his way was much more subtle and just as effective. He had wound Lord Hockley up tighter than a spring when he and Sophie had been fighting their obvious attraction to one another, by hinting in every way possible that he had designs on her whenever the pair of them collided. Nothing chivvied a reticent suitor into action like a love rival as he supposed he was testament. Ned would still be in denial about his feelings for Izzy if *Daniel* hadn't arrived in Whittleston.

'So you have set your cap to her?'

'Maybe.' It wouldn't hurt to make the doctor suffer a bit, any more than it would hurt to throw out a few crumbs to put the village off the real scent of his own romantic intentions. If Izzy was going to turn him down, which the pessimist within fully expected her to do, he would rather nobody else know of his humiliation and defeat.

'I'm surprised,' said Dr Able with a curt edge to his voice, 'only I was convinced you only had eyes for Isobel.'

Good grief! Of course it would be his blasted eyes again! 'Do I look like an idiot, Sam?' He hoped his dismissive chuckle sounded more convincing than his friend's casual questions had. 'A man would have to be mad to want to shackle himself to Izzy.' Mad with jealousy. Mad with lust. Mad with love and longing to have for ever with the blasted menace.

'Oh, I don't know…' Nowhere near ready to give up on Rose, Dr Able tried to sell him on the idea, oblivious to the fact that Ned was already sold. 'She has lots of delightful qualities and she's a stunner. You'd have to go a long way to find a woman as pretty as Isobel.'

A ridiculous statement when there wasn't a woman alive who held a candle to the minx.

'That's as maybe...' Ned finished checking the reins and set the horses on their way with a gentle slap. 'But I think I'd prefer to take my chances with Rose.' And then, purely because it tickled him to toy with the man a bit more he added, 'But if you're mad enough to want Irritating Izzy, then you, my friend, are welcome to her.'

Isobel was too upset to concentrate on all the assembly. Thanks to overhearing Ned's cutting words outside the cake tent while she was still in it, she was, frankly, devastated. Even hours afterwards, she still couldn't quite believe that someone who had proclaimed her to be his best friend could be so cruel.

Irritating Izzy.

Irritating Izzy who a man would have to be mad to shackle himself to.

'Do you mind if we move?' Beside her as they hovered near the refreshments, Sophie looked a bit green, making Izzy feel guilty for neglecting her so. 'The smell of that salmon is turning my stomach.'

'I thought morning sickness was supposed to be confined to mornings, hence the name.' She blinked at her gaping friend blandly, trying to put a brave face on things even though all she really wanted to do was go home, curl up into a ball and cry.

'How did you know?'

'Because obviously I am a genius.' Isobel flicked her gaze towards the protective hand on Sophie's tummy and rolled her eyes. 'And because you've been rubbing your belly constantly like an overprotective mother for weeks.' Then she beamed. It took every last bit of her strength. 'Congratulations by the way. I've wanted to say that for weeks too, but I was doing the unthinkable for Whittleston and respecting your privacy.'

'Thank you.' Her friend smiled shyly then glanced around furtively. 'Do you think anyone else knows?'

'Perhaps not *everyone*.' She forced a smile to soften that blow. 'There's always an idiot in every village, so I am sure there must be one here too who is too stupid to have worked out the obvious.' She glanced around too as if looking for one, hoping Ned would be there so that she could point the finger at him, until her gaze fixed onto Mr Bunion. 'Ah…there he is.' With perfect timing the stinky solicitor's clerk wiggled his fingers in what he likely thought was a seductive wave because he thought Isobel was interested.

'Our resident idiot is resplendent in puce tonight to match his complexion, I see.'

Instead of laughing at the insult, Sophie sucked in a breath. 'And talking of resplendent… Be still my beating heart…'

Isobel followed her eyes and sucked in a ragged breath of her own.

'Ned's shaved,' said Sophie, nudging her, 'and, oh, my goodness indeed, as isn't he handsome?'

As there was no denying that, she nodded, lost for words. She was so accustomed to his beard, she had quite forgotten what a strong, angled jaw he had. The straight proud nose, or that he had cheekbones a Roman statue would be proud to own. Towering over everyone in the striped and perfectly fitted waistcoat she had had made him, paired with the smart black coat she had insisted upon which emphasised his broad shoulders and with the typically Ned-like unfussy knot tied in his expertly starched cravat, he had a presence that drew every eye. Such an effortlessly masculine presence that he far and away outmanned every other man in the room.

Drat him to hell.

Almost as if he sensed her staring, his eyes found hers across the crowd and she quickly looked away in case her pain showed and the tears fell. She would certainly not give him that satisfaction. Not tonight and not ever.

Tonight, she would treat him with all the cold disdain the traitor deserved.

Tomorrow he would be cut from her life.

Snip-snip.

Slash-slash.

And she would never speak to the wretch ever again.

With an odd look, he started towards her but was halted by Mrs Fitzherbert, who gave him a thorough inspection through her quizzing glass as she prodded and poked him like a prime piece of beef. He endured that with surprising and un-Ned-like good humour until Rose swooped in to steal him, threading her arm through his possessively, claiming him as hers before the entire room in case any other lady present had ideas.

Thankfully Isobel didn't any longer. Any fanciful ideas she might have had now lay shredded and bloodied on the floor. Stomped on by that big oaf's huge boots until they died a painful death. Which was precisely what she wished upon him at this precise moment. Preferably at her hands.

'Lucky Rose,' said Sophie in a whispered aside as she nudged her. 'It seems her broken heart has mended, though who can blame her. Well done,

Izzy, for pairing them. You truly are a matchmaker *par excellence*.'

Because of course he had shaved for Rose.
Set his cap to Rose. Preferred to take his dratted
chances with Rose.

Rose the *beautiful*.

The flash of jealousy was as instantaneous as
it was instinctive and infuriated her to the point
that the rest of the room disappeared in a thick,
green fog through which she could see only them.
Rose simpering with undisguised desire for the
big oaf she had no right ogling, and Ned smiling down bewitched as if the sun rose and set
with the woman currently clinging to him like a
limpet. Stomping on Isobel's already bludgeoned
heart still further, as if he'd quite forgotten that
not hours before he had twirled his finger in her
hair, told her it looked lovely in a flirty manner
and been the most attentive gentleman towards
her all day.

Right up until the moment he had shown his
true colours and called her Irritating Izzy.

Irritating.

Izzy.

As if she were nothing more to him than an
annoying fly to be swatted.

Not a friend. Certainly not a best friend. And

most definitely not someone who reciprocated her feelings in any way, shape or form.

That rejection sliced like a blade.

How dare he toy with her emotions like that?

As bitter tears pricked her eyes, and ready to murder both Rose and Ned with her bare hands for their treachery, Isobel muttered a pathetic excuse to escape her friend and scurried to the retiring room to calm down. Ten minutes later, when that didn't work, she splashed some water on her face and decided some fresh air might be in order. Perhaps a brisk march around the village square might help dislodge the spiralling panic that had gripped her guts and the pain strangling her heart? Or maybe she should simply go home where she could lick her wounds in private now that this assembly—this stupid, parochial assembly that she had always adored—suddenly felt more oppressive than her father's house.

She dashed out of the retiring room and straight into a broad chest.

'I believe this dance is ours.'

Isobel had been in such a blind panic to escape that the sound of Daniel's voice so close to her ear made her jump. Mortified in case her devastation showed, she wrestled with her dance card and attempted to scrutinize it.

'Is it?' She had no memory of pencilling his

name in or even any recollection of him asking, or anyone for that matter, because she had been so lost in a pit of despair, but before she could argue, he took her hand.

'It is now.'

Rather than call him out on his boldness or flee wailing into the night, and to give her something else to do rather than seething or grieving at the sight of Ned and the woman who did not irritate him, she allowed the Lieutenant to lead her to the floor. That he had claimed her for the first waltz also came as a shock, because the first she realised that that was what the musicians were playing was when he tugged her into his arms.

'You look beautiful tonight. The most beautiful woman in the room, actually, which I suppose, by default, makes me the luckiest man here too.'

She managed to muster a stiff smile. 'I bet you say that to all the girls, Lieutenant Healy.'

'I thought we had agreed that you would call me Daniel.' He twirled her so fast, she lost sight of Ned and his floozy for a moment.

'Did we? I forget.'

'No, you didn't. You are making me sing for my supper exactly as you should.' He chuckled and tugged her a little closer. 'But as a trained soldier, I should warn you that I love the thrill of the chase.'

'What makes you assume that I wish to be caught, Lieutenant?' Rose had dragged Ned to the buffet and was shamelessly feeding him cake.

'Ah—I see how it is.' He was gazing deep into her eyes with such impertinence she was sorely tempted to step on his toes to make him stop. Then step on them some more while she imagined that they were Ned's toes she was crushing into dust with her heel. 'My sister is right and you are head over heels in love with your jealous farmer.'

That snapped her attention back to him. 'I beg your pardon?' She tried to appear more amused than affronted and feared that she failed on both counts because he laughed. 'Rose is quite wrong. I couldn't be more delighted that she and Ned have found one another.'

He twirled her again so that she had to face them. 'Rosie and Ned are in cahoots, Isobel. Simply to fool you. They have been since the first day they met.'

She felt her nonchalant smile waver but still pretended to be more intrigued by his comment than hurt by it. How many more things had Ned been lying to her about? How many more games had he been playing at her expense? 'In what way are they in cahoots?'

'Ned went along with your matchmaking

machinations simply to please you and stop you directing them elsewhere, and Rose did the same, at least for his benefit. In reality, she realised that you harboured feelings for him and decided that the only way to make you admit them was to make you jealous.'

'I refuse to believe that your sister is that cruel.' Even if Ned was. Were they both laughing at her behind her back? Had they both been laughing at her all this time? 'You jest, sir.'

'Rosie isn't cruel, she's a hopeless romantic who worked out that Ned was hopelessly in love with you from the outset.'

Now the Lieutenant was being cruel. 'He really isn't.' Because to Ned she was Irritating Izzy. The bane of his life.

'He is and I can prove it.' He manoeuvred the pair of them towards Ned and Rose. 'He watches you incessantly. He has been your loyal bodyguard all day in case I got too over-familiar, and each and every time he catches me flirting with you his fists clench as if he is imagining what it would feel like to wring my neck or pummel me to paste.'

If only...

'Now you are being fanciful, Lieutenant, as I have always been more of an irritant to Ned than a...' She was almost winded by the force with which he tugged her close and spun her while he stared covetously at her lips.

'Watch his hands, Isobel, not me.'

Powerless to do anything else, she did and gasped to see that Ned's fists were indeed clenched by his sides. Then they clenched some more as Daniel's hand slipped from the middle of her back to the small of it as he twirled her right past him.

While she scrambled furiously to digest what she had just seen and then make sense of it in view of what she had overheard, Daniel had whisked her to the opposite side of the floor, only so that he could waltz her past them again.

This time she saw Ned's eyes narrow as his fists clenched, then watched him watch her with all the intensity of a man who could not tear them away. Even when Rose whispered something to him, he seemed oblivious of her presence.

Behaviour all so at odds with what he had said to Dr Able that it made absolutely no sense.

'If that is not a man consumed with jealousy for the woman that he loves then I'm a farmer, Isobel.' The music ended and the Lieutenant lifted her hand and pressed a lingering kiss on the back of it. 'Now, the big question is, do you feel the same about him or do I actually stand a chance with you?' His smile was teasing, already accepting and she found herself smiling at him in return, suddenly giddy as foolish hope sprang once again eternal.

She shook her head. 'You don't.'

'I thought as much, and Rosie said as much—but you cannot blame a chap for trying. Because I meant what I said, Isobel Cartwright, despite your heart lying so obviously elsewhere, you are still the most beautiful woman in this room.' He wrapped her arm around his and escorted her back to where his sister now stood with Sophie, Rafe, Mrs Fitzherbert and a grinning Archie.

But there was no sign of Ned anywhere.

'He's gone,' said Mrs Fitzherbert without pre-amble. 'He took one look at old Smug Chiselled Chin here, kissing your hand as if he meant it, and he stormed out with a face like thunder, so fast he's probably halfway to London by now.'

'Oh, for goodness' sake!' Unsure whether to kiss him or kill him for being so terminally exas-perating and difficult, Isobel picked up her skirts to dash after the brute. So fast herself that she did not witness Rose and Daniel, Sophie and Rafe, Mrs Fitzherbert and even Archie patting each other on the back in hearty celebration of a job well done.

Chapter Eighteen

❦

Ned's boots tore over his most useless field in a blur. He was furious at himself.

Furious at her for choosing that lieutenant over him. Furious that she was still hell-bent on leaving like she'd always planned. Furious at Archie for the sowing the seeds in his mind that encouraged him to attempt to fight for her. Furious at himself for hoping, dreaming, dressing like a dandy and blasted shaving for the minx!

Furious, too, for practically announcing it to the whole, nosy, meddling blasted village in his stampeding jealously! For making himself look like an idiot as a result. For wearing his heart on his sleeve. For wanting what he knew better than to want in the first place!

But most of all he was furious at his stupid, aching heart for beating only for her.

Her!

The infuriating menace!

What a lovesick blasted fool he truly was! And now the joke was on him because he'd have to endure the pity of the entire village for goodness knew how long until he could convince them that he was over it, when he knew already he would never be over it.

Never be over her.

Heaven help him!

If the moon had been out, he'd be howling at it for his reckless stupidity, but instead, while the last of the amber rays of the sunset lingered to mock him further for daring to reach for the stars, he settled for flinging himself on *their* stump and staring out at the river despondent. As this was likely where it had all started, right back when who knew when, it seemed fitting that this was where he had to acknowledge that it had all ended too.

The end of an era.

The end of their friendship.

The end of the dream he had been too scared to dream until it was too late to do anything about it.

He dropped his head in his hands, wishing he could turn back time at least enough that he could erase today, then instantly froze because he sensed her.

'What do you think you are about, Ned Parker, dashing off like that without telling me? And before you even had the decency to say hello to me too.' She sounded upset and that made two of them, but he still had his pride. At least for now he hoped he still did. Izzy wasn't stupid and she'd likely piece it all together by tomorrow anyway and by then he might have thought of a way out of the humiliation and heartache fate seemed to have decided he was doomed to suffer.

'Well, Ned?' All the flesh on his back tingled to let him know she now stood less than a foot away, and knowing her, she'd be all arms folded and indignant. 'Why are you here and not there?'

In case his face called him a liar and proved how wretched he felt, he refused to turn around and stared for all he was worth at the horizon. 'I wasn't in the mood for all those people, Izzy. Not after a whole day of them. I'm sorry.' As the tentacles of grief and despair were already wrapping themselves around his vocal cords, threatening to choke him, he stood ready to bolt. 'But don't let my unsociable tendencies spoil your evening. Go back and have fun as I'm off to bed. Some of us have a long day of work ahead of us tomorrow and I've squandered enough time on your nonsense already. I'll need the early start to get it all done.'

As his feet moved to escape, she caught his arm and just that touch set his misguided nerves jumping with need. 'I need to ask you an important question first, Ned, and I'd appreciate a frank answer. The frankest in fact, because it concerns my future.'

'Then it can wait till tomorrow, Izzy.' Because if she wanted his blessing for her and her smarmy lieutenant tonight, he just didn't have it in him. He tugged his arm from her grip and started towards home. 'There's nothing that needs saying tonight that can't be said better in the morning when I'm rested.' After he had raged, regrouped and licked the worst of his wounds in private. 'We both know that my temper is always at its worst when I'm tired.' Except he wasn't tired, he was broken.

'I need to know if you are in love with me, Ned.'

His feet paused while he panicked. 'Don't be daft. Have you gone soft in the head, woman?'

'Everyone seems to think that you are, but I need to hear it for myself, Ned. From you.' Her hand grazed his elbow again and he flinched. 'After overhearing you call me Irritating Izzy, I won't dare to hope otherwise.'

Dare to hope? Had he heard that wrong?

He must have, surely, because Izzy…

Against his will, his body turned and he searched her face for any clue that this wasn't goodbye. It was every bit as wary and wretched as his own. There were tears in her lovely eyes and they looked so vulnerable, as if she feared that she was the one mistaken. That he was going to reject her. 'I need to know…do you love me, Ned?' A single fat tear spilled over her long lashes and it humbled him to realise it was the first one he had ever seen her shed.

'I might do.'

'Might?' Her laugh was nervous, her eyes swirling with an emotion he could not fathom but wanted to hope matched his. 'I think you are going to have to be more specific. Only I overheard you telling Dr Able earlier that you preferred Rose to me and you called me Irritating Izzy and…'

He winced at the hurt in her lovely eyes. 'I was lying…trying to save face. Hoping he wouldn't realise how I truly felt.' He huffed at his own inarticulateness. 'What if I did love you, Izzy?' He took a tentative step towards her, his heart hammering so hard in his chest it was a wonder it didn't burst out and bounce along the riverbank.

'Then I might feel the same.'

'Might?' It was his turn to laugh without humour. 'What sort of flighty answer is that, woman?'

She steeled her shoulders, all bravado till the last despite the tell-tale tear. 'The only sort you are getting from Irritating Izzy, you big, impossible oaf, until you bare your soul to me.'

'Well…all right then…' He supposed someone had to break the deadlock, so he choked out the words in his heart and hoped that they were the right ones. 'In that case, of course I love you, although God only knows why because you're a pain in my backside too. If I'm being totally frank…' He couldn't stop the hopeful smile from blossoming. '… I've probably always loved you but just was too stupid and stubborn and scared to admit it to myself before now.' He reached out and used his thumb to swipe another tear from her lovely face. 'You're my everything, Izzy.'

'And you are mine, Ned.' She threw herself at him, half laughing, half crying, wrapping her arms around his neck and hugging him tight. 'You've always been my everything, you difficult, gruff and surly curmudgeon.'

He hugged her back, so overcome with elation and relief there were tears in his eyes now too. 'At least I'm not scruffy any more. That has to count for something.'

'No…you're not.' Her fingers traced the contours of his face, her plump bottom lip trembling slightly as she bit down on it. 'About that…' She held him out at arm's length and shook him ineffectually by the shoulders. 'It turns out that you are too damn handsome without your beard so I am going to have to insist that you grow it back forthwith in case some other woman gets ideas in her head and tries to steal you away from me!'

'Make your mind up, wo—' She squashed his giddy chuckle with a kiss.

It was short and sharp and utterly perfect, but nowhere near enough.

'Now what?' She stepped back, shy and uncertain and utterly beguiling as a result because she had never let anyone but him ever see her that way. 'Do we head back to the assembly and face the music after we both charged out of it in such a hurry? Or do we...um...?' Her gaze dropped to his mouth again before she wrenched it back to his eyes and shrugged. 'As you can probably tell, despite knowing you for ever, I'm new to all this being-in-love-with-you malarkey, and so now have no earthly clue how I am supposed to behave around you. Isn't that silly?'

He shook his head and gave in to the urge to cup her cheek, touch her hair, smooth his hands down her arms until they locked snugly around her waist. 'We'll work it out. Between us we always work it out.'

'And until we have a battle plan?'

He kissed her nose, then rested his against it. 'We do what we always do but just add a bit of kissing now and again.'

'I like that plan. I like that plan a lot.'

Chapter Nineteen

Isobel went willingly into his arms when he opened them and sighed against his mouth when Ned pressed his lips to hers. Straightaway her body rejoiced at the contact and wanted more, but as he seemed to be in no hurry, she allowed him to set the pace. Revelling in the myriad of sensations that only the soft brush of his mouth could elicit.

Unlike every man who had ever kissed her in the past, Ned's hands remained on her waist and seemed content to remain there while his mouth explored hers. Even when he deepened the kiss all they did was pull her gently closer, then closer still until they touched almost from head to toe.

She could feel his desire resting hard against her midriff. His heart beating against her breasts. The heat of his big body radiating through their clothes to warm hers as the river breeze played with her hair and cooled her back. All so utterly perfect and romantic she felt like she was floating in one of her girlish fantasies, cocooned in the strong arms of her prince.

With reluctance, she allowed him to tear his mouth from hers, only to have it do more wicked things to her nerve endings when it trailed across her jaw to her ear, then down her neck. She heard herself moan her encouragement while her hips arched of their own accord against his in invitation.

'I want you, Ned.' Isobel only realised that she had spoken that thought aloud when he pulled back to stare intently down at her, his irises so dark with desire they took her breath away. The molten heat in them emboldened her to repeat herself. To offer herself to him entirely. 'I want you now. Here.' Because she couldn't wait until they made their way back to his house and here was their spot.

He closed his eyes and released a ragged sigh before he nodded, smiling. 'Thank God…because I don't think I could stand not having you now too.' His next kiss was needy. Thorough. Sublime. His big hands splayed over her bottom, then slowly, ever so slowly, explored the short distance between her buttocks and her breasts, moaning his pleasure at the weight of them in his palms.

At the way her nipples puckered from just one caress beneath the inconvenient barrier of her gown.

As if he realised that her skin needed to feel his, he helped her shrug off his coat, then chuckled as her clumsy fingers wrestled with the buttonholes of his waistcoat while his fought the laces at the back of her gown. They were hampered further by the ever-deepening twilight, but somehow the fall of the night and the gradual emergence of the stars only added to the intimacy and rightness of the moment.

Isobel took her own sweet time relieving him of the waistcoat she had made him, using it as the excuse to explore his upper body properly while she kissed him, marvelling at the muscles that a lifetime of working the land had honed to perfection beneath the soft linen of his shirt. Then, to torment him and eek out this precious moment still further, she insisted on doing it all again under his shirt before she removed that too and looked her fill.

He was, for want of a better word, magnificent. So tall, so broad, so powerful and yet not the slightest bit intimidating. She traced his mouth with her index finger before trailing it down his chin and his throat. Although that wayward finger wanted to continue straight downward, she forced it to meander across his chest so that she could gently scrape her fingernail over his nipple simply to watch it harden like it had been when she had caught him sleeping in his bath. Then lower, to follow the arrow of dark hair on his abdomen and through his navel until it reached the waistband of his breeches. 'I've never actually seen a completely naked man before.' She smoothed her palm over the front of his falls, enjoying the way his Adam's apple bobbed and his breath became erratic as she learned the long, thick shape of him. 'Which is probably just as well as there isn't a hope that any average man's physique could compete with yours.'

He laughed at that, embarrassed by the compliment, tried to shrug it off but still watched her reaction intently as she unbuttoned him and finally revealed that part of him, laughing some more when her eyes widened.

Good gracious but he was…big. 'I did wonder if everything would be in proportion. No wonder Lusty Lavinia took you under her wing.'

She must have done a poor job of hiding the brief flash of concern that he might just be too big, because he pressed a soft kiss on her lips and smiled against them. 'I promise I'll never hurt you, Izzy, so please don't worry.'

'I know that.' And she did. For all his imposing solidity and his outwardly intractable character and quick temper, the big brute was as soft as down inside. He would rather die than hurt a fly and he loved her.

Loved her! The most irritating fly that had ever been in his ointment.

Who saw that coming?

Although with her erstwhile enemy hindsight, she wasn't shocked she had missed all the signs. She had adored Ned for eternity—but hadn't realised that the adoration she had felt as a child would obviously have morphed into that of a woman over time. As much as she loathed to make Ned right about anything, right here, right now, in this place, she realised this was fate.

A bubble of laughter escaped as she attempted to fight the rest of him out of his tight breeches only to nearly topple them both over in the process. Laughing too, he steadied them both before he toed off his boots, stepped out of his breeches and kicked them away.

'My turn.' As naked as the day he was born, and despite his body ripe with desire, Ned stepped back and folded his arms as if he had all the time in the world, the wretch, when she was desperate. 'Take every stitch off.' His gaze raked her body. Worshipped her with his eyes. Set every nerve on edge in excited anticipation. 'Slowly.' She adored the silky timbre of his deep voice thickened with need just for her. 'Start with all fifteen of those hairpins because I swear I've never seen anything as beautiful as you with your hair unbound.'

Because she could see that it pleased him, for once Isobel was only too happy to comply with an order. When the first wild tendril fell upon her shoulder, his jutting manhood twitched. By the third, he had to touch her, winding his fingers in a fat curl that bounced near her breast and torturing them both as he played with it against her nipple.

He lost them both in a decadent kiss after the last pin fell, leaving her breathless when he stepped away, then stood in awed silence as she peeled out of her dress and unlaced her stays.

It was Ned who eased the final barrier of her chemise from her shoulders and then tugged it until it puddled around her feet. He swallowed as he took in her nudity, all the love and desire he felt for her fully exposed in his eyes as his hands travelled the same path as his gaze wandered. 'I knew you'd be beautiful.' His hand skimmed her curves from hip to breast, leaving fire in his wake. 'You've always been the most beautiful thing I've ever seen.'

When he next kissed her it was with reverence, and with their lips still fused he lifted her into his arms and continued to kiss her as he carried her to their tree stump and gently laid her on it.

As he covered her with his body, it opened for him like a flower, already ready. So libidinous all of a sudden Isobel barely recognised herself, and so desperate to be joined with his there wasn't the space for a single rational thought in her head. Yet despite all her earthy protestations, he still made her wait while he kissed every bared inch of her skin from top to bottom, lingering over her breasts as his teeth teased each needy tip until she could barely stand it. But that was nothing compared to the sensual torture he wreaked when his tongue dipped between her legs and loved the most sensitive spot on her body. A spot she had been oblivious of for five and twenty years came alive as he kissed it and rendered her a writhing, nonsensical and shameless wanton begging for release.

He sensed that, robbing her of it as her hips bucked to kiss her mouth again so that she tasted herself, filling his hands with her aching breasts, that part of him hard and insistent against the soft curls at her entrance, teasing them both. Torturing them both with denial before his lips nibbled their way down her body again to that throbbing, humming, needy bud of nerves that told her that her body was on the cusp of something wonderful. So close and yet still so far away.

She tunnelled her hands in his thick hair when

he kissed that again, forcing herself not to beg him to hurry because she somehow understood that the journey to wherever it was he was taking her was as wonderous as the destination. Stunned that her body felt so much when it never had before, revelling in the way something built inside her with every intoxicating flick of his clever tongue and praying for the end at the same time because each new sensation was too much. Too new. Too overwhelming.

Yet, as much as she craved it, when that shuddering release came, it surprised her and she cried out into the night sky, calling his name like a benediction as wave after wave of ecstasy pulsed from her core and ricocheted out along every nerve and sinew, blinding her with stars. Excruciating bliss so all-consuming that it rendered her powerless.

Boneless.

Mindless.

Anchorless as she tumbled off the edge of the earth into the abyss.

Until Ned caught her and brought her back to earth. Kissed her as he tenderly edged inside her. Filled her completely. His heart beating rapidly against hers in perfect harmony, hers rejoiced at all of it, because he was her everything and she was his. And when she assumed that he had already introduced her to all the pleasure in the world, that nothing could surpass what she had just experienced and that this part of the act was for him and him alone, he stared deep into her soul. Used his big, powerful, gentle body to love her from within and then took them both soaring to the moon.

Chapter Twenty

❧❦❧

A shaft of sunlight found his eyelids and forced them open. It would have been a painful, rude awakening if the pillow beside him hadn't been covered in a tangle of golden girls and Izzy's delectable, bare peach of a bottom wasn't nestled snugly in his groin. Beneath the weight of his arm around her middle, the rhythmic rise and fall of her ribs told him that she was still fast asleep. It was a state of affairs which suited him just fine because for the first time in for ever he was perfectly content with his lot despite the clock on the mantel telling him that it was already eight. It wouldn't hurt his spoiled animals to have their breakfasts a few hours late, after all Sunday was supposed to be a day of rest and all work and no play had made Ned a very dull boy indeed.

He snuggled closer to the menace in his arms, quite prepared to hold her for the rest of the day if she failed to awaken, burying his nose in her curls. She sighed, muttered something genuinely nonsensical and stretched like a cat. He knew the exact moment she came to, because she suddenly stiffened and held her breath, letting it all out in one big whoosh before she twisted in his embrace, smiling shyly as she desperately tried to tug the tangled bedcovers trapped under his body over her gloriously bare and deliciously sensitive breasts.

He supposed the gentlemanly thing to do was to release the sheets so that she could cover her modesty. But, seeing as he was a farmer and not a gentleman, he propped himself up on one elbow so that he could trace his fingertip over the furthest one. He offered her his most sinful smile when the juicy, raspberry tip hardened before his eyes.

'Morning, beautiful.'

And she was.

The sight of her all nude and rumpled on his mattress, her lips still swollen from his kisses, looking every inch a woman who was thoroughly sated fair took his breath away.

'Morning, handsome.' She smiled as he bent to kiss her and was still smiling when he rolled back onto his elbow so that he could bask in the wonder of this moment some more before he seduced her all over again.

However, to his horror, her lovely smile began to quiver and falter almost straightaway and all at once she was up like a shot. In her haste to escape him, she perched on the edge of the mattress with her back to him while she scrabbled for the discarded eiderdown, then made some odd, choking, snorting sounds as she wrapped it around her body.

'Izzy, what's wrong?' Because she was scaring him.

'Nothing…n-nothing whatso…e-ever.' As something equally as disturbing seemed to be happening to her shoulders, which were quaking slightly as she battled to keep them rigid, Ned quickly rolled to the edge of the bed himself in time to catch her hand before she fled the room.

'Izzy?' He had to physically cajole her to turn around and when she did it frightened the life out of him because she wasn't so much crying as sobbing uncontrollably. 'Oh, good grief, what did I do?' Now that there was no use hiding it, she crumpled, burying her head in her hands as she wept. 'Did I hurt you?'

Consumed with guilt he tried to gather her close but as her posture was so rigid and he was still seated, all he managed to do was hug her hips as she stood between his splayed legs. 'Tell me what I've done, Izzy?' Because Ned was buggered if he knew.

Frantically, he ran through all the events of the night before while he tried to soothe her. It might have been a while since he had been with a woman, but he was pretty certain that she had enjoyed the way he had made love to her beneath the stars. All the signs had pointed to it at least and she had been quite vocal in her pleasure as she had come undone twice in quick succession on their tree stump.

After that, there had been a lot of giggling and heavy petting on the way back to his house, some very heated kissing in his kitchen before he had relieved her of her dress again, and she had certainly moaned and sighed and writhed some more when he'd had his wicked way with her on the kitchen table. And when they had finally made it to the bed where he had been quite content to sleep he was so exhausted, he might well of dreamt it, but he was convinced it had been Izzy who had awoken him in the small hours so that she could have her wicked way with him. Had something else occurred that he had no memory of? Had he done something despicable in his sleep?

It had to have been something pretty despicable to have caused all this, because she was in a veritable spasm now, wheezing and shuddering and spilling noisy tears all over the place.

He gently shook her to try and get her to look at him. 'For the love of God, woman, please tell me what I've done?' When that didn't work, he carefully prised her hands from her face and held them tight. 'Please.'

'You...y-you...' She yanked one hand out of his grasp and used it to point a quaking finger at him, filling his heart with dread. 'You loved me.' Her face contorted as she snorted and choked some more. 'You *loved* me.'

'And?' Ned threw up his hands wishing he knew what to do or what to say.

'And that's never happened before!' She grizzled into the eiderdown momentarily and then wagged her finger some more. 'I never knew it was meant to be like that. I n-n-never knew it was meant to be so perfect and so special and... and...and...' She flung her head back this time to cry and continued to do that until he could stand it no more.

So he stood and caught her face between his hands and angled it to his. *'And?'*

'And I wish I'd waited for you, Ned! I wish I hadn't let those other two idiots anywhere near me and I'm furious at myself for not s-s-saving myself for you!'

He realeased a sound which was part laughter and a greater part relief and cuddled her close, swaddling her like a baby as he dragged her onto his lap, stroking her riot of hair as she wept against his shoulder. 'Oh, for goodness' sake, you've gone completely soft in the head now, woman.' And he loved her all the more for it. 'Whatever nonsense happened in the past, it's best left there. It has no place in the here and now and certainly none in the future.' He kissed her nose, her tears, her mouth.

'If anyone should castigate themselves for any foolishness in the past it should be me. I never should have shut you out, Izzy. I should never have abandoned you to your awful father all alone. Never should have pushed you out of my life after my father died and the flood happened and I thought my world imploded because you are my world. I'm livid at myself for allowing something as trivial as pride to come between us but I was so ashamed that I had nothing, Izzy, I just couldn't face you. And I'm furious that I kept shutting you out afterwards when I should have let you all the way back in—we were both lost. Lost for two long years and we didn't need to be. I loathe myself for that but I'll be grateful for ever that you were too stubborn and too persistent to not completely give up on me. Especially as my father was right, he knew we'd get there in the end.' He kissed her head, her nose, her quivering, blubbering mouth some more. 'But trust the pair of us to take the most convoluted route around to get to this point, but we are here now and that is all that matters.' She smiled at him through her tears, tried to speak and her chest, shoulders and jaw went into spasm again. 'Why don't I go make us some tea and we'll drink it back in bed?'

She shook her head laughing. 'Your tea is awful. I'll make it.'

He followed her eiderdown-clad body into the kitchen where they both smiled at Falstaff, who was snoring his head off on the knotted, hopelessly crinkled pile of clothes they had torn off one another as they had stumbled inside. His dog refused to budge from them and pretended to remain asleep as Izzy wrestled her pretty evening gown from beneath him. While the kettle boiled, Ned laced her into it, and then they sat together, holding hands and smiling soppily at one another as they drank the tea.

She was in the middle of pouring him a second cup when they both heard a distant commotion outside in the yard. 'Is that banging? Is someone here?'

'Sounds more like an animal to me.' Ned strode towards the door and flung it open in time to hear a familiar honk coming from the direction of his barn. 'Oh, dear God, no...'

As he hurried out, clad in only his unbuttoned breeches, Izzy followed and they both stopped dead when they saw what the problem was. Old Nick had decided to return and was doing his best to peck his way into the barn this time, instead of out of it. Only this time he had brought along a friend.

Izzy, of course, was instantly charmed by the sight. 'That must be Mrs Old Nick.' She wrapped her arms around his arm and sighed. 'No wonder he wanted to escape all those weeks, he wanted to be with his sweetheart.'

'Oh, for goodness' sake! As if swans have sweethearts.'

She slapped him playfully. 'Swans mate for life, Ned, and Old Nick's clearly an old romantic—like you.'

Such a romantic, the ungrateful bird took one look at him and instantly starting hissing and flapping his wings in anger, and then thwacking his lethal beak back against his barn door with such force it sent a spray of splinters flying.

Izzy, of course, thought that adorable and practically melted. 'He's brought her here so they can make a nest together.'

'Romantic or not, that feathered monster is not moving back into my barn under any circumstances. Not when his blasted wing works and there are miles of perfectly serviceable riverbank he can use instead like all the other less troublesome swans do.'

'Stop being such a curmudgeon, Ned.' She let go of him to walk towards the birds, crouching as she made cooing noises at them in the daft belief that she and the satanic Old Nick might somehow now be friends. 'It's nesting season and she's probably desperate for somewhere to lay hers.'

He jogged beside her and spread his arm to encompass the vista. 'Then behold the perfect spot. They can pick any stretch between here and the Cotswolds to raise their devil chicks.'

'A baby swan is a cygnet, Ned, not a chick.'

'That's as may be but as Dr Able rightly pointed out and we've both learned through bitter experience, swans aren't pets. If they want to live alongside humans, then the King can have them, seeing as he owns all the blasted things, but they are not living in my barn.'

The menace gave him one of her I've-decided-to-ignore-you looks, slid open the bolt and flung open the barn door just to spite him, then sighed again in contentment as Old Nick and his sweetheart waddled inside. Within seconds, the ungrateful fowl was pulling apart a hay bale to build himself a house.

Ned would have argued, but Izzy was already kissing him to soften the blow. 'At least let them stay until the eggs have hatched. Please, Ned. For me…' She kissed him some more then sashayed back to the house, beguiling hips undulating. 'Would it help if I stayed till Tuesday to help settle them in?' She shot him a saucy look over her shoulder that forced him to chase after her.

He caught her around the waist. 'Tuesday you say…?' He was already hard just thinking about it.

'Well seeing as Tess had a family emergency and this place is a good mile away from all the prying eyes in the village, it seems a shame to waste the opportunity, doesn't it?'

'It does.' He nuzzled her neck, ready to seize the opportunity right this second and she wriggled out of his arms.

'I need to pop home first and collect some things.' She gestured to her crumpled evening gown. 'This isn't exactly suitable for feeding your pigs.'

'A fair point.' He gestured to his bare chest.

'Let me put a few more clothes on and I'll come with you.'

'Have you gone soft in the head, Ned?' Her expression was appalled. 'At least if it's just little old me I stand some chance of sneaking in and out again while most of the villagers are in church, but you stick out like a sore thumb. And although I am thoroughly ruined, I'd rather not be publicly ruined, thank you very much and if they see you, with me dressed like this, we'll have our *indiscretion* splashed all over the front page of the *South Essex Gazette*.' Then she smiled a very naughty smile indeed. 'Give me an hour and I'll happily be indiscreet with you again.'

'So long as it's only an hour and you come back via the bakery as I'm starving.' He shooed her with his hands, and she shooed him right back.

'Go feed your barren pigs, who are doubtless also starving.'

Chapter Twenty-One

Isobel practically floated home grinning. She had taken the fields on purpose rather than the lane to avoid all the villagers on their way to the Sunday service at St Hildeth's, and thankfully never saw a soul. If she had, she'd have had no idea how to explain the scandalous, crumpled state of her dress or her wild mane of loose hair because all her hairpins were scattered in Ned's meadow by the river. She hadn't had the where-withal to try and find them in the dark after they had made love for the first time, nor hunt for her stockings or her stays. At the time, it had been a miracle that she could stand after what he had done to her, because her head had been spinning and her heart so full she had felt as though she were drunk.

Drunk on love.

Another giggle escaped at that fanciful thought

because at least she now knew why Sophie and Mrs Fitzherbert smiled smug, secret smiles whenever any vague mention of wifely duties came up. For it turned out that if the man doing the dirty deed was the right one then it wasn't a duty at all. Thanks to Ned, she was looking forward to a lifetime of doing her duty.

A fanciful thought that made her stop and think that perhaps she was assuming erroneously again? Ned might well have repeatedly told her how much he loved her last night and this morning, but at no point had he mentioned anything about marriage. He certainly hadn't proposed or even hinted at a future, even when she had offered to come to stay for the next few days. And drunk on love and dizzy from her splendid introduction to passion, she hadn't thought to seek proper clarification of his intentions.

Should she have?

She shook her head to banish that idiocy. Ned wasn't like any of the others. So what if he hadn't gushed about wedding her after he had bedded her, he was a man who needed the time and space to come to his own conclusions. And, perhaps selfishly, she wanted a proper, heartfelt proposal and didn't want to have to cajole one out of him. Unless…

Instinctively her hands covered her belly because unlike the other wastrels she had been intimate with, Ned hadn't taken any precaution to prevent planting a baby inside her. Not once in all of their many splendid joinings yesterday. Maybe that was unintentional? Mistakes made in the heat of the moment?

Although even that didn't add up because Ned was a farmer who knew how such things worked and she was pretty certain Lusty Lavinia would have taught him how avoid an insurmountable problem that would shackle him to her for ever?

Which meant that he had been well aware of the risks and had taken them anyway, and she was doing him disservice by doubting him.

Of course she was!

She was only doubting him because she had been let down so many times in the past, when he was nothing like any of them.

Thank the Lord!

He loved her.

Loved *her*!

So obviously she and Ned were going to spend eternity together.

Her cheerful, optimistic equilibrium restored, Isobel dashed the last few yards across the field, climbed the little fence that separated it from the back alleyway adjacent to her house and practically skipped towards the kitchen door. Only to stop dead at the unexpected sight of a wall of unpleasant yellow blocking the other end of it. The unmistakable shade warning her that it could only belong to her father's new curricle.

Ned sluiced the soap from his body, trying to tell himself that the frigid water from the pump was more invigorating than painful. After an impromptu tussle with Delilah in the pigsty, to get a tick out of the old sow's hind leg, he wanted to be clean for Izzy's imminent return. Just in case she was eager to be as immediately indiscreet as he was. He certainly hoped she was, as even all this cold water was doing nothing to dampen his ardour.

Beyond the gushing and gurgling, he heard someone and stopped pumping, hoping it was her, only to see Archie was tearing down the path towards him, waving his arms frantically. 'Ned! You need to come quick!'

'What's happened?' Instantly on alert, Ned ran towards him, shrugging on the clean shirt he'd grabbed before his ablutions as he went.

'It's Isobel.' Archie bent double in a panting heap before him in the yard. 'Her father's disowned her! He's throwing all her stuff into the street.'

'What the...?' Ned didn't wait for the lad to

catch his breath or explain further, he had to get to her. His mind already conjuring all manner of scenarios of what that vindictive bastard was doing to humiliate her in full view of the village. All Ned's fault, of course, because he let her go back alone after he had convinced her to spend the night. Thanks to him she had walked into an ambush and was suffering the consequences unsupported. He hoped she had made it back into the house to change before Cartwright had darkened his own door. If she hadn't, and she was still a walking scandal in all the clothes she had left him in, it didn't bear thinking about.

But think about it he did, all the way there, castigating himself for all his failings and once again not being there in her greatest time of need.

His lungs were burning as he reached the outskirts, but like a man possessed, he pushed harder until he saw the gathered crowd. From the shocked expressions and furtive whispering, he knew without seeing it for himself that old Cartwright had made her a spectacle.

'Get out of my way!' Ned barrelled into the gossiping villagers uncaring, then elbowed every single one of them out of his path in his panic. 'Izzy!'

The scene before him was almost as bad as his worst imaginings and, of course, the entire village seemed to be gathered in disparate arced clusters to witness it, all staring wide-eyed as George Cartwright spewed venom from the threshold of his front door.

'You spent the night with a man!' He threw a bundle of clothes outwards and an explosion of petticoats, stockings and stays exploded on the dirt. 'Filthy harlot! You are dead to me! *Dead* to me!'

'Enough!' Rafe blocked Cartwright's view, his palms raised and his expression thunderous. 'You've said and done enough!'

Behind him, and equally as incensed, was Lieutenant Healy who was gathering up all of Izzy's unmentionables shaking his golden head in outright disgust at the vindictiveness of the man. Next to him was Dr Able, also trying to calm the fool down but Cartwright was unappeasable and grabbed more things from the hallway behind him to fling into the air, spewing more venom about his daughter as he did so.

As much as he wanted to kill him with his bare hands, Ned scanned the sea of faces searching for her, expecting to see her pale and crying again in her shame, and needed to comfort her more than he needed to kill. But when his eyes finally found her, she was anything but.

Stood in her crumpled gown between Mrs

Fitzherbert on one side and Sophie on the other, her stance was defiant, her lovely face disdainful amidst her riot of love-mussed curls. On the ground around her feet appeared to be the amassed contents of her life—clothes, fabric, cottons, cushions, hairbrushes and shoes were scattered everywhere.

'You are dead to me!' Cartwright lunged and was restrained by Rafe and The Chin, his eyes bulging from his purple face and spittle flying from his vile mouth. 'I will never speak to you again!'

'For a man who has said that at least fifty times already, you still seem to have plenty to say.' Izzy's rebellious tone echoed in the ensuing silence. 'What beggars belief, though, is that you think that I care for I can assure you that I am as done with you as you are with me.'

'Har—'

'Finish that word and it will be the last you ever say!' Ned pushed his way past the last of the crowd and stalked towards Cartwright, his fists clenched ready to break the bastard's jaw.

He looked Ned up and down, took in the damp, untucked shirt and pointed an accusing finger at him. 'She was with you, wasn't she! You're the filthy dog she spread her legs for!'

Clearly Izzy had misguidedly thought to protect him with her silence as the whole crowd instantly gasped and began to mutter.

'Thanks to you she is soiled goods! She debased herself with a low-life Parker!' Cartwright had the audacity to spit at him then. 'Wasted herself on a nobody! The filthy har—'

The rest of that word got strangled as Ned grabbed a fistful of the man's cravat and yanked him out of Rafe and the soldier's grasp to smash him against the wall of his own house.

He pulled his arm back fully intending to smash the man's toxic jaw to smithereens, revelled in the way Cartwright's eyes widened as he recoiled in fear, when he felt her hand on his shoulder. 'He's not worth it, Ned.' She sighed as she gently held him back. 'And you're better than this. You've always been better than him, kinder than him and more decent than he could ever possibly comprehend, so please don't stoop to his level now.'

'He's a bully, Izzy. I've stood by for years and let that happen, but I'm damned if I'm going to stand by now.'

'He has no joy in his soul, Ned, and wouldn't know love if it slapped him in the face. He's pathetic, is what he is, nothing to me and I am done with him.' She smiled as she tugged him away. 'He's my past and like all things in the past, as a wise man said to me only this morning when I thought that it mattered, is best left there.'

For her and her alone, he allowed Izzy to drag him away from her snarling father, but just a few yards away, the spiteful fool couldn't resist one more poison barb when he assumed Ned would not retaliate. 'You're welcome to the harlot!'

It was all the excuse he needed, and he charged back to Cartwright like a bull at a gate despite all Izzy's attempts to stop him. Terrified, like all bullies her loathsome sire was a coward at heart, when Rafe and Lieutenant Healy stepped aside so that he could receive the pasting his thoroughly deserved, Cartwright darted inside his house and tried to close his front door. Ned shouldered it open with such force the man fell on his behind, then began to use his feet to shuffle backwards in the hope that he could escape.

He couldn't and squealed like one of Ned's Tamworths as he was hoisted from the floor by his lapels and dragged unceremoniously back out into the street so that the whole village could witness his comeuppance.

He wanted to hit him so badly, he could taste it, but knew the second that he gave in to the temptation he wouldn't be able to stop. There was just too much pent-up fury for what this monster had done to the woman he loved to not end up killing him in cold blood. So instead, he used his strength to lift him in the air, and while Cartwright's feet flayed and he begged for mercy, Ned carried him towards his curricle, and like a sack of potatoes tossed him in it.

As the fool cowered some more as he scrabbled up on the seat, Ned took great pleasure in climbing up on the stoop to loom over him. 'Chelmsford is welcome to you, you snivelling, malicious, pathetic, bullying bastard! And mark my works, Cartwright, and mark them good.' He grabbed the man's cravat again and twisted it until his face reddened. 'You set one foot in this village again I will tear you limb from limb and feed your putrid entrails to my dog!'

Because you could have heard a pin drop, everyone heard Cartwright whimper, then watched transfixed as Ned tossed him the reins, jumped down and pointed the way out of the village. 'Go! Now! Before I change my mind.'

And Cartwright did, his head bowed as the amassed villagers parted like the Red Sea to let him pass, then jeered him as he did.

Chapter Twenty-Two

'And good riddance to bad rubbish!' Mrs Fitzherbert waved her cane in the air as her father's curricle sped out of the village, then she turned to Isobel grinning. 'Well, I think that all ended rather magnificently, don't you? Thank goodness this all happened before we all went into church, else I'd have missed it.' Then she cackled and slapped Ned heartily on the back. 'I thought he was going to soil himself, he was so afraid, so well done, you! That was a splendid effort of controlled but brutal masculine force! I haven't had so much fun since we barricaded the road against Rafe here last winter.' Then she waggled her cane at him. 'It goes without saying, though, that I expect you to do the decent thing and put a ring on this young lady's finger. She's waited long enough for one and I, for one, am all done with all your shilly-shallying.'

Mortified, Isobel rushed forward. 'Don't listen to her, Ned.' This really wasn't how she wanted to be proposed to. On sufferance and under pressure on the back of a scandal. 'It doesn't matter.'

'Doesn't matter?' Now it was him that was appalled. 'What is that supposed to mean?'

'It means that everyone should have *a choice*, Ned.' She willed him to understand with her eyes that she was prepared to wait until he was ready. 'To marry or not as they see fit. It shouldn't be foisted upon them and it certainly shouldn't be done because one of the party feels beholden and…'

He did not let her finish her sentence and threw his arms up in the air his quick temper already gone. 'Is that your unsubtle way of telling me that you don't want to marry me? Because if it is, you have another think coming, Izzy. I'm not the sort of man you can have your wicked way with and then cast aside.' He slapped his chest, clearly holding the entirely wrong end of the stick. 'I'm just like Old Nick, I am! I mate for life!' Then he gestured like a madman around him. 'If you're leaving this blasted village, then I'm coming with you, and the least you can do after you've stolen my heart and ruined me for anyone else is wait for me to sell my farm so that—'

'Good Lord, but you are exasperating!' She

shook him by his ridiculously broad shoulders, smiling. 'I don't want you to sell your farm, idiot! I love that farm. All my most treasured memories are there.' Like the beautiful one they had made last night. 'I can think of nothing I would like more than to make my home there with you.'

'Well, make your mind up, woman!' He was still too angry for the significance of those words to sink in. 'For years you've been waffling on about how much you want to leave Whittleston and now you suddenly want to stay. I'll not be your gaoler, Izzy. Not in a million—'

She had to kiss him to shut him up.

'He was my gaoler.' She pointed to the racing dot of yellow haring towards Chelmsford at speed. 'You were right—it was never Whittleston I wanted to escape from. It was there.' She tilted his chin towards her father's oppressive house. 'That isn't the case any longer.'

His etched outraged frown softened. 'So you'll marry me, then?'

'Of course I will, you big oaf.'

'And that'll be enough?'

'More than enough.'

'Then can the pair of you get to the church now and get it over with?' Mrs Fitzherbert wedged her wizened face between them. 'Only I have fifteen shillings on you being married this May and I'd be devastated to lose them to Dr Able, who has you down for the first week of June.'

Because of course the village had opened a book on them.

'Yes! Do it today!' That came from Archie, who was clapping his hands with glee. 'I'll be your Best Man, Ned.'

'You can borrow my ring,' added Sophie, prising hers off. 'So long as I get to be the Matron of Honour.'

'Now see here—' The Reverend Spears, still in his cassock and carrying his prayer book, pushed his way to the front of the crowd. '—as the Lord's appointed shepherd of this motley flock, responsible for your spiritual health both here and in the hereafter, I feel duty bound to state that it is morally wrong to use the sacred institution of Holy Matrimony to win a bet. Furthermore, as it states in ecclesiastical law, no marriage can take place without the Banns being read so there will be no more talk of an illegal and hasty wedding today, no matter how much the prospective bride and groom undoubtedly need one. Should an immediate wedding be required...' he coughed uncomfortably as he glared at Isobel's middle '...under the circumstances, Ned would need to ride to the capital to procure a special licence.'

'What poppycock.' Mrs Fitzherbert waved

her cane at the Reverend. 'She was born here in Whittleston and she'll be wed here in Whittleston and I shall be giving her away.'

'Then the Banns shall need to be read on three consecutive Sundays and that is that.' The Reverend set his jaw. 'And these two will need to act with a bit more decorum while they wait for that to be done.' He looked them up and down and stared heavenward, muttering a prayer for their impatient and libidinous souls.

'Well, of course they will. In fact, Isobel will be moving in with me so that I can chaperone her while they wait. For propriety's sake.' A lofty declaration Mrs Fitzherbert ruined by winking at the pair of them. 'And as today's Sunday service was delayed by that blithering idiot...' she gestured towards the now empty lane ahead '...it strikes me that you could read the first of those essential Banns today, couldn't you, Reverend?'

'The lengths some people will go to win a bet in this village are staggering.' It was Dr Able's turn to grumble.

'Nobody likes a sore loser.' Mrs Fitzherbert was unrepentant. 'But if you wish to recoup your losses, Doctor, then you should know that we've opened another betting book on you, and I see no reason why you cannot wager upon who you believe your future bride will be while the odds are so favourable. At least then you can have some influence on the outcome and can only blame yourself if you lose to me again.'

'I beg your pardon!' Now it was the local physician's turn to be aggrieved. 'You've all opened a book on me as well?'

'Indeed we have, and I put fifteen shillings on you and Rose while the odds were ten to one after the way the pair of you cosied up together during that card game.' As both the good doctor gaped incredulous and Rose blushed profusely, the riling old lady beamed from ear to ear. 'And I'm not the only one who saw it. Lord Hockley is so convinced he's sensed a frisson between you he's bet thirty.' That done, Mrs Fitzherbert glared at the vicar again. 'But back to today's happy couple. Are you going to read those blasted Banns today or not?'

'Well… I suppose I could, so long as the prospective bride and groom are willing.' The vicar waggled his prayer book at them all. 'They cannot be coerced.'

As all eyes swivelled to them, Ned nudged her. 'I'm willing if you are, Izzy.'

'I've never been more willing in my life.'

'Then lead the way, Reverend.'

Ned took her arm and wrapped it possessively

around his and together they followed the gathered crowds towards St Hildeth's, smiling at one another as they entered the churchyard. Not caring one whit that he was wearing just his untucked shirt and breeches and she was still in the crumpled evening gown that she had worn the night before.

As they crossed the threshold, happier than she had ever been in her life, Isobel's yanked her big brute's arm at the doorway of the church and forced him to stop, then made a great show of sniffing the air. 'Didn't I tell you that I smelled rose petals in your future, Edward James Parker. Rose petals and wedding ca—'

He smothered her glib comment with a searing kiss, not caring that he was supposedly a private man who preferred to keep himself to himself or that the entire congregation had twisted in their pews to watch them. By the time he stopped she was breathless, and he was grinning smugly down, much too aware of the devastating effect that he had on her heart and her body.

'Even a stopped clock is right twice a day, Izzy Cartwright, so don't let it go to your maddening head.' Then he traced her face with his finger and sighed. 'And don't let it go to your head that I shall be counting down those days to all the rose petals either, menace. I'd marry you right this second if the vicar would allow it.'

'Which I won't,' shouted Reverend Spears, reminding them both that everyone could hear them as well as see them. 'The Banns will be read thrice, in accordance with the law, irrespective of your obvious indiscretion.'

'It's only three weeks.' She traced her own finger over Ned's cheek and the quarter inch of stubble which already dusted it. Then against his ear, in a saucy whisper just for him, she set out her stall for the precise sort of lover he could expect in her. 'With a proper battle plan, and some effort on your part, I am sure that we can fit a great many subtle *indiscretions* into three whole weeks. Even more if you finally relent and hire a farm hand.'

He smiled against her mouth, then turned to the congregation without a moment's hesitation. 'Does anyone here want a job?'

* * * * *

COMING SOON!

We really hope you enjoyed reading this book.
If you're looking for more romance, be sure to
head to the shops when new books are
available on

Thursday 30th March

To see which titles are coming soon, please visit

millsandboon.co.uk/nextmonth

MILLS & BOON®

Coming next month

A MANHATTAN HEIRESS IN PARIS
Amanda McCabe

A song drifted up to them from the open windows of the lounge, a waltz tune, and Jack gave his head a little shake and smiled down at her. "Shall we dance, Miss Van Hoeven? Last chance for a waltz with the ocean under our feet, bird girl."

"Yes, I believe we should," she said, something poignant and bittersweet piercing her heart. He took her hand and twirled her into the dance, smooth and natural and perfect, just like before.

As the music ended, they swirled to a stop, the stars a glittering blur over her head. He raised her hand to his lips. She reached up with her other hand to touch his face, marveling at his rare beauty. He made her feel so safe with his quiet strength, even as she was dizzy with so many strange feelings—feelings she'd never had before, never even imagined except in music.

"Eliza," he whispered, and then he did what she longed for. He kissed her.

She went up on tiptoe to meet him, twining her arms around his neck to keep from falling, tumbling down from this dream. He caught her around her waist, pulling her even closer to him.

How well they fit together! Their mouths, their hands, their whole bodies, so right. She parted her lips and felt the tip of his tongue sweep over hers. He tasted of champagne, of something sweet. Light, enticing, and then the kiss turned frantic, hungry, full of burning need.

Until she heard a crash of a door slamming, a burst of drunken laughter, reminding her sharply of where they were. Who they were.

He stepped back, his arms falling away from her. She shivered, suddenly so very cold, so sad, so out of breath and confused. She didn't know where to look, what to say, what to think. She only knew that something, everything, had utterly changed.

Continue reading
A MANHATTAN HEIRESS IN PARIS
Amanda McCabe

Available next month
www.millsandboon.co.uk

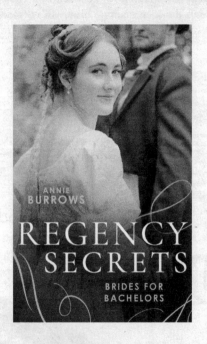

JOIN US ON SOCIAL MEDIA!

Stay up to date with our latest releases, author news and gossip, special offers and discounts, and all the behind-the-scenes action from Mills & Boon...

 @millsandboon

 @millsandboonuk

 facebook.com/millsandboon

 @millsandboonuk

It might just be true love...